DENTON LITTLE'S
DEATHDATE

ALSO BY LANCE RUBIN

Denton Little's Still Not Dead

DENTON LITTLE'S DEATHDATE

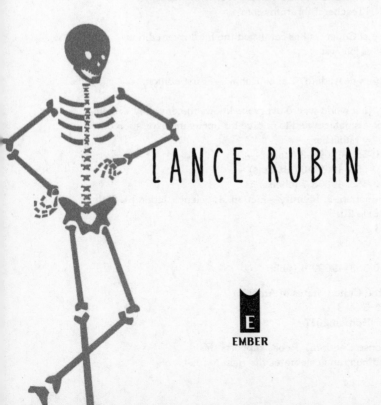

LANCE RUBIN

EMBER

Text copyright © 2015 by Lance Rubin
Cover art copyright © 2017 by Mathieu Persan

All rights reserved. Published in the United States by Ember, an imprint of Random House Children's Books, a division of Penguin Random House LLC, New York. Originally published in hardcover in the United States by Alfred A. Knopf, an imprint of Random House Children's Books, New York, in 2015.

Ember and the E colophon are registered trademarks of Penguin Random House LLC.

Visit us on the Web! randomhouseteens.com

Educators and librarians, for a variety of teaching tools, visit us at RHTeachersLibrarians.com

The Library of Congress has cataloged the hardcover edition of this work as follows:
Rubin, Lance.
Denton Little's deathdate / Lance Rubin. — First edition.
p.   cm.
Summary: "In a world where everyone knows the day they will die, a teenage boy is determined to outlive his upcoming expiration date."
—Provided by publisher
ISBN 978-0-553-49696-3 (trade) —
ISBN 978-0-553-49697-0 (lib. bdg.) —
ISBN 978-0-553-49698-7 (ebook)
[1. Death—Fiction. 2. Identity—Fiction. 3. Science fiction.] I. Title.
PZ7.R83128De 2015
[Fic]—dc23
2014008677

ISBN 978-0-553-49699-4 (pbk.)

Printed in the United States of America
10 9 8 7 6 5 4 3
First Ember Edition 2017

For Mom and Dad,
who taught me it's okay to laugh
about serious things,
and
For Katie,
who cracks me up about all kinds
of things all the time

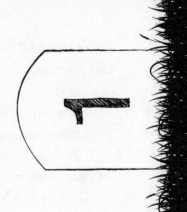

I don't think this is my bed.

It's hard to know for sure, as my head is in excruciating pain, but there's something about this bed that doesn't feel like me. It's got extra fluff.

This is disappointing. I had a very clear vision for how the day of my funeral would start, and it involved waking up in my own bed. I would yawn and stretch like a well-rested comic strip character as the smell of bacon wafted up from downstairs. *There's so much bacon down here!* my stepmom would shout.

But instead, I'm swiping at my skull to make sure there aren't any knives sticking out of it as I listen to the voice of some lady who's not my stepmom talking about something that is not bacon. "Nothing yet," she says, from out in the hallway. "Yes, trust me, I know this is important."

Ow. Something's lumped up under my back. Possibly

my old faithful companion, Blue Bronto. Maybe this *is* my bed after all!

Nope.

It's a pink koala.

I have never owned a pink koala.

"Well, I'm doing everything I can," the woman in the hallway says.

Of course. It's Paolo's mom. I'm in Paolo's house.

I make a halfhearted attempt at sitting up, and as the room slowly spins, I look around. My eye lands on a poster for the National Sarcasm Society. LIKE WE NEED YOUR SUPPORT, it reads under the logo.

This is not Paolo's room.

It's a room I've been in approximately three times before, the room of Paolo's older-but-not-by-much sister, Veronica. So: I just woke up on the day of my funeral in my best friend's sister's bed. This was never part of my plan.

"Denton . . . Are you awake in there?" Paolo's mom says from just outside the door.

I shoot back down and pull the blanket up over my head. She doesn't seem to care that I'm in her daughter's room, but I'd prefer to hide.

"No, he's still out cold," she says as she walks away.

I shrug the blanket off, noticing a Band-Aid on my right index finger. I have no idea why it's there. I must have hurt my finger.

At least my critical thinking skills are firing on all cylinders.

I need to mobilize. I turn onto my stomach, and my face mashes deep into the pillow, getting a full-on blast of girl smell. The scent—a mysterious amalgam of soap, peaches, and . . . mint?—travels up my nasal passages and slams into my brain.

Wait.

Veronica's face appears in my mind, speaking as she gets within kissing distance: "It's just because I feel bad for you."

I remember. I made out with my best friend's sister in my best friend's sister's bed last night. That's incredibly exciting.

But waitasecond. I have a girlfriend. A girlfriend who is not Veronica.

I lift up the covers and look down at myself. My plaid shirt is unbuttoned. Thankfully, I am still wearing jeans. But pants or not, I have completely betrayed my girlfriend, Taryn. Who I really like. Her face pops into my brain: "You're really cool and great and fun, but I don't think I can do this."

Hold on.

Did my girlfriend dump me last night? I put my hands on my face and joggle my head back and forth, hoping to ease my brain-pain and settle my thoughts into some logical arrangement.

She totally did.

I made out with Veronica and got dumped by Taryn last night. Hopefully not in that order.

My headache pulses. My mouth is sand.

"Don't be *ridiculous*," I hear Paolo's mom say in a sharp tone. "He's just gonna mess this up." Her intensity is sobering, but only for a fleeting second.

Time to go. I roll to the other side of the bed. A rotting-fruit smell collides with my nose, and I vomit. Right on Veronica's pillow.

Oh man. Through throw-up tears, I see an almost-empty bottle of peach schnapps on the carpet near the bed. Gross.

I hear a scary buzz from under the covers, and I spring into action, legs scrambling wildly as I propel myself back against the thin metal columns of Veronica's headboard. Approximately two seconds later, I realize the buzz was my phone, and not some sort of hostile bug.

I am a cool, manly dude.

Hey you awake yet? Paolo has texted.

Yes. You in your room? I text back, wondering if he's writing to me from across the hall. As I wait for a response, I push the vomit-pillow onto the floor, where it lands amongst a tiny village of bags and crates, detritus from Veronica's first year at college. She just got home a few days ago.

Ha no we got school today bro, Paolo texts. *Well you don't haha.*

Right. Of course I don't.

Because my funeral is at 2 p.m. this afternoon.

For the first time since opening my eyes, I don't think about what I'm doing in this room, what happened last night, or when the construction crew in my brain is going to let up.

What I think is: *Tomorrow is the day I'm going to die.*

I don't mean to be dramatic about it. Well, I do, because I think it's funny and it makes people uncomfortable, which I like, but it's really not that dramatic.

People have known that tomorrow is the day I will die since I was born. Just like almost everyone else in the world knows the date when they will die, thanks to the group of doctors, scientists, statisticians, and astrologers led by the Nobel Prize–winning, featured-in-every-science-textbook-ever Herman Mortensky, who pioneered the field of Astro-ThanatoGenetics (ATG).

Is it still weird and anxiety-provoking that my death-date is tomorrow? Hell to the yes. But do I need to get movie-preview-voice-over-guy intense about it? Probably not. Which isn't to say people shouldn't feel bad for me if they want. In my entire senior class at MHS, there are only three kids with deathdates during high school, and one of them is me. The other two are Ashley Miller, who died from a weird brain thing during our freshman year, and Paolo, my best friend, whose deathdate is twenty-six days after mine. Delightful coincidence, right? Best friends dying within one month of each other! I'd think that, too, if I didn't know that our close deathdates are a big part of why we became friends in the first place.

During our first week of kindergarten, I was minding my own business in the book corner, reading a story about this bear that bakes a birthday cake for the moon, when suddenly this slightly chubby, smiley little guy was looking over my shoulder. (I guess I was also a little guy at that point, but you get the idea.) At first, I was annoyed, like, *Let me read in peace!* But then he said, "The bear should give the moon a cake for his deathday, too," which struck me as the funniest thing ever on so many levels, just the wisest, most insightful words I'd ever heard. (In retrospect, it doesn't hit quite as hard, but to a kindergartner, it killed.) (Pun maybe intended.)

We cracked up for a long time, and then we started talking about deathdates. "My mom told me you're an Early," Paolo said. An Early is anyone whose deathdate comes before the age of twenty-one. "Yeah," I said, looking down at the carpet. "Me too!" he said. I was elated. I'd never met another Early before.

So there we were: laughing at the same things and both on the road to being dead before even leaving the public school system. If that's not a solid foundation for friendship, I don't know what is.

My phone buzzes again, and this time I'm only terrified for the briefest of milliseconds.

Everyone is talking about your funeral, texts Paolo. *Gonna be a good turnout dude! Hope you're feeling ok haha man you were WASTED last night. So proud.*

So I can now definitively say that this horrible head-ache/dry mouth/overall badness of feeling is a hangover. My first ever, how exciting. And just in time.

I've had the past week off from school, though of course I could have stopped attending way before that. But then it would have been me hanging out in my empty house or with my parents when they're not at work. No thanks! At least Paolo's played hooky with me the past few days, both because he's a good friend and in anticipation of his own earthly departure. (I remember now that he said he was going to school today to "build some good buzz" for my funeral.)

Most people spend their DeathWeek doing the things they most love to do. For people my age, that often amounts to a crazy spring-break-style marathon of mind-lessness. I'm not against that, but it's not exactly my style, and drinking has never really appealed to me. It was only Paolo's strong persuasive abilities ("Don't you wanna know what it feels like?") that finally convinced me to ditch our original plan to go movie-hopping (one of our favorite pas-times, already featured earlier during my DeathWeek) in favor of hanging around in Paolo's house and enjoying the now-gone peach schnapps. (As well as, apparently, the now-gone Veronica.)

I don't know if I should feel encouraged that most of my high school will be at my funeral or nervous or what. If we're going to be brutally honest, people are probably "talking about my funeral" because they're excited it's going to get them out of eighth period and end the school day early.

There's also the whole Veronica-Taryn situation. If this is that "blackout drunk" thing kids are always talking about, I'm not a fan, as it would be helpful to go into my funeral knowing who I made out with, who I broke up with, and anything else I did that's awesome/horrible.

What exactly happened last night? Paolo's mom had told me earlier in the evening that she would give me a ride home so that I could spend my last guaranteed night of life in my own bed. I had planned to start my funeral day—today—with a morning run to clear my head. That's not happening. Not to mention that my stepmom is probably freaking out that I chose to sleep somewhere other than under her roof.

"Okay, Dent . . . You awake yet?" Paolo's mom says from just outside the door.

"Morning," I say. "I'll, uh, be out in a minute."

"Oh!"

I realize now she was actually speaking to the door of Paolo's room, across the hallway. Until I just responded from Veronica's room. My b.

"Didn't know you were in V's room, sorry about that!" she continues, sounding as chipper and friendly as ever. Why *she* is apologizing to *me* for my being in her daughter's bed, I have no idea. Until I remember that my dying tomorrow may be a strong incentive for people to treat me well today.

"Not a problem! Just wanna, uh . . ." I'm staring at Veronica's semi-ironic Smurfs pillowcase lying on the floor.

Some of my throw-up has caked into Papa Smurf's beard. " . . . make the bed and stuff."

"Sounds good. I have some Tylenol out here, in case you need it."

"Okay, great. Thanks, Cynthia."

I hobble out of bed, make it to the bathroom, look in the mirror, dislike what I see, splash water on my face, try to barf some more in the toilet, sort of succeed, grab some toilet paper, wet it, attempt to clean up Veronica's pillow, sort of succeed, decide instead to take the pillowcase off, throw it into the closet, return the bare pillow to Veronica's bed, and make said bed, feeling a sense of victory when the comforter reaches all the way past the pillows, making it seem like I'd never even been here.

As I survey my work, I notice a piece of paper on Veronica's nightstand. *Off to work,* it says, in Veronica's delightfully feminine and loopy handwriting. *That was fun. Kinda. Make my bed please. See you at the funeral.*

I smile at this note, the kindest words Veronica has ever directed at me. I've always thought our aggressive banter masked a genuine affection for each other. But I am wrong about a lot of things. So it's possible these words, and our making out, came purely from a place of pity.

And why not? I pity me, too. I've spent so much of my life trying to be one of those guys who are so *chill* and *cool* with everything that happens, able to roll with anything, my death most of all. I've prided myself on impressing people with how mature and accepting I am of my situation. ("Wow, you have such a great perspective on it; it's really amazing.") After all the hours of death counseling, I'd come to think that, as my death got closer, I would only grow more accepting—more resigned to my fate. But in this moment, with my funeral hours away and Veronica's note in my hand, I don't feel very *chill* or *cool* about any of it. Emotions mingle with my still-very-much-existent hangover, overloading my body's circuitry. I throw up on Veronica's comforter.

3

"Well, look who decided to come home and spend some time with his family on his last day," my stepmom says to me seconds after I cross the threshold of our house, as if she's been perched by the door for hours, a patient eagle waiting to sink its talons into an unsuspecting fish. "It's already past eleven."

"Hi, Mom," I say, failing in my efforts to keep out any guilty inflection. "Sorry I ended up staying at Paolo's last night. I really meant to come back here. But then we . . ." I rifle desperately through my brain-files for any shred of last-night memory I can safely insert into this sentence.

"Oh," my stepmom interjects, "I talked to Cynthia this morning. I know all about what went on in that house."

Yipes. Care to fill me in?

"And I understand," she continues. "Don't like it, but I understand. Apology accepted, my sweet son."

"Thanks, Mom. And this isn't exactly my last day; we've got all tomorrow to be together, too, so . . ."

"Yes, but we don't know *how much* of tomorrow we have. You could be gone minutes after midnight tonight."

"Thanks for the reminder."

"Oh, Denton," my stepmom says, starting to get a little tearful and bringing me in for a huge hug, which is actually not unwelcome at this moment. "I never wanted this day to come. I love you so much."

"I know. I love you, too."

My stepmom sniffs my neck. "You smell like liquor."

"What?"

She pulls back to look at me, her hands on my shoulders like they're a steering wheel. I can tell she wants to lecture me on the dangers of underage drinking but realizes that's pointless. "You look terrible, Denton."

My stepmom has never been as chill as Paolo's mom (I'm required to text her any slight change in my plans, our house has a strict no-junk-food policy, and I had to wait until I actually turned seventeen to watch R-rated movies), but I think that's because she cares about me so much. She's insanely supportive in a bajillion ways, which, considering I'm not her son by blood, makes me feel lucky.

"I'm really fine, Mom." Which is almost true. The combination of the repetitive, involuntary cleansing of my system and Paolo's mom's magical Tylenol has worked wonders.

"Well, go take a shower. We'll eat in a half hour."

"Are you rhyming on purpose?"

"What?"

"Guess not."

"I have to go check on your father," my stepmom says, and she glides deeper into the house and up the stairs to their bedroom. I find myself staring at the framed family photo, taken years ago at my aunt Bess's wedding, that sits on the white table in the foyer. I've always enjoyed trying to find some resemblance between my stepmom and me that might convince people we're actually related.

I was convinced myself for a number of years, until my dad sat me down for a little talk when I was eight and told me that my biological mom died giving birth to me. It sorta blew my mind.

"Wait, so who's my mom?"

"She died."

"Yeah, no, but I mean, who's the lady I know?"

"Oh, Raquel, right, she's your stepmom. I got married to her when you were three."

"But some other lady had me."

"Right."

"Were you married to that lady?"

"Cheryl, yes, I was."

"Did you love her?"

"I did, yes."

"Was it sad when she died?"

"It was."

My actual mom's deathdate fell on my birthdate, which is poetic in a way, but mainly just sad. Some days I feel guilty and responsible for my mom's death. My dad did imply that my conception was "sort of an accident," but he also said my mom was really excited that she would have a second child before she died. Apparently, she was nervous up until the moment I was born, though, worrying that she would end up dying from complications before I came out or that her deathdate would also be mine.

Once I knew the deal, I wanted to stop calling my step-mom Mom, but my dad said that wasn't an option. And I'm glad he did. For all intents and purposes, Raquel is my mom, and I love her like one. In fact, anytime someone even utters the word *mom,* it's her reddish-brown, chin-length hair, her jangly pendant necklaces, and the per-petually hopeful yet disapproving expression on her face that come to mind. At her most annoying moments, does it occur to me that my actual mother might have been more relaxed, more like Paolo's mom? Sure. But at the end of the day, Raquel's my mom. And I feel bad for her that she's about to lose a son.

"Dentooon," my stepmom calls from upstairs in her typical singsongy way.

"Yes?"

"Do you need help picking out what to wear?"

"Nope, I'm fine," I half shout so she can hear me. "I'm just gonna wear my suit. Like we talked about."

"You and Raquel talk about suits?" says my older brother, Felix, suddenly appearing, in a suit of his own.

"Always."

"Us, too. Sometimes I'll give her a random call be-tween classes just to talk about button variations. But then we end up talking for hours, I miss class, and my professors get mad at me."

I'm ninety-six percent sure he's joking. "That's lame. I feel like law school should be more supportive of your right to discuss menswear with your stepmom."

"I know, right?"

"Yeah."

"How are you doing?" He pulls me into a hug.

"I'm all right."

Felix is nine years older than me, and I honestly don't know him that well. I was eight when he went away to college, and he's only home about five days a year. That's not an exaggeration. Partly because there's this ever-present, low-level friction between him and my stepmom (his stepmom, too), but also because he lives in the city and is always busy. I feel flattered that he's here now. I assumed he would make it to my funeral, but I really wasn't sure.

He pulls himself back to look at me, almost fully replicating my stepmom's pose from moments ago. I feel like it's going to be a popular one today.

"It's gonna be okay," he says, staring into my eyes with an intensity I don't think I've ever seen from him. It makes me uncomfortable. "You know that, right?"

"I . . . guess so. . . ."

"Wait, look at me."

"Okay."

"Life works in strange ways sometimes."

"Right." He means well, but it's irritating. "Kinda easy to say when you're gonna live to be sixty-two, but right."

"Yeah, I know. This is a challenging time. Let yourself feel that."

"Can you not lecture me right now?"

"I'm not lecturing; I'm trying to help you. I'm sure your death counselor has told you—"

"My death counselor is a weird-smelling old dude!" Who happens to have been genuinely helpful to me in the past months. But I'm eager to end this conversation any way I can. Anger is not something I do often or well, so I usually greet it like a moth that's landed on my shirt: shake it off shake it off shake it OFF!

"Whoa, all right, Dent," Felix says, his hands in the air. "It's all good."

"I need to go get dressed," I say, avoiding his eyes and heading up the stairs. I guess even as you approach the end of your life, your family can still annoy the crap out of you.

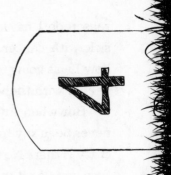

As I unbutton my shirt and get ready to shower, my mind travels back to some well-worn territory: How am I going to die?

It is a question that has kept me up many a night, occupied many a daydream.

I read that during the first years of the Deathdate Movement, the government offered up the option to learn how your death would happen, but it proved to be accurate only seventeen percent of the time, so they scrapped it. Bummer.

Because sometime tomorrow, I will cease to be. And, man oh man, do I wish I knew how. Car accident? Trip and fall? Stung by a bee and it turns out I'm allergic? Infected by some Ebola-like virus? Mysterious brain thing à la Ashley Miller?

Or: straight-up murdered?

With my health records all perfectly normal, what

reason do I have to believe I *won't* be murdered? If I was sick with cancer, for example, I'd be pretty confident in how I was going to die, which would maybe give me a sense of ease with the whole thing. No murder here! Just cancer!

But when my grandpa Sid was growing up, as he has never been shy to tell me, nobody knew how *or* when. How crazy is that? No time to mentally prepare, no way to make sure you do all the things you want to do before you die. In a Time with No Knowledge of Deathdates, I could see how getting cancer would be an advantage of sorts. It would either warn you of your upcoming death, giving you time to get ready, or it would scare you into appreciating your life and then not kill you.

Then again, I've known my deathdate my whole life, and have I done all the things I want to do? Not really. "I just want to live a normal life." That's always been my party line on my premature death, even dating back to the August afternoon when my dad and stepmom first told me about it.

Parents are advised to let children know their death-dates around age five, old enough to comprehend things but young enough to accept information without overthinking it. (I guess in our family, "You're gonna die young" got first dibs over "That's not your actual mom.")

"So, uh, Denton," my dad said as I sat on the couch with Blue Bronto, the first and best stuffed animal I ever owned, on my lap.

"Are we eating lunch soon?" I asked.

"Yes, of course. Absolutely. But, uh . . ."

"Oh come on, Lyle," my stepmom said, plopping down next to me. "Denton, do you understand what death is?"

"Yeah, when people aren't alive anymore."

"Right, that's right. And it doesn't have to be a scary thing at all. It just is."

"Okay."

"Well, your death is going to happen when you're seventeen years old."

"I'm five."

"Right, you're five now, so that's . . . a long while away. We just wanted to tell you now. And if you ever have any questions about it, you can always ask me or your dad, okay?"

"Okay." I ran my hand down Blue Bronto's tail. "How do you know?"

"What?"

"How do you know I'll die then?"

"Well, they know when everybody will die, sweets."

"Except for the undated people," my dad said. "Those are the people whose, uh, blood is unreadable by the ATG tests. Just comes up blank. Possibly because of a gene defect."

"What is a jeans defect?"

"Oh, that's . . . ," my dad said.

"Lyle, you're just confusing him," my stepmom said. "Look, when you were born, they took some of your blood and a couple of your hairs—"

"Ew."

"And then they used those, along with the time and date you were born, and some other things—"

"A genetic map of your DNA," my dad said, "as well as one of my DNA and of your, uh, well . . ." (In retrospect, I realize he was starting to refer to my biological mother's

DNA here but then remembered I had NO KNOWLEDGE WHATSOEVER of her existence.) "They have these people who are really good at math and probability, called statisticians, who have this highly advanced thing called a risk assessment model, which, you know, gets thrown into the mix." My dad rubbed at his right eye under his glasses. "And then they know."

"When will you and Mom die?" I asked. "Before me? Or after?"

My stepmom looked up toward the ceiling, blinked three times, and took a deep breath. My dad shifted his position on the couch. "After, sweetie," my stepmom said. "We'll always be here with you."

"That's good," I said.

"It is," my dad said. "And, uh, Dent, now that you know this, we support whatever choices you make, like if you wanna go skydiving, or if you just wanna skip school some days, or . . . you know . . ."

"Lyle, he has no idea what you're talking about. Don't—"

"I don't wanna skip school," I said.

"Oh. Of course. Sure," my dad said.

My stepmom ruffled the hair on the back of my head; my dad looked down at his feet.

"Is now lunch?" I asked.

We had alphabet chicken nuggets.

Soon after, I became obsessed with death, with the science of AstroThanatoGenetics, with thinking about how it would happen for me. Yet, at the same time, I never wanted my early death to make me different, to force me to live some rebellious life I wasn't actually cut out for. Sure, I could have been riding motorcycles off rooftops while shooting heroin into my veins, but it freaked me out too much. I couldn't *die* before seventeen, but I could become paralyzed or go into a coma or do permanent damage to my brain. So, nope, reckless wasn't for me. I just wanted to be normal.

But now I stare around my room—at the black-and-white squares on my bedspread, the meaningless trophies from elementary school soccer leagues, the crowded shelves of books and movies, the bulletin board photos of me and Paolo, and me and Taryn, and me and my family—and I wonder if I've done this perhaps a little too normally. I'm not leaving any legacy to speak of: no novels written or inventions invented. (I have written a couple of dinky songs on my guitar, but I keep forgetting to record them.) I'll just be another name on the list of unexceptional people who lived and then died in a suburb of New Jersey. I could have done so much more.

What was the point of normal? Did I think that by blending in with the crowd, maybe Death wouldn't see me?

I'm sliding off my socks when my phone buzzes in my pocket: a call, not a text. It's Taryn.

"Hey."

"Oh, hi! I didn't think you were going to pick up." Taryn sounds like she's been crying. "'Cause of the funeral and everything."

"Yeah, I can't really talk long. What's up?"

Taryn is silent.

"Hello?"

"Hi, yeah, I'm here. You sound a little mean."

She's right, I do sound kinda mean. But there's definitely no way to correct that because now I'm annoyed and self-conscious about how I sound. "Sorry. It's the day of my funeral and you dumped me last night, so you'll have to pardon any meanness."

"What did you just say?"

"You'll have to pardon my meanness."

"Do you think I dumped you last night?"

"I . . . Yeah, I mean, I think I remember you dumping me last night."

"I didn't dump you, Denton. I just wouldn't, you know, *do it* with you. You were too drunk."

It is my turn to be silent.

"Which is maybe stupid, but I didn't want our first time to be like that," she adds.

I can't keep up with the information being fired my way. I am disoriented, I am ashamed, I am an idiot.

"Right . . . No, me neither. I didn't want that either."

"No, you really did."

This is so pathetic. My first time drinking alcohol, and I apparently morphed into the jerk from the after-school special, pressuring his girlfriend to have sex with him. "I . . . am so sorry, Taryn. I was really drunk, I guess, and I don't remember . . . much of that." My mind is racing to catch up with the present moment. Why did I assume she had broken up with me? Thanks, peach schnapps. "I'm sorry I was pressuring you, that's so lame."

"No, I mean, I'm sorry I disappointed you. I feel lame, too. I know I probably should've just done it because there's not much time and everything, but I just felt like it should be more special than that. You know?"

"Yes, yes," I say. She should know that I am the undisputed winner of the Lame Award. "Of course I know, and I think you're right."

"Okay, thanks. Because you were saying things like 'Don't you think I'm cool and great and fun?' and—"

"Wow."

"—and I need you to know that I think you're the most cool and great and fun; it just—"

"Tar, it's really all right. I understand, we don't have to keep talking about this."

"You were just kinda messy."

"Oh man. Well, yeah, new topic."

"How was the rest of your night? You get sick?"

"Uh, it was . . ." I made out with Veronica! And I'm not broken up with Taryn! This is so bad. Or maybe I've misremembered that, too. "It was dumb. I got a little sick this morning." On Veronica's pillow! I feel Blue Bronto judging me from the bed.

"Ew, sorry, that sucks. I guess I'd be angrier about the whole thing if you weren't gonna . . ."

"If I wasn't gonna what?"

"You know."

"Oh, if I wasn't gonna die tomorrow?"

"Don't say that."

I laugh. "Why shouldn't I say it? I am dying tomorrow."

"I don't like to think about it." She is crying. "I wish you were at least going to make it through prom."

I can't decide if that's flattering or the most selfish thing

I've ever heard Taryn say. "Well . . . I mean, I *might* still be alive tomorrow night when prom happens, but . . . yeah, well, no, I won't be going to prom. Sorry."

Taryn sobs.

Part of me wants to sob, too. I wish the prom committee had been a little more compassionate when they chose the date for this year.

"Hey, it's okay. I very like you, remember?" I say in my boyfriend voice, hoping an inside joke will make this better.

Taryn and I have been dating for more than seven months, and I'm still kinda surprised we're a couple. The first two and a half years of high school, I knew her only as the girlfriend of Phil Lechman, the fastest runner in the school and a teammate of mine on the cross-country squad. He's also kind of a dick. So when Taryn would be at some of our meets, cheering Phil on at the finish line, I never paid much attention. Sure, she was cute—in her tall, gawky way—but her attachment to Phil deemed it likely that she was as lame as he was.

And then, my junior year, I saw the spring musical *Cabaret.* About halfway through, I realized that the actress playing the sad main character was *Phil's girlfriend.* I was blown away. Her performance was so funny, ballsy, and sophisticated. I couldn't stop thinking about it.

So when cross-country season started senior year, I was still a little starstruck. After one of our first meets, I caught Taryn standing alone by a tree. Without any clear plan of what to say, I walked over to her.

"So. *Cabaret,* huh?"

"What?"

"Very good. I very liked it."

"Ha, what?"

Somehow she was able to see past that train wreck of an introduction, and we found ourselves on a consistent "How's it going?" basis—at meets, in the hallways—and sometimes I would sneak in a joke, too, which, to my surprise, she'd actually laugh at.

I started nursing an impossible crush, looking forward to every cross-country meet, pretending Taryn was there to cheer for me. Until she stopped showing up at meets. This was disappointing, but potentially awesome. Because, sure enough, she and Phil had broken up.

"Get it!" Paolo started chanting in my ear every day during class. "It's Dent time!" It still seemed painfully unrealistic—going after Phil's girl, thinking she would have any interest in me—but having less than a year of life left can be a big motivator.

Cut to early October, the school variety show. Taryn had mentioned once in passing that she'd be performing a song in it, so I decided I would, too. "You can be in one of the big numbers," Ms. Donatella said when I stopped her in the hallway, "but I can't just give you a solo number. I've never even seen you before." And then I told her when my deathdate was.

I sat up there with my guitar, singing and playing a ridiculous song I'd written just for the occasion, something designed to be airtight in its ability to charm and garner immense sympathy: "I'm Gonna Die This Spring (So Let's Make Out Tonight)." As I left the stage, I bumped right into Taryn, who was waiting there in the wings, smiling nervously and looking at me in a way she never had before.

"I very liked that," she said.

We made out that night.

And many other nights.

Because of my deathdate, it got real serious and real committed real fast. Like, we've talked about the wedding we'll never have, about possible kids' names we'll never use. And I'm into that. *Have a monogamous relationship* was high on my bucket list. But, even so, now that I'm almost dead, part of me wonders if the sow-my-wild-oats route might have been the way to go. It's probably the same part of me that thought it would be okay to make out with Veronica last night.

"Dentoooon!" My stepmom's shouting from downstairs pierces our cell-phone bubble. "Have you showered yet? Come on! We need to eat!"

"Okay, I'll be right down!"

"You have to go," Taryn says, with more tears in her voice.

"Yeah. To be continued."

"I have to go back to Spanish class, so I won't be able to pick up if you call."

"Oh right, you're in school right now."

"Yeah, we don't all get to skip today."

"Taryn, I get to skip because I'm gonna be dead tomorrow. Geez."

"Sorry . . . I'm sorry. I'm just . . . sad."

"I know, I know, we'll talk at the funeral."

"Okay . . . I love you."

That's the first time she or I have ever said that.

We always said we'd only say it if we really meant it. I should say it back, but how do I know if I'm truly in love with her?

"I love you, too." I think I mean it.

She says nothing, but I hear the sounds of smiling on the other end of the line.

"Really?" she says finally.

"Really. I'll talk to you later, Tar."

"Bye, Denton."

I hang up. I am simultaneously impressed and disgusted with myself. After one phone call, I'm able to cross three things off a bucket list I never would have written.

Act like a drunken asshole? Check. Cheat on a girlfriend? Check. Say "I love you" without being sure I even mean it? Check.

I do realize that approximately zero percent of this should matter to me right now.

I'm going to *die* tomorrow. According to my death counselor, around now is when I should be feeling either profoundly depressed or beginning to exhibit signs of reckless, life-endangering behavior.

So why the hell am I still invested in these small, ordinary, seemingly insignificant details?

I'd say it's probably an attempt at keeping myself distracted from the dark chasm looming in my future. But with all this Taryn business, I feel terrible and guilty and unworthy and generally like I do want to die. So maybe I'm on the road to depression after all. I head to the shower.

I've only been to four funerals, but that's enough to know that I don't want my self-eulogy to be like the ones I've seen: weepy, nostalgic, and self-congratulatory, sort of like a cringe-inducing Oscar speech. So I've constructed one that I think is sharp and funny, with a lot of heart toward the end. I've also thrown in some advice to the human race to appreciate what they have. Because no one really does. I figure if a sweet guy like me gets a little intense, it'll be very effective. "Oh wow," they'll say. "That was a real wake-up call."

I'm running through it during my Last Shower Ever, trying to get the delivery just right, when I see something weird on my thigh.

It's a reddish-bluish-purplish Rorschach splotch of a bruise, and it makes my breath catch in my chest.

It looks like I've bumped into a desk or table really hard, but I don't remember doing that. Maybe last night during SchnappsFest. But under closer examination, it doesn't look like a normal bruise; it's peppered with electric red dots. "It's okay, it's okay," I say to myself as I scrub at the splotch, not actually expecting it will do anything.

But it does do something. In one swift but orderly motion, the red dots shift around on my thigh, like the rotation of players in a gym class game of volleyball. I poke again, entranced by this touch screen on my leg. I dig in a little harder with my fingers, trying to will some pain out of the splotch; if it hurts, then I can convince myself it's just a strange bruise.

But it doesn't hurt.

I am panicking.

If it's not a bruise, then it's probably the first visible sign of some blood disorder that, even at this moment, is deploying troops throughout my body, gumming up the works, making me almost dead.

After so much time devoted to thinking about how I'm going to die, I now have a very legitimate scenario staring up at me from my thigh. You'd think I'd be relieved, but instead I'm in a state of shock, with one message circulating through my brain, pounding in time with the water thumping against my back:

This is it.

This is it.

This is it.

The beginning of the end.

This is actually happening.

I stare at blue tiles.

I breathe.

As if from another galaxy come the medium-frequency

tones of my stepmom's voice, and I know I'm running later than late.

Shower off.

Suit on.

I stare at myself in the mirror.

This is what dying looks like.

I adjust the knot on my lucky purple tie. I fork my fingers down either side of my head, first flattening and then messing up my dark brown hair. I always thought my nose was a little too big, but now I've come to enjoy the added character it brings to my face. I look good, and I can suddenly see myself the way I imagine everyone at this funeral will see me.

Denton Little. Funny, sweet Denton Little. Handsome but not too handsome. So charming and likable that in seventh grade, he technically won Most Likely to Succeed before teachers decided it seemed like a cruel joke to print that in the yearbook. He would have grown up to do so many great things. . . .

My capacity for self-pity is growing by the minute.

I take out my phone and search for *purple splotch on thigh*.

I'm greeted by scores of message boards, linking my condition to everything from burst capillaries to food allergies to an underground conspiracy to thin skin to a bad tanning bed experience to leukemia to, as was my suspicion, a blood disorder. None of the entries mention red dots, though, and a lot of them mention symptoms I don't have, like itchiness. My splotch is not itchy. Yet.

My stepmom calls up to me once again, and this time her voice has anger around the edges. I haven't made much progress on a self-diagnosis, but let's be real: it might be more helpful not to know.

Downstairs, the mood is a bit frantic. Felix and my dad are already sitting at the kitchen table, looking fancy and suited, and my stepmom is flitting around the kitchen in one of her nice green dresses. This is the Last Meal we will have together, just us, and my tardiness has dictated that it will be a quick one.

Surveying the landscape of the table, I notice all of my favorite foods ever. Even though this is a universal pre-funeral tradition, I'm surprisingly touched.

My dad stares at me as I devour a stalk of my step-mom's famous broccoli with curry powder (it's good, trust me). "How you doin', bud?" he says, pushing aside the newspaper he'd been reading.

"All right," I say. "This is weird."

"Really? I watched your mom make it, same recipe as always."

"What? No, not the broccoli. I mean *this*, today . . . Everything."

"Oh right, right."

Should I be upset that my dad seems less alarmed about my dying than he does about the possibility that my stepmom's broccoli might not be up to par? My dad is great, but he's always had an inability to process and acknowledge upsetting things. I've only seen him cry twice in my life: once, nine years ago, when a few stealth tears trickled down through his gray stubble during Felix's high school graduation and another time when he messed up his knee real bad during a game of tennis. (That second one might not even count because those were pain-tears.)

"Mom, this food is awesome," I say, mouth full of mac and cheese, and hummus, as she continues Tinkerbelling around the kitchen. "Why don't you sit down?"

"What dressing do you want?" she asks. "Balsamic? Oriental sesame?"

I can't express how incredibly little I care about salad dressing at this moment. Seeing that splotch has brought me into this strange headspace where I'm noticing more things. Like my dad's glasses are dark brown and not black, as I'd always thought. Maybe these are new? And the kitchen table is so solid. I spread out my fingers, like I'm palming a basketball, and push against it.

"Your hand okay?" asks my dad, with a small, labored chuckle thrown in for good measure. It's my least favorite habit of his, fake-laughing at things he doesn't understand.

"No, this table . . ." Someone made this. "It's just really cool."

"I brought them all," says my stepmom, finally sitting down with us, too many stupid salad dressing bottles in her hands. "What's this about the table?"

"Denton thinks the table is cool," Felix says.

"Well, thank you, Denton, I agree," says my stepmom, ignoring or missing the snarky tone in his voice in favor of being genuinely touched that the table she chose more than ten years ago has finally been validated.

"This whole kitchen is great." In this moment, it's like the nerdy-girl best friend who the protagonist abruptly realizes is, in fact, his superhot dream girl. Why did I never appreciate this kitchen?

"It really is!" my stepmom says, looking around like a kid in Disneyland. "Oh! By the way"—she grabs an envelope off the counter behind her—"this came for you." She slides it toward me. "No address. Someone must have left it in the mailbox."

"Ooh, nice, that's old-school," I say. Possibly my Last Piece of Mail Ever.

The envelope is blank except for a small typewritten *To Denton* on the front. I'm thinking it's from Taryn or Paolo. "If this is a love note," I say as I open it up, "I'm not reading it out loud. FYI."

It's not a love note.

I'm staring down at a huge-fonted message that reads:

DENTON
YOU ARE GOING TO DIE. SOON.
WATCH OTT

My brain stops.

I'm not sure what's more unsettling, the message's content or the choice of Comic Sans font. I hold it up for all to see.

Everyone is silent and still.

"Ohmigod," my stepmom says, one hand to her mouth.

"Yeah," I say. "Kinda messed up."

"Kinda? What— Who do you think would send this?" she says. "Do you have enemies?"

"I mean . . ."

"Well, look, it's true, right?" my dad says. "This message is just stating what we already know, really."

"This is a death threat, Lyle!" my stepmom says.

"But he already knows he's going to die soon. That's not news."

"It says, 'Watch out'!"

"No, technically it says, 'Watch ott,'" Felix says. "A nine-word message, and this person couldn't be bothered to spell-check. I love that."

On the plus side, this means the splotch on my thigh might not be what's going to kill me after all.

On the minus side, I might be murdered.

"Oh, Dent," my stepmom says.

I liked it better with just the splotch.

"I don't know if you should be leaving the house anymore, sweetie."

"Mom . . . I have to. It's my funeral." But part of me thinks she might be right. Silence hovers for a solid five seconds.

"It's gonna be okay, Raquel," Felix says. "Dent will be okay."

"I will," I say. Though tomorrow is, in fact, the one day that's fated to be very Not Okay.

"We love you so much, Denton," my stepmom says, in tears now.

"We really do, bud," says my dad.

"Thanks, guys," I say, pushing aside the death letter. I try to eat another bite of stuffing, but it won't go down, so I spit it into my napkin.

Here's what you can expect to experience at your funeral:

You will be overwhelmed by the sheer number of people there. You will see friends you haven't seen in years, including Randy Regan, who moved away in second grade to Colorado. Your family and extended family and extended family's family will be there, and they will shower you with attention and praise and pity and love. Everyone else will shower you with these things, too. You will be the star, but not in a way that you'll be able to fully enjoy.

Your girlfriend will try to get a moment alone with you, but it will only last three minutes before you're interrupted by an oblivious cousin and forced to head back to the celebration. Your girlfriend will seem angry with you, but you'll know she's really just upset about the whole death thing, and you'll promise her that you'll have time alone after the funeral, which you do genuinely want. You will wonder if you'll get to sleep with her during that time alone. You will wonder if you'll die a virgin. You'll wonder if you're a jerk for thinking about sex right now.

You will be thankful your best friend is there; he is supportive and great without acting like a freak about it, which makes him something of an oasis in the desert of people surrounding you. As expected, you will see almost everyone from your high school class, and it will weird you out, because you can't ever imagine another occasion where you would invite literally every person from school. You'll remember, for an instant, that in less than a month, your best friend will be going through this exact same thing. You will feel bad for him. You will feel bad for yourself. Occasionally, that death threat from earlier will pop into your head, and you will stare around the room in a paranoid fashion, trying to figure out who wrote it. You will search the crowd for your best friend's older sister, both dreading and fiercely anticipating the run-in, as if she were the result of an important quiz you took last week that you honestly have no idea how you did on.

You will quickly realize that one-on-one conversations at your own funeral—or, as many will choose to call it, your Final Celebration—are largely unsatisfying, especially when they're with Willis Ellis, the biggest stoner in your grade. ("Hey!" "Hey!" "I'm so sorry about today, my brother. I'm really gonna miss you." "Thanks so much, man." "Always crackin' your funny jokes in class and stuff." "Yeah, thanks, I'm glad you're here." "Yeah, of course, dude. How have you been?" "Oh, fine, I guess. You know, school, hanging out, getting ready for this." "Yeah, yeah, it sucks so much. You going to prom? Gonna be crazy!" "Nah . . ." "Oh, right, yeah . . . Sorry, man.")

You will use the restroom, and, after peeing, you will check out the reddish-bluish splotch on your thigh and see that it has gotten bigger. Or has it? You won't be quite sure; maybe it's expanding, maybe you're imagining things. Ultimately, you will push thoughts of the splotch out of your head so that you can try to enjoy this funeral without having a full-on panic attack. You will have a bizarre encounter with Don Phillips, the vaguely slimy man running the show at the Phillips Family Celebration Home, and he will engage you in a matter-of-fact discussion about your coffin until you kindly redirect him toward your parents and wonder how a man in charge of funerals could be so lacking in social grace.

After the requisite amount of mingling, people will be asked to please sit down in the hundreds of chairs set up in the celebration home's huge ballroom. You will be seated with your family at a table at the head of the dance floor, and the official ceremony will begin. Your family is not very religious, but they are somewhat spiritual, and the service will be conducted by Bert Hemling, an old college friend of your dad's, who is now some kind of respected Buddhist priest or something. Bert will talk about you and what a great kid you are and the story of how, when you were five, for about three or four months, you carried around an eggplant wearing construction paper clothing, which you had named Charles. You will think, This *is a story that gets told at my funeral?* Then things will get deeper as Bert explains that your body will die, but you will not; your energy will never die, and you may be back, even a week from now, in the body of a rabbit or a chipmunk or a squirrel (you will wonder if there's a reason Bert has limited your reincarnation possibilities to three fairly similar rodents), and even though you know he's talking about you, you will have trouble connecting these concepts with yourself, trouble believing that those ideas will be highly relevant very soon. You also will have trouble embracing the idea that coming back as a chipmunk is a good thing.

People will begin their eulogies. You will find yourself enjoying what everyone has to say about you but not fully recognize the portrait that is being painted. You will know that a certain amount of hyperbole comes with these speeches, but everyone will sound so genuine that you will truly believe you have touched all these lives and that you will be Remembered Forever. And maybe you will. Your girlfriend will deliver the fifth eulogy, and, though she'll be a bit over-the-top dramatic ("This is going to be the biggest loss I've ever experienced"), you'll be glad the crowd gets to see this charismatic girl say such loving things about you.

By the ninth or tenth eulogy, you will find yourself getting antsy, thinking that there should be a limit to how many of these there are; even Millie Pfefferkorn, the sweetly odd girl who lives down the block and who you're barely friends with these days, will take the mike. If you're feeling restless, you can't imagine how everyone else is feeling. As if in response to this thought, your best friend will get up and, like a breath of fresh air, deliver a eulogy that is closer to a stand-up set. ("Do you know this guy actually flosses every day? I've always been so intimidated by that.")

Then your brother. His eulogy will be sweeter than you expect but will still leave much to be desired; certain parts will seem embarrassing in their lack of specificity, as if this were the mailman and not your brother speaking about you. Just as it dawns on you that your self-eulogy will be coming up soon, your parents will take the microphone and wreck you. Your dad will, of course, be keeping it together, but your stepmom will be struggling to get out any words, and you will understand for the first time how very hard this will be for the two of them, how maybe you have it the easiest out of everyone. Soon you will be sobbing, and it will occur to you that this is the most emotional you've been since the family dog died five years ago, when everyone sat together in that tiny room in the animal hospital, completely losing it as Dash, already in some far-off place, was injected with a lethal something in front of you. You will remember how you thought at that time that Dash's death was especially painful because you didn't know his deathdate in advance. Since it's so expensive to determine deathdates for animals, your family hadn't the slightest idea when he'd be gone. *If we knew this was coming,* you'd thought, *we wouldn't be so sad right now.* But now, here, you're thinking that maybe knowing wouldn't have made any difference. Your parents will be wrapping up their speech, saying how proud you have made them, how much you will be missed, what an incredible person you are, how happy they are to have known you, and how they are sure you will always be with them. It will be almost too much to take, and you will be focusing all your energy on reining in the sobs that are trying to escape your throat when you will realize you are being called up to give your self-eulogy. You will stand up a little shakily and walk toward the microphone, fumbling in your pocket for your speech, which you will realize is not there. It will not be in your left pocket either, or in your back pockets, and you will then remember exactly where you left it: on the dresser in your room. You will stand at the microphone, staring into the faces of almost everyone you have ever known, your mind swimming with fragments of your speech, and you will prepare to speak.

Or, at least, that's what I experienced. Your funeral might be different.

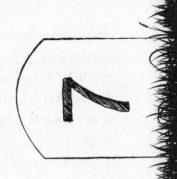

As I stand there about to eulogize myself, I spot Taryn with her parents in the second row of chairs on the left, and on the other side of her is Phil, that toolbox track star she used to date before me. And—it's worth mentioning—the guy who took Taryn's virginity. She says they only slept together twice, but that's two times too many, as far as I'm concerned.

She doesn't necessarily look happy to be sitting next to Phil, who is for once without his trademark fedora, but she hasn't moved to a different seat either. And Phil is leaning toward Taryn and laughing about something. At my funeral. Nice. If I didn't know his deathdate was many years from now, I might contemplate killing him. Murder wouldn't work, but I could at least put him in a serious coma.

Okay. It's time for me to talk about myself to all these people.

"Hello, hey, hi, everybody." I notice a bunch of my

elementary school teachers about seven rows back. Mrs. McGeehan, Mrs. Pond. That's really nice. "Thanks so much for being here. This is obviously an incredibly weird day all around, and it's, uh . . . it's just . . ." Even the parts of my speech I remembered two minutes ago are now nowhere to be found in my brain folds. All I can remember is that I wanted to be sorta angry. But that's not helpful. "It really means a lot to me that you all are here. I wrote a whole thing out, obviously, because this is an important day and these are my last words, so to speak, but . . . um . . . I left it on my dresser in my room. At home. Whoops. So bear with me—"

"I can run home and get it for you! I'll go!" My stepmom is already up out of her seat, headed toward the exit like a crazy lady.

"Mom, no. Please don't, I'm fine," I say into the microphone.

"This is important!" She continues her bouncy run away from me. I have no idea how we've so quickly gone off the rails.

"My mother, everybody!" I say, presenting her, trying to work with this moment, as if it's a bit we had planned together in advance. There's mild laughter from the crowd, but mainly confusion. "Mom, honestly, I think I remember most of it." A lie. "Please don't leave right now. During my funeral."

I seem to have said the right thing, and my stepmom walks back to her seat.

"Yeah," I say, refocusing my attention onto everyone else, "my mom loves me." Big laugh from the crowd. The tension has been defused, and we are back on track. And of course it's a big laugh; these people are probably ready to laugh at anything even slightly resembling a joke. That's why Paolo's eulogy went over so well (except for the joke he made about getting all of my coolest Blu-rays once I'm dead, which I found a little depressing). I am feeling confident. "And I love her." The crowd gives a quiet sitcom-style "Awww."

"And I love my dad. And I love you guys. And I love Maggie, my favorite lunch lady." Another nice laugh. I can't see Maggie in the crowd, but if I could, I'm sure she'd be shaking her sixty-something-year-old head back and forth and smiling like, *Oh, Denton, what'm I gonna do with you?*

"And I love the school lunches, for that matter! I will miss them most of all." Huge laughs. I'm on fire. "Like, everyone's always complaining about school lunches and how much they suck, but can we just agree that they have a certain charm?" I have no idea where I'm going with this, but there is yet more laughter, and I'm enjoying it. "I mean, honestly, everyone's always complaining about everything. Like, the stupidest stuff. Like, please, let's just take this in for a second: I am going to die tomorrow. So could you not, like, complain about all the homework you have? Or that your computer's really slow? Like, can we have some perspective on this?" This is a close approximation of a section of the speech that I had written, except here I think I'm saying the word *like* too much. "People are like, 'Oh man, my life sucks. I didn't get a part in the spring musical.' And I'm like, 'No, MY life sucks because tomorrow I won't even HAVE a life!'" I'm expecting this to get a huge laugh, but there is only silence. "Right? Right?" I am struck by the sudden realization that comedy and anger may, in fact, be closer together on the map than I thought, as I've found my way from one to the other surprisingly easily. Many faces in the crowd seem to be saying, *You poor bastard.*

"I, uh . . . Sorry, sorry. I thought that would be funny. That wasn't in the speech I wrote. Maybe you should have run and gotten it after all, Mom. No, please sit down, don't actually get it." My stepmom sinks back into her seat. "But thank you.

"What is there to say, really? I mean, I don't want to die. Who ever wants to die?" My attention is diverted to a man in his late forties standing alone in the back of the room. He's shifting back and forth from one foot to the other as he stares at me. "Well, I guess suicidal people wanna die, when they're depressed and stuff. But that's a chemical thing happening in their body that's not their fault." That man is kind of freaking me out. Do strangers often show up at random funerals? Is that a thing? "I know not everyone believes that, but it's what I believe." What am I even talking about? I need to ignore that dude and get back on track. "So . . . yeah. I guess my point is, I've had a good life, and I want all of you to have good lives." All of a sudden, I fully grasp the idea that tomorrow I will be nonexistent. It takes my breath away.

"I won't be here tomorrow. Please remember me. Remember to live. I don't care if your deathdate is in a week or seventy-five years from now, please appreciate the people in your life." I'm spouting weird Hallmarkisms that don't even make sense, but I truly believe what I'm saying. "I appreciate the people in my life. I appreciate my amazing parents. Thank you, Mom and Dad, for being the best. And I have a great older brother." I find Felix, sitting right next to my parents, and he gives me a tiny brotherly nod. "He is smart and funny and . . . even though he's busy a lot, he always makes time for me." Sorta. "And I appreciate that." Felix smiles.

"And I appreciate my friends. Paolo, thank you for being the best friend a dude could have. You always crack me up. I'm really sorry you'll be dead in a month, too. Maybe we'll hang out in the afterlife. Or wherever. As chipmunks. We'll be the new Chip and Dale. Not like the male dancers. I mean like the . . . cartoons." That got weird for a second. "Or, you know, maybe we won't be reincarnated at all. Maybe we'll go to some place with lots of other dead people, where we can see everyone we've been missing. Like, I'll see my grandma Sarah. And Mima. And my great-grandparents. And maybe I'll even get to meet my biological mother. Who would obviously never be as great as you, Mom. Anyway, I have no idea, but the point is, Paolo, you rock."

"GAY!" someone shouts.

"Uh . . . I, uh, also want to thank all the guys on the cross-country team," I say as I watch three adults beeline toward the seat where the "GAY!" came from. "You guys are the best. I don't know what I'd do without you. Running with you guys was always so fun and great."

Fun and great? I'm listening to the crap coming out of my mouth as I'm saying it, and it's true enough, but it's the exact shit I promised myself I would never say.

And yet. I can't stop.

"Oh, and Taryn! My girlfriend. Pretty, awesome Taryn. Pretty and awesome and pretty awesome, too." I smile at her. "Wordplay," I acknowledge. I pretend not to notice that as I directed my attention toward Taryn, Phil was leaning over to snicker something in her ear. "You are . . . simply . . . the greatest girlfriend that ever was. I very like you very much." Taryn is smiling, tears running down her face. "Correction: I very love you very much. Yes, that's right! I said it, folks! The L-word! All we need is that, right?"

I've never been less in control of my words.

Maybe this is why everyone's self-eulogies always suck so much; maybe it can't be helped. Maybe everyone is suddenly gripped by a love for everything and everyone, by an overwhelming desire to hang on for dear life. I am everything I don't want to be up here, and this makes me angry. I rebel against my urge to keep repeating how beautiful life is.

"And, Phil," I continue, "I just want to say that I don't like you. I have this reputation for being such a nice guy, a really good guy, so people think I'll just put up with lameness. But I really don't want to. You're a tool. You were the worst part of being on the cross-country team, and I hope you excluded yourself from that nice thing I just said about everyone else on the team. Because it didn't include you. You suck."

That felt kinda good.

"And to the guy who yelled out 'GAY!' earlier—you know, during my funeral—I'm sorry your penis is so small. I really am." Laughter. Applause. "I'm sorry for everyone in this high school who's derisively said anything like that to me or to anyone. Unlike me, you will live, but your lives will be much sadder than mine."

This feels great but also dirty, like maybe this isn't the

way I should be saying goodbye to the world. I don't care. If I have to die tomorrow, this is what I deserve today.

"And, Mrs. Donovan, if you're out there, I gotta say, you are mean. You're a mean lady and a terrible teacher. I think I actually know less about calculus because of you. We talk about how much you suck a lot, but we would never say anything to your face because we are terrified of you. So, there it is. You could consider therapy, maybe? I don't know, just spitballin' ideas here."

Somebody on the side yells, "Woo!"

"I don't want to be a dick, you guys. In a way, I'm glad for the mean people. Adversity makes us who we are, you know? But I just want to be real about it. I want us all to be real. The realest people that ever were. Really. Because life is now. These moments are all we have. You know?" I'm getting freakin' deep.

"Because all this . . . I mean, the SATs are not real." I catch a glimpse of my parents, who are looking at me as if I just produced a shockingly huge fart. "I mean, they're real, they're fine, you should probably take them, but are the SATs what life is about? No! I sure as hell didn't take them!" I really wanted to, actually, just to see how I would do, but then on the testing day, I accidentally drove to the wrong testing center, and by the time I made it to the right one, it was too late.

"What is real is us. We are real. Friends are real. Love is real." And just as I say that, I finally spot Veronica in the crowd, standing amongst all the folks in the back behind the chairs. There she is, in her red Friendly's waitress uniform. We have this moment of direct eye contact, and a chill goes down my spine. That has to have been some kind of sign. Right as I mention love, I find Veronica?

"You're real, Denton!" somebody shouts.

"Yeah, Denton!"

I look back to where Veronica was standing and she's no longer there. Seeing as I can't even remember basic details about what I did last night, I'm not sure I have any right to be telling these people how to live. Probably time to wrap this up. Way beyond time.

"So, um . . . thank you. Seriously. Please stick around for the dance party. Otherwise . . . see you never! Denton Little OUT!"

I've flung my arm up in the air triumphantly, and now it's just hovering there, and it suddenly occurs to me that maybe you're not supposed to applaud at funerals, or maybe no one wants to applaud, and maybe I should leave the podium before the crickets get too loud.

But then the crowd erupts, with all of my friends and classmates spontaneously jumping to their feet, total standing ovation. They chant my name. My parents look appropriately sad and happy and everything, but I also see in them a whiff of disappointment, as though they maybe expected my self-eulogy to have gone a little differently. Paolo catches my attention, wildly gesturing and pointing behind me, and for a split second, I think he's warning that someone is trying to kill me.

Of course he's not; he's just reminding me about the huge bucket of candy we set up for the end of my eulogy, to either add to the joyous celebration or save it in case I totally bombed. ("Those things always end on such a sad note, dude. Why does it have to be that way?" "I know!") I grab the huge yellow plastic bucket from behind the wooden party divider thing and start lobbing handfuls out into the crowd. They're loving this. I am some sort of demented sugar god, raining gifts upon my disciples. The power goes to my head a bit. I spot Phil, looking like a sullen little boy, and I am inspired. I try to whip a peanut butter cup at him really hard, but my aim is off, and it nails Taryn in the face.

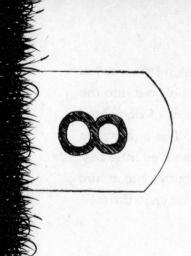

I'm glad the dance party portion of my Final Celebration is limited to two hours, because if it were up to me, we'd bypass it altogether. It's an old-fashioned tradition that was way more popular in the decade or so after deathdates first became mandatory, and my stepmom seems to think that if we don't do it, she'd be depriving me of the full death experience. "I'm telling you," she's often said, "Sheila Hammer's Final Celebration party—my sophomore year of college—was one of the best nights of my life." Gonna go out on a limb here and assume Sheila might have had a slightly different take on it.

To add insult to injury, the DJ my stepmom hired is pretty lame. I'm like a pioneer person headed west, except instead of being weighed down with ropes and supplies and rations, I'm buried in plastic novelty crap. And instead of heading west, I'm doing the Cha-Cha Slide. (Hop two times!) I'm wearing a glittery green top hat, extra-large sunglasses, and—around my neck—two glow-stick neck-laces, one disco ball, one neon blue whistle, and one faux-blingy dollar sign. I like to think I'm being hilarious and wearing all of it ironically, but I guess from an outsider's perspective, it's impossible to tell; probably everyone thinks they're wearing this stuff ironically. Whoa, that feels like a profound realization about humanity.

I'm still juiced from my self-eulogy but trying not to think too hard about it. "That was amazing! You said the word *penis* in your eulogy," Paolo said, standing amongst a sea of people, moments after I left the microphone. "And then you ended it with 'Denton Little OUT!' So incredible, I might have to steal that next month for mine."

"I said that?" I asked. "It's kind of a blur."

"You definitely did, dude, and it was amazing."

Now Paolo is dancing right next to me, working his classic moves, which have always seemed like a strange but charm-ing parody of how an old, slightly sleazy man might dance. At this moment, they seem to be effective; Lucinda Delgado and Danica Riegel are cracking up at everything he's doing.

Paolo leans over to me. "Are you seeing this?"

I high-five him. "They both seem really into you. You still crushing on Danica?"

"Yeah, I think so. Her breath smells like walnuts!"

"Is that . . . a good thing or a bad thing?"

"She must have eaten walnuts before your funeral! Maybe during!"

Paolo and I have at least one sort-of miscommunication like this a day, and it is a huge part of why I love him.

"All right, evvvverybody," the DJ says into his micro-phone, sweating profusely under the terrible fluorescent lights, which have remained on the whole time. "We're gonna slow things down a bit now. Dexter and his girlfriend are gonna head to the center of the dance floor, and then I wanna see all you other couples come on out and join them."

"DEN-ton," my stepmom shouts. "Not Dexter, DEN-TON."

As a poorly written pop ballad starts to play and I wonder why this DJ didn't think to get my opinion on what I'd want to hear for my Last Slow Dance Ever, I look around for Taryn, who told me she was going to the bathroom at least ten minutes ago.

"Come on up here, Dexton, and start us off."

"Uh . . . hold on a sec," I say to SweatyMan as I weave a path toward the ladies' room. There's a line of seven or eight girls and women, but Taryn isn't one of them. Maybe she's inside?

"Hey, guys," I say as I politely skip to the head of the line. "I mean, ladies."

"Hi, Denton," some of them say, in identically sunny, sympathetic voices.

"You can go ahead of me if you really have to go," says Millie Pfefferkorn, the one closest to the bathroom door. She's wearing a bright yellow headband and a patchwork Raggedy Ann dress. Her parents are both lawyers who make a lot of money, but you'd never know it from her clothes.

"Oh. Thanks, Millie, I don't. Have to go."

"I thought maybe you'd want the women's room experience before you died."

"Hmm. Okay. I'm looking for Taryn. Is she in there?"

"Taryn who?" Millie asks, not fully making eye contact. I can't tell if she's joking. I turn to the other females in line, like, *Are you hearing this?* They give me compassionate looks, which probably have more to do with my death-date than my current interaction with Millie.

"Taryn my girlfriend."

"Oh, Taryn Mygirlfriend. I've never met her. I thought you meant Taryn Brandt, that girl you've been going out with." Millie grins in the subtlest way possible, more in the eyes than the mouth.

Millie and I were pretty close friends up until sixth grade, when we drifted apart due to natural causes, so I'm familiar with her strange brand of humor. She means well, but she has a poor handle on what jokes are appropriate for which occasions. Which may have contributed to our drift.

"Yes, all right, but is she—"

"Did you like my eulogy?"

The underwhelming pop song has hit its bridge, and I've pretty much given up hope that Taryn and I will make it in time. I'm in a mild panic.

"I did, I did." I stare at the bathroom door, willing it to open and reveal Taryn. "But—"

"Did you like the part about the summer of Fog? You remember that?"

I did like that part, and I do remember that. There was one summer, either before or after first grade, when Millie and I used to play outside with the other kids on our block. One afternoon, Ryan, our four-year-old neighbor, found this frog hopping around near the gutter in the cul-de-sac. "Fog!" he called to all of us. "There's a fog over here!" Our gang was instantly charmed by the tiny amphibian, and the magical part was, Fog kept showing up all summer, as if he genuinely enjoyed our company, too. This magic came to a grinding halt—as most magic does—on a humid, yellow day in August, when Ryan's despicable older sister Marita deliberately ran over Fog with her bike. "Look, now the street's all Foggy!" she said as she rode away. We were devastated, and in a moment of courage and inspiration, I said we needed to have a postmortem funeral for Fog. I led the ceremony and delivered a truly heartfelt eulogy, which remains, to this day, one of the proudest moments of my life. Come to think of it, my eulogy for Fog was probably better than the eulogy I gave for myself. That's sad.

"I really should find Taryn, Millie, and if she's not in the bathroom, then—"

The bathroom door opens, and I am standing face to face with Veronica.

"Taryn's not in there," Millie says.

Veronica and I stare at each other with the electrifying intensity that comes from sharing an awesome, terrible secret. Her dark hair is in a ponytail, and her waitress getup somehow makes her curvy body look better than ever, in a way that a skinny girl would never be able to pull off. Her brown eyes burn into mine. Something important is happening.

"Nice accessories," she says as she takes one large step to the side and walks away.

Right. I have completely forgotten that I am dressed like a person who shops exclusively at Oriental Trading.

"Thanks," I say, following after her and placing my

giant-person shades on the nearest chair. "Wait up, wait up."

Veronica stops, but she doesn't turn around. I am forced to walk past her, unless I want to talk to her back. Which I don't.

"Hey," I say.

"Hi," she says, giving me a look I am not liking, one that is akin to *Why are you talking to me right now?*

"Um . . . I'm glad you're here."

"Yeah. I came right from work." She gestures half-heartedly at her apron. I don't know why I'm so charmed by it.

"Yeah, well, thanks."

Veronica looks at me like, *Can I go now?* I have to admire her consistency; even at my funeral, she's not very nice to me.

"I just wanted to, uh . . ." I am midstammer when I feel a hand on my shoulder and see a mass of light brown hair out of the corner of my eye.

"Where have you been?" Taryn asks. "You missed our slow song!"

"*I* missed it? I went looking for *you!*" My five necklaces jostle around in the excitement.

"What are you up to?" Taryn says, eyes bouncing back and forth between me and Veronica. I can feel my face starting to turn red. Everything's normal. Behave as if everything is normal.

"Oh, you know Paolo's sister, Veronica, right?"

"Yeah, of course. Hi," Taryn says, brushing a strand of hair behind her ear.

"Hey," Veronica says. She gives her best attempt at a smile as she fidgets with the pocket of her apron.

"I was actually at your house last night, but you weren't there," Taryn says, making small talk.

"Oh yeah?"

"It's a nice house," Taryn says.

"It is, right?" I add, wanting everyone to get along. "Great architecture."

"I got home later," Veronica says, her attention drifting off to the dance floor behind us. "Work."

I bounce along to the music, maybe too enthusiastically. "Okiedokie, well, wanna go dance, Tar?"

"Sure," she says.

But, even though (or maybe because) she's visibly uncomfortable, Veronica won't let me get off that easily. "It's funny, Denton actually said you guys broke up." She's laughing a little, but her eyes are aimed at me and doing whatever the opposite of laughing is.

Oh right. Veronica isn't being very nice to me because she sees that Taryn and I are still a couple. Meaning I'm the asshole who tricked her into becoming the Other Woman last night. But I'm not an asshole, I swear! I'm just a moron!

"He did?" Taryn is not pleased. "Yeah, well, he was . . . confused."

"I'll say!" I say loudly, in a way that instantly feels inappropriate.

"What do you mean, I'll say?" Taryn asks, alarmed.

"Oh, what? Nothing," I say. "Just 'cause I was so stupid drunk."

"Oh. Right."

"This guy," Veronica says. She's doing this thing I've seen Paolo's mom (well, her mom, too) do a couple of times: to compensate for anger, she ends up smiling in this big, unnatural, fake-seeming way. It's terrifying.

"Yeah, I'm an idiot," I say, hoping that something or someone will save us all from this sauna of awkwardness.

And the next moment, an unlikely someone does: Taryn's freckly friend, Melanie, who, for maybe the first time ever, I'm glad to see. (Melanie's hated me ever since I knocked her out of the fourth-grade spelling bee by knowing there are two c's in *moccasin*.)

"Hey, girl," she says to Taryn, adjusting the neckline of her neon pink dress. "Everything okay?"

"Uh-huh, just talkin' about Dent and his shadiness," Taryn says, mussing up my hair.

"How's your face?" Melanie asks, pointing to the bright red welt I inadvertently inflicted on Taryn's cheek with my poor peanut butter cup aim.

"Oh, it's totally fine."

"Complete accident," I say, giving the cheek a quick kiss.

Melanie looks skeptical. "That's what abusive husbands say."

"You know you're at my funeral right now, right?"

"Whatevs. Let's dance, girly!" Melanie says, pulling Taryn away.

"Are you coming, Dent?" Taryn says.

"Yeah, definitely. I'll be over in a second. Veronica was just . . . finishing telling me a story."

Taryn looks at me a beat longer, enough for me to understand that she's frustrated and it's my fault, before she's yanked away by Melanie.

Veronica hasn't walked away, but she isn't saying anything.

"I'm so sorry. I really thought Taryn broke up with me, you have to believe that. I wouldn't have . . ."

"Wouldn't have what?"

I might be more straightforward about all this if I had a clearer sense of what we did.

"If I had known I was still with Taryn, I wouldn't have . . . done . . . what we did . . . last night."

"You wouldn't have played Scrabble with me?"

"Did we play Scrabble last night?"

"No."

"Oh. Okay." I'm not enjoying this game. "I mean, I wouldn't have . . . made out with you last night? And I'm sorry."

"Made out with me?"

I see Paolo nearby, trying to get a read on what's happening.

"Yeah, I—I think I did. I mean, I know we did. I . . . remember something."

"Probably hallucinations from all that drinking."

"Does alcohol make people hallucinate?"

"You tell me."

"This cryptic thing you're doing isn't very cute. I mean, I'm not sure if you heard, but time is kinda valuable for me."

You know how sometimes you think you're saying something witty and appropriate and it's only when you see how someone responds that you start to question whether it was either of those things?

"Denton," she says, disgust written all over her face. "I'm sorry your deathdate is tomorrow, I am. Because I think you're a good guy. Or I used to anyway. But you've got a lot of growing up to do." And she walks away.

It's my turn to be pissed. "Well, great! Thanks! When will I do that, Veronica? Huh? I don't have time to do any growing up! I don't get that time!"

Veronica turns around. "Calm down, D. I'll see you at your Sitting." Then she continues to walk away.

"You know, you're only one year older than me, V! College has made you really pretentious."

She stops in her tracks, turns around, and walks back to me. I'm excited to hear what she's going to say next.

"By the way, Denton," she says, leaning in so close that I can smell her girlness blended with the smell of the french fries she'd been serving that afternoon, "we didn't make out last night. We slept together. Okay? We had sex. Remember? You drunk idiot."

I'm without words.

"So. See you later." And she is gone.

Paolo sidles up beside me. "Man, I know what it means when she gets that look. How much money do you owe her?"

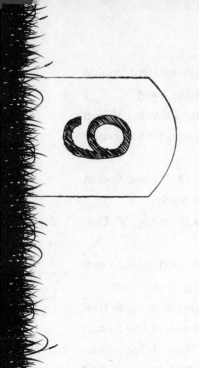

It's a surreal feeling when you realize you are everything you've always tried so hard not to be. I never wanted to be a lying, cheating, sleep-around type of dude. I thought I was a romantic; a writer of sweet notes; a buyer of hilarious, well-thought-out gifts; someone who wanted to wait to have sex until it was Really Right. But whether I've been this way all along or whether I have death to thank, this much is indisputable: I *am* an asshole. A non-virgin asshole.

"Wait, so seriously, do you owe her money?" Paolo asks.

I'm not sure if I should tell him about me and Veronica. There are two ways to think about it. Either *Oh, I'm gonna be dead soon anyways, so I might as well not tell Paolo that I boned his sister.* Or *Oh, I'm gonna be dead soon anyways, so I should just tell Paolo that I boned his sister.* Maybe he'd cheer me on. But there's bound to be some weirdness, and I don't want that in these last hours.

"Oh, uh, well, yeah. I owe her ten bucks."

"Ten bucks?" Paolo says. "V's freaking out like that over ten bucks?"

That is kinda low. "I mean twenty bucks. Twenty-five bucks."

"Still. Calm it down, lady."

"Yeah. Totally."

We stand side by side, taking in the festivities celebrating my death.

"So this is a trip, huh?" Paolo says.

"I don't think it's fully hit me yet."

He puts his arm around me, hand on my shoulder. "Wherever you go, I'll be there in a month. Just remember that."

This is cold comfort to me. Because, really, where are we even going? In spite of whatever I said during my self-eulogy, I've never fully been able to embrace the idea of the afterlife as this place where dead people can all hang out together and have fun.

"So if you forget anything," Paolo continues, "your toothbrush, phone charger, whatever . . . just let me know, and I'll be able to bring it for you."

"Oh, cool, thanks, good to know. I'll leave a little duffel bag you can put all the stuff I forget into."

"Sweet, I love duffel bags."

"Me too."

If someone overheard our jokey conversations, they'd think we were idiots. But what we love to do is have conversations where we're talking *as if* we're idiots. It's a subtle, but key, difference.

"Actually, could you lend me a few of your duffel bags?"

Paolo asks. "I won a couple new ones on eBay yesterday, but I'm gonna need some backups."

"Absolutely. I'll lend you my duffel bag press as well so you can make your own. It's great for emergencies."

"Oh, that is gonna change my life. Thanks, dude!"

I laugh. Paolo laughs.

"Duffel bags," I sigh.

"Duffel bags."

We sit in this moment that suddenly feels representative of our entire friendship. It's sad. I don't want to sit in it anymore.

"I should get back to Taryn. She's—"

"I think Taryn will be okay without you," Phil says, appearing from behind Paolo's shoulder like he's been waiting for the perfect opportunity to interrupt. His trademark fedora is back.

"Oh. Thanks for the input," I say. Whatever this is, I'm not in the mood for it.

"Great speech, Little. Really appreciated all the nice things you had to say about me. Right, Tooch?"

Another one of our cross-country teammates, Eric Vertucci, stands nearby. He's generally a nice guy—except for when he's around Phil—so he seems confused about how to respond. He settles on a quick bounce of his thick eyebrows.

"Look, Phil, I . . ." It was much easier to call him a tool when I was standing at a microphone in front of tons of people.

"What's the big deal?" Paolo says. "He called you a tool because you're a tool."

"Nobody asked you, dick-lick!" Phil gives Paolo a little shove.

"Come on, stop!" I say, sounding even to my own ears like a whiny little kid.

Phil gets all up in my face. His breath smells like tuna fish.

"Like you're gonna do something about it? A wuss like you?"

I say nothing. I wonder how Taryn dated this guy for three years.

"I know you were aiming that PB cup at me. Too bad you have the throwing skills of a three-year-old girl."

Can't argue with him there. "Get out of my face," I say.

"You know that once you die, Taryn and I are getting back together? Right?" How painfully insecure does a guy have to be to say this to someone who is about to die? "Where do you think she was just now, when you couldn't find her? She was with *me*."

Whether or not these things are true, my predominant thought is that I've never punched a human being before (although that makes it sound like I have punched animals) and this might be a good time.

I ball my fingers up into a fist.

"Yo, Lechman," Eric Vertucci says, hands on Phil's shoulders. "Not here, man."

Phil looks around, notices various concerned, disgusted faces, maybe hears the judgmental mumbles. ("No class whatsoever." "Geez, it's his funeral, dude.")

"Yeah, okay." Phil takes a couple steps back. "Not here." He adjusts his fedora.

I go to straighten my tie and realize I'm still wearing many novelty necklaces.

"You're lucky you're dying, Little."

"And you're lucky you can run fast," I say, trying my best to quickly assemble some kind of comeback.

"You threatening me?" Phil takes a step toward me.

"No, no, I meant it like, since you have no other skills or talents to fall back on in life."

"What?"

"It didn't fully make sense, never mind."

Phil stares me down a beat longer. "See you soon. Let's hit it, Tooch." He saunters off.

Well, somebody just shot to the top of the Death Threat Suspect List.

"Sorry, dude," Eric Vertucci says, lingering a moment longer before following Phil. "Bye, I guess."

"Oh man!" Paolo says. "You were way too nice to that guy in your eulogy."

"Yeah. I was seriously about to punch him just now."

"Ah, I thought so! Man, that would have made my life." Paolo awkwardly punches the air twice. "Who's the dick-lick now, dick-lick?"

"You think all that stuff he said about Taryn is true?"

Paolo takes way too much time to answer. "Nah, dude, he was just talkin' smack."

"Hmm," I say.

"Honestly, I'd be more worried about that whole 'See you soon' business."

This is all kinds of disturbing. I don't want Phil to be the reason my life ends.

And I certainly don't want him anywhere near my rapidly approaching Sitting.

I know different people and cultures have varying approaches to death, so in case you don't know about the tradition of the Sitting, here's the deal: whilst waiting for death, you sit. You generally end up in a room of your house, probably the family room (ideally not the living room because the irony of that is too hilarious and stupid), where you're joined by your immediate family and whoever else has been invited: cousins, aunts, uncles, grandparents, girlfriends, best friends, and so on. Everybody communes and celebrates and waits for something to happen.

And something always happens.

Heart attack, stray bullet, seizure, fallen bookshelf or tree, stabbing, tornado, tumble down the stairs, strangling, drug overdose, fire, aneurysm. Not to mention the basics: old age, cancer, pneumonia, other fatal illnesses. People have gone to great lengths to try and survive, but you just can't. This guy, Lee Worshanks, in Pennsylvania, spent years working on what he called a Safety Room, the perfect place in which to spend his deathdate: ideal temperature, rubber walls, dull-edged furniture, the works. When the Big Day rolled around, the room's complicated security system somehow malfunctioned, and Lee found himself locked out. After hours of failed attempts to get inside his perfect room, he went a little nuts. He ended up electrocuted by some kind of circuit panel in the basement. So pretty much every possible variation on death in a house has happened to at least someone in the past few decades.

But you don't know what that variation is, and you

don't know when in the day it will happen. That's why the Sitting has always seemed insane to me. Who would ever want to be sitting in a room with their family for twenty-four hours straight? How is that anybody's idea of a happy way to die?

I asked my stepmom a little while back if we could do my Sitting on a beach somewhere, and for a second, it seemed like she was going to agree. But then she must have envisioned a terrifying land shark chomping off my head, because she shot me down hard-core. I sorta get it.

Being in your house inspires some blind hope, a feeling that nothing bad could actually happen in that sacred space of familiarity and comfort. It's a healthy delusion, giving you the false sense that you have some control over your fate.

Not only that, but there are some places where you're straight-up not allowed to be on your deathdate. Airplanes, for example. Sometime in the first few years after Astro-ThanatoGenetics went public, people began to realize that it was ludicrous to allow someone onto a plane on the day they were going to die. Suddenly the odds of that plane going down go way up. Even though the deathdated would be the only ones killed, there'd be plenty of potential for others to be injured, paralyzed, maimed, traumatized, etc., so the airlines in the US banded together and created a no-flying-on-your-deathdate policy.

Insanely enough, the number of plane crashes in the country dropped dramatically. There have still been exceptions involving the undated or tourists (the US, UK, and Germany are the only countries in which learning your deathdate is mandatory), but all in all, it's a smart policy. And a nice demonstration of why a Sitting makes sense.

Though there's danger aplenty at Sittings, too. There's the story where the woman sat for a while with her family, then went outside to get a quick breath of fresh air, her husband accompanying her as a bodyguard of sorts. They weren't outside longer than two minutes when a drunk driver swerved onto the sidewalk straight into them. And this was a sunny weekday afternoon. She died in the hospital three hours later, and her husband, whose deathdate wasn't for another *twenty-one years,* went into a coma that I think he's still in to this day. So. Yeah. You understand why you might err on the side of not leaving home at all.

But ultimately to Sit or not to Sit is a very personal decision.

Since I'm dying young, it means, technically, I still answer to my parents. And it's hard to argue with your parents. At least, it's hard for me to argue with mine. I feel bad; they're losing a son. I don't need to add the worry and anxiety of not knowing where it'll happen.

So that is why I will be having a Sitting.

But I'm not looking forward to it.

"Yo, dude, wanna head back to the dance floor?" Paolo asks. "Danica's dancing alone, which is clearly her inviting me to jump on it."

"Clearly." I should get back to Taryn, but I feel compelled to give my splotch a peek, see how my death is progressing. "I think I'm gonna take a quick jaunt to the bathroom, so I'll just meet you over there."

"Oh, I gotta go, too. I'll come with you."

"But I think it's a one-person bathroom."

"I'll just wait by the door. What's the big deal, you gonna rub one out or something?"

"No, no." I haven't told anyone about my death splotch yet, but Paolo may as well be the first. "I . . . uh . . . well, yeah, just come with me. It's not a big deal."

"Okay . . . I don't want to see your junk, if that's what this is about."

Alone in the bathroom, I nervously unzip and lower my pants.

It's worse than I imagined.

My entire right thigh down to my right knee looks like it's been soaked in wine, and the electric red dots are everywhere. I run my hand up and down my thigh, and the cavalcade of dots rearranges itself in perfect formation. I peek under my boxers and see that the splotch extends all the way up my right hip, narrowing to a sharp point, like some jagged stalagmite.

"Stay calm, Denton, stay calm," I say quietly. "It doesn't hurt, it's okay."

"You all right in there, brozer?" Paolo asks.

"Eh" is all I can manage through the door.

"Should I come in?"

"I dunno," I mumble.

"Whoa, shit, man, has the dying started? The door's locked, lemme in!"

"Okay," I say, starting to raise my pants and go for the handle.

There's a karate grunt, followed by a loud bang against the door.

"Ow," Paolo says.

"Are you okay?" I open the door and usher Paolo quickly inside.

"I was trying to kick it down," he says, shaking the pain off his foot. "In case you were dead."

"Thanks, man. But this is what I was freaking out about." I show him.

"Oh wow, yeah." I can tell he's trying to downplay his reaction, but he's shocked and fascinated by what he's seeing. "Did you fall or something?"

"No. I noticed it this morning. I have no idea. Have you ever seen anything like this?"

Paolo is looking closely at my leg, and even though it's in the most clinical, doctorlike way, I can't help but hear in my head the shout of "GAY!" from earlier.

"No, definitely not. I mean, maybe it's some sort of weird STD?"

"No, it's definitely not an STD," I say, maybe a bit forcefully. But holy crap, is it? Did Veronica give me some rare disease that's going to be the thing that kills me? Did we even use protection last night? I have to believe I would have used a condom, even drunk. Right? Moron, Denton, moron!

"Ease up, Sparky, I was joking."

"Yeah, I know," I say, trying to conjure up a chuckle.

Sweaty DJ's voice reverberates on the other side of the door: "Everybody, let's get out here for one last song for Dante, really show him our love now."

"Last song," Paolo says. "Shit, we gotta get you out there."

Amazingly enough, one of my favorite songs of all time starts playing, but I can't fully take it in.

"Okay," I say, "but . . . do you think there are STDs like this, though?"

"I don't know, dude, maybe. Wait, why . . . ? Did you have *sex*?"

"What?" I've been caught off guard, and I'm doing a terrible job of playing it cool.

"Oh my good golly, DUDE. You had sex? Last night? I thought you and Taryn didn't have sex!"

"Quiet down."

"But you totally did!" Paolo says in a loud whisper. "You be stealthy! Oh man, that is amazing. Congrats! I'm so happy for you guys."

"Yeah, well . . ."

"And it happened at my house, I'm honored."

"Right. Um. It wasn't . . ."

"It wasn't at my house? Where did you do it? You guys are crazy!"

"No, no, it wasn't . . ."

"It wasn't good?"

I want to tell him that it wasn't with Taryn, but the words aren't coming. I haven't lied yet, though. Not exactly.

"It's never good the first time. Never. When I did it with Jasmine that time, it was like mice stuck in glue." He gives an exaggerated shiver.

"Ew, what?"

"It was bad, dude, so don't worry. But this thing on your leg, huh? Maybe Taryn did STD you, I don't know."

"She didn't STD me, okay?"

"What's with those dots?"

"I don't know. They move," I say as I show him.

"Whoa, cool! Can I try?"

"I . . . No, stop stroking my leg."

Someone knocks on the door. "Dent . . . ?" asks Taryn. "Are you in there?"

My attention is distracted, because right as she knocked, the splotch began to expand before our very eyes.

"Whoa," Paolo says.

"Oh, hey, Tar," I say. "I am. Sorry, I'll be out in a sec."

Like a bloodstain in the movies, the death mark blossoms down my calf in a way that would almost seem beautiful if it wasn't so damn freaky.

"Is . . . Paolo in there with you, too?"

"Um . . ." This would be a stupid thing to lie about, as it will be pretty obvious once the door opens. "Yes. We were just . . . chatting in here."

"Oh," she says, five long seconds later. "Well, we were all out here worried about you. Want to join us? I wanna dance with my boyfriend at his funeral."

"Of course, of course," I say. I pull up my pants. Paolo is still staring at my leg, mesmerized.

"That was incredible," he says.

We come out of the bathroom to find not just Taryn but my stepmom and dad, too.

"Hey, guys, sorry about that," I say. "We weren't making out in there or anything."

Taryn's face changes to one of surprise and mild shock. "What? Why would you be making out in there?"

"What did he just say?" my stepmom says to my dad.

"Oh. I thought . . ." I seem to have misjudged the situation.

"It's okay, Denton," my dad says, with a look of such compassion and understanding it would break your heart. "We're just glad you're all right."

"Yeah, no, I know, but really, we were just talking in there. About movies."

"Lots of cool movies out right now," Paolo agrees.

I don't want to tell my parents about the splotch yet. It would only make them worry more. (I realize that's absurd, considering I'm dead either way. But.)

"Okay, so . . . I think Taryn and I are gonna . . ." I gesture to the dance floor.

Taryn is giving me a playful look with squinty eyes that is also kinda serious, like, *Who are you?*

"Yes, fine," my stepmom says, waving us off. "Go, go, but, Dent, people are starting to leave and they want to say goodbye to you, so make sure you do."

"You want me to say individual goodbyes to everyone that came?"

"Well, they're here for you!"

"All right, all right," I say, grabbing Taryn's hand and steering us toward the scattered, bouncing bodies. I wonder if she can feel that I'm no longer a virgin, the guilt radiating off my skin.

"Were you guys really talking about movies in there?" Taryn whispers into my ear.

"Definitely not," I whisper into hers. "I found something weird. I . . . I'll show you later."

She pulls her head back, eyes big. "Is everything okay?"

"Not sure, but don't worry."

I give her a spin, then bring her close, just as the song key-changes into its final triumphant chorus.

"I do worry," she says. "I can't help it." Her hazel eyes are glassy and concerned.

I think of what Phil said, that they'll be getting back together once I die.

"Hey," I say. "Did . . ."

"Did what?" Her eyebrows slope sweetly together.

"Ah, never mind."

I go in for the kiss.

A hand lands on my shoulder. "Excuse me. Denton?"

I turn and I'm staring at the handsomish, pockmarked face of that man who was standing in the back during my eulogy. He seems nervous. I want him to leave.

"Uh, yeah? I'm kinda in the middle of—"

"Hi. Um . . . You don't know me, right?"

"I don't . . . What?" I exchange a look with Taryn.

"Sorry, that was a strange way to say that. I wasn't sure if maybe your dad had told you about me or . . . showed you pictures."

"Oh. No, I'm sorry. Not that I remember." WTF.

"Right, right, okay. I'm Brian Blum." He holds out his hand, and I reluctantly take my arm from around Taryn and shake it. "I, uh, knew your mother."

"She's right over there, if you want to talk to her." I point to Raquel across the room, in mid-conversation with Taryn's mom.

"Huh?" The man's head spins really quickly to look. "Oh no, no, not— I mean your actual mother."

The music around me fades.

The people around me disappear.

Other than my dad and brother, I've never met a single soul who knew my mom. But this man says he did.

"You knew my mom?"

"Yes."

My biological mother. We are on sacred, uncharted terrain.

I turn to Taryn. "Do you mind if I . . ."

"No, of course, of course," she says, which I know must be hard because this is our Last Dance Ever.

"Come this way," I say to him, and lead us to a less obvious corner of the room. The song has ended and people are entering that postparty milling-about phase. We don't have much time to talk.

"Sorry to pull you away from . . . ," Brian Blum says.

"It's okay. I mean . . . Well, so, what do you mean you knew my mom?"

"Yeah. Right. So." He looks around, then back at me. "I mean exactly that. Your mother, Cheryl, and I were very close."

What's this guy getting at? "Like . . . you were her boyfriend?"

"No, no, nothing like that. Well, actually, at one point, we . . . But, no, we had a very close friendship, is all. I was the doctor who delivered you, did you know that?"

I beg your pardon?

"When you were born, I was the ob-gyn. I thought your dad might've at least told you that. You've grown up a lot since then." He lets out an awkward chuckle.

So. Much. Information. Hold the bad jokes please, mister.

"What . . . But . . . didn't my mom die giving birth to me?"

"Ah, I was there for that, too, yes, but look, obviously you know that at midnight tonight, your deathdate begins."

"Right."

"You need to be careful."

"What?"

"I don't know how to say it other than that. There may be strange characters lurking about, people with bad intentions, and you should just keep your feelers on high alert. Trust no one, especially if they're associated with the government. You get me?"

"Not really. Are you saying you think I'll be murdered?"

"Here." He reaches into a pocket of his jeans. "If anything happens, if you feel you're being followed or you see anything weird, just call me at this number."

He extends a business card toward me, and I'm reaching out to grab it when a hand ushers me back.

"Okay, no, no," my stepmom says, steering me out of the card's reach. "Please keep your cards away from my son."

"Oh, hi, I'm Brian." He puts the card in his other hand and re-extends his right to shake. "I knew Denton's mo—"

"I know who you are, Brian, and that's all well and good. But Lyle doesn't want to see you, certainly not here."

Brian lowers his unshaken hand. "Okay, look, I understand where Lyle's coming from, but can't he walk over here to tell me that himself?"

"No, he can't," my stepmom says.

"What are you guys talking about?" I ask.

"Don't worry, sweetie."

"With all due respect," Brian says, "it's been almost eighteen years. And Lyle hasn't forgiven me yet?"

"Guess not. You should leave."

"This is for Denton's own good!"

"I really don't want to have to call the cops."

Brian Blum looks desperately back and forth from me to my stepmom. His eyes hold on to me, like he's trying to will some nonverbal message into my brain. I try to understand, but I don't speak Silent Weirdo.

"Sorry," I say.

Brian's eyes drop down to the ground. He looks back up. "All right," he says, then turns and slowly walks out a back door of the celebration home.

"Mom," I say. "What the hell was that?"

"Well," she says, still watching the door Brian exited out of. "I think you should ask your father. And watch your language."

"Excuse me," one of the celebration home staff members says, grabbing a chair from behind me and my stepmom so he can passive-aggressively fold it and stack it, oh so subtly hinting that it's time for everyone to leave.

You would think they might not do that for funerals, but they do.

A river of people streams over to hug me final goodbyes. I go into autopilot, hugging everyone and saying sweet things, while the rest of my brain struggles to find some solid ground.

Trust no one.

This is for my own good.

It's been almost eighteen years, and my dad still hasn't forgiven him.

I try to extract some meaning from all this.

Did Brian intentionally kill my mom? Because maybe that would be worthy of eighteen years of unforgiveness.

I always imagined today would be a time for closure, for resolution, but instead, my head swarms with a million questions I would never have known to ask yesterday.

"Trust no one?" Taryn asks as we sit in my small silver car, parked at "our spot," a sandy hill that overlooks all the streets and lights of a neighboring town. We like that it's kind of a funny throwback to the 1950s, when teenagers would park up at Make-Out Point or Lovers' Lane or Sex Mountain or whatever.

"That's what he said."

"So you literally can't trust anyone? Not even your mom and your dad?"

"Well . . ."

"Are you supposed to not trust me?" Taryn asks, pulling me closer.

Phil's words pop into my head: "She was with *me*."

"No, I think I can trust you," I say.

"You think you can?" Taryn scoffs, but her tone is playful. She puts her hands on either side of my face. I lean in closer and kiss her. Our tongues touch, and hers is strangely cold, like she's been eating a Popsicle. I feel a tear land on my cheek. We stop for a moment.

"This sucks so much," Taryn says. "I hate that the day we finally say 'I love you' is the day before you dehhh." The word *die* gets caught up in a sob. I pull Taryn close, over the gearshift thingy, as she quietly convulses. I'd forgotten about our *I love you*s.

"I hate that, too," I say.

"You're just my favorite guy."

I feel my heart beating through my shirt.

"Thanks, Tar."

"And, I mean," Taryn goes on, "who's gonna come to this spot with me?"

"Well. Hopefully no one."

"Ohmigod, of course," she says, about ninety-eight percent convincingly. "No one."

Down below us, two cars nearly hit each other, their tires screeching.

My pocket buzzes, and I see that my stepmom has texted: *Sorrry about befor. Maybe youu and Dad wll have tume to talk lator> ? Have fun w T and P. xoxoi.*

It makes my heart ache, and not just because my stepmom has the texting abilities of a five-year-old.

"Who is it?" Taryn asks.

"My stepmom. She said maybe me and my dad can talk later."

"Oh, that's good."

I tried to talk to my dad at the celebration home, but he was settling money stuff with Don Phillips, and I had to get going to stay on schedule. The rest of my pre-Sitting evening has been carefully planned and divided: Taryn time, then Paolo time.

"It would be pretty annoying to die and never know what that guy meant."

We hear a plane fly overhead.

"Isn't it crazy that that's how it used to be?" Taryn says. "Before people knew?"

"What do you mean?"

"Like . . . before people knew when they'd die, it could just happen anytime. And you had *no idea*. Probably so many unanswered questions. And you could be anywhere: in the supermarket, in school taking a test, or, like, in the bathroom even. No prep time whatsoever."

"Yeah." Though I'm not convinced all this prep time is a helpful thing.

"And then you couldn't even go to your own funeral."

"Yeah . . ." I'm also not convinced I really needed to be at mine.

"It's just weird to think about."

"Definitely." My arm is still around Taryn, my hand rubbing her shoulder.

Here's the funny thing about my state of mind right now: in spite of the immense guilt I feel about Veronica, I am still very much hoping that Taryn and I will have sex. Maybe that makes me an even bigger asshole, but there it is.

Now is probably the moment to make my move.

Problem is, I can't get all that stuff Phil said out of my head. I'm sure most of it is untrue, but it's kinda gnawing at me.

"What's up?" Taryn says, sensing something's wrong and looking up at me. There's glitter on her lips.

"Well . . ." Ah, fuck it. There's no time. I go in for the kiss, surprising Taryn, who lets out a pleased little yelp.

We make out. Lots of tongue wrestling and deep nose inhales. It's good.

I will ask her about Phil when we're finished. Definitely.

I guide Taryn over from the passenger seat onto my lap, pulling the little bar underneath the driver's seat so it slides back to give us more room.

It's not that big a deal that Taryn was with Phil instead of slow-dancing with me. I'm sure there's a logical explanation.

My hands find their way to Taryn's legs. I trace a path up and under her dress.

"Oh, Denton," she says.

"Oh, Phil," I say.

Taryn abruptly pulls back and stares at me.

"What'd you just say?"

"What?"

"You totally just called me Phil."

Oh my holy shit, I did.

"No, I . . ." Whoops. "Yeah, okay, I guess I did."

"That's really weird," Taryn says, awkwardly crossing back over to the passenger seat, bumping her head. "Ow."

"I know," I say. "But Phil said some stuff to me at the party. About you. And it's kinda driving me nuts."

"Oh no," Taryn says, slowly leaning forward with her forehead cupped in one of her hands. "I'm sorry, Dent. He's being . . . really difficult."

"Yeah, well, he said you guys were getting back together after I died. And that you were with him when I couldn't find you for our slow dance."

"Okay," Taryn says, rising back up, looking into my eyes. "I promise you, Phil and I are not getting back together. We're just not. As for the slow-dance thing, I was with him for some of that, but I feel horrible about it. You don't deserve that, Dent."

Not gonna lie, my stomach drops when she says she was with Phil.

"It's just, well, first of all," she continues, "you embarrassed him in front of, like, two hundred people. Which I get because he can be a dick, so that's whatever, but he's already in a bad place to begin with. Because of his dad and everything. So I was trying to be there for him, just for a few minutes."

"He looked like he was in a great place to me, laughing and joking all over you."

"His dad has pancreatic cancer, Denton. He dies—"

"In two months, I know, Tar. May I remind you that I die TOMORROW!" I surprise myself with how loud I am, like when you start a car and the stereo is still blaring from the last time you drove it. "Maybe even in a few hours."

"Whoa. Okay. Sorry." Taryn stares out the passenger-side window.

The proverbial clock ticks.

"Sorry," I say.

"You've never yelled at me before."

"I know." I have almost no experience with sexual intercourse, but I'm guessing this doesn't count as foreplay.

"Denton, I love *you,* okay?" she says into the window, emotions in her voice.

"I know. Could you look at me? Please?"

Taryn slowly turns back to me, eyes wet.

"I just have a lot going on in my mind right now," I say, "and it's all getting mixed up and intense. But I love you, too." The more I say it, the more it feels like I really do mean it. "And I just want to be with you. Is that okay?"

Taryn silently nods. I lean over and touch her cheek as I kiss her.

She kisses me back, and we are at it again, even more charged than before.

I start to pull Taryn back over to my seat. Her hands fumble around with the button of my pants.

There is a *tap tap tap* at my driver's side window.

It startles the crap out of both of us. I turn my head to find a policeman peering in.

Talk about a boner killer.

I push the window button, but it does nothing, and I remember that the car has to be on first.

Car on.

Window down.

"Hello, sir," I say into the scraggly face of this white-haired cop.

"Evening, kids," the cop says, with an annoying grin. "License and registration?" I fish around in my pocket for my wallet and ask Taryn to get the registration out of the glove compartment.

"Um, hi," Taryn says, ignoring my request as she leans forward and tentatively waves at the cop. I hope she's not trying to seduce him to get us out of a ticket, because that could get awkward.

"Oh." The cop looks worried for a second, then his

wrinkly face lights up. "Look who it is! Phil-Phil's little girlfriend!"

"Hey there," Taryn says, radiating discomfort. "Um, Phil and I actually broke up, a while ago."

The cop looks at me and scrunches up his mustache in thought. "Hwell . . . on to the next, right? Heh heh!" He seems disingenuous, like he's putting on some kind of performance for us. "Philip is my grandson," the cop explains in my direction, all of the mirth instantly drained from his voice. "Damn good kid."

Are you kidding me? Of all the cops in town, we get the one who's the grandfather of my girlfriend's ex?

"Of course," I say, angling my head in GrandpaCop's direction without making full-on eye contact. "Yeah, we, uh, run together. Ran together. Like . . . on the team . . ." I trail off pathetically.

"May I?" he says, grabbing the license I've been holding this whole time. "Dinton Little . . ." He pronounces the e in my name like it's an *i*. "Hey, you're that kid who's dying tomorrow, aren't ya? Yeah, here's your deathdate, tomorrow. Sorry to hear that."

I wonder if Phil has told him all the mean things I said at the funeral. "Thank you, sir," I say.

"And you, my sweet," he says, hitching his head to get a better look at Taryn, "are looking lovely as ever. Like a daisy in the summertime."

"Thanks, Grandpa Ford." Ew, she called him Grandpa. And his name is Ford.

"Now. I'm gonna have to ask you to get out of the car, Dinton."

I stop breathing for a few seconds.

"What? Why?"

"Don't worry, I'm not gonna bite ya."

I look over at Taryn. She shrugs.

"I just, uh . . . Don't you need, like, a reason? Or a warrant or something?"

"Well, the government has the deathdate statute, surely you know about that. Gives me the right to search someone within seven days or less of their deathdate, 'case they're planning on committing some crimes before they go. You know, steal some money for their family, that sort of thing. You can look it up on the Net."

"I promise you, I'm not planning—"

"Or," GrandpaCop says, flipping my license through his fingers like in a bad card trick, "you can stay in the car, and I'll take you to jail, spend the night. Maybe you'll die there."

This man is officially horrible. Taryn looks mortified.

I open the door and step out. "Just stand right over here," GrandpaCop says as he shines his light in my eyes, then down my body. "So, got any theories on how you're gonna die?"

"Not really," I say. My eyes land on the gun holstered at his waist.

Trust no one.

"You feeling anything strange now?" GrandpaCop asks, flashing his light around more, giving me a pat-down. "Got a fever or anything?"

"No, I don't think so."

"'Cause sometimes people get sick, get a virus or something, that's how they die."

Is he referring to my splotch? How could he possibly know?

I feel suddenly brave. "Nope, other than being frisked by a cop for no apparent reason, feeling great."

"Huh." GrandpaCop stares at me. "Phil was right about you. Think you're some kind of rebel." So Phil did tell him about me. Great.

"No, sir."

"Well, li'l rebel boy . . ." His hand slowly moves down to his holster. "You seem clean." He rests his hand on his hip. Phew. "You're gonna have to go somewhere else, though, to do whatever it is you two were doing up here—don't worry, I won't tell Phil-Phil." This guy is gross. "'Cause you're trespassing on private property."

"Yeah, okay," I say, getting back in the car, eager to get as far away from here as possible.

"Have a good last night, Dinton," HorribleGrandpaCop says as he hands me back my ID, all soiled with his fingerprints. "A pleasure seeing you, young lady. Drive safe now."

"Bye," Taryn says quietly.

I want to yell, "Suck it, Ford!" as we pull away, but instead I just nod.

The old couch in Taryn's basement isn't quite big enough for both our bodies to lie down on, so my legs are draped off the side. Her legs extend out into the air as she lies on top of me. We are kissing. Passionate, sloppy, end-of-the-world kisses.

Taryn's parents are upstairs watching an NBA play-off game, and we know that they know what we're doing down here. It's not as good as "our spot"—where parents are not within a twenty-foot radius—but it'll do. Taryn's mom insisted we take down some ruffled potato chips and a bowl of onion dip, both of which sit untouched on the coffee table.

That unsettling run-in with Phil's grandfather certainly didn't help my attempts to clear Phil from my mind-palate. Taryn seemed genuinely shocked by the whole thing ("His grandpa always seemed so sweet . . ."), but my paranoid thoughts are running rampant. Did Phil sic his grandpa on me? Was Taryn involved in setting me up? Or is Grandpa-Cop one of the people Brian Blum was warning me about?

"You okay?" Taryn says, lifting her face up away from mine. The welt I gave her earlier is almost gone, just a small raised pink circle.

"Yeah, of course, why?"

"You seem a little out of it. Should we not do this?"

"No, we should, we absolutely should." I pull her face back into mine, but she resists.

"Dent. I really am sorry about Phil." I can tell she means it.

"I know," I say. "Let's not talk about it anymore." And we're making out again.

In our messing around up till now, Taryn and I have pretty much done everything except for sex. But we were both in agreement that we didn't want my death to rush or pressure us into having sex early, that it should happen organically.

In retrospect, this seems really dumb.

We should have had sex, like, one week in, and then maybe we would have had time to get good at it and right now the prospect of doing it wouldn't seem so terrifying. Another plus to this idea is that I would have lost my virginity to Taryn and not to Veronica.

"Whoa," Taryn says. She's just slid my pants off and is staring wide-eyed at my purple, dotted leg.

"Oh. Yeah. That's what I was telling Paolo about in the bathroom."

"What . . . what is it?"

"I dunno. Maybe a blood disorder? I completely understand if you're turned off and don't want to—"

Taryn pushes me back down on the couch and kisses me harder than ever. I feel like that's partly to erase the image of my splotchy leg from her brain, but that's okay.

She takes my tie off as I unbutton and take off my shirt.

I help Taryn slide her dress up and over her head.

I run my fingers up her bare back.

We are nearly naked. I am once again in the present moment.

"Should we . . . ," I ask.

Taryn nods solemnly.

"Okay, let me just . . ." I grab my pants off the floor and dig around until I find my wallet. When I was twelve, I had a camp counselor named Eli who showed us how he always kept a condom in his wallet, and this struck me as the most badass thing ever. This guy was ready to have sex *whenever.* I later learned that it's usually the guys who don't have sex a lot who keep condoms in their wallets, but I could never quite erase from my brain the idea that this is an awesome thing to do.

However, the condom that's been in my wallet for months is no longer there. Because, duh, Denton, you probably used it last night. Feck.

"What are you getting from your wallet?" Taryn asks in a jokingly coy voice. She knows exactly what I'm getting (or trying to get), because she found it in there once, and it's become a running joke between us. Like "Why don't you take your wallet out?" or "Let's go inside and . . . have a look at your wallet."

"I am getting . . ." Stall with a joke! "My school ID out. I'd like one student-priced ticket, please."

Taryn laughs, even though I realize it sounds like I've made some weird prostitute joke.

"What *else* is in your wallet?"

"Well," I say, "I . . . don't know. What else there is. I, ah, this sucks—I think I just threw out the condom last week because it had expired."

"Oh," Taryn says.

"Yeah."

"What do you mean, you think?"

"No, I mean, I know. I threw it out, and I meant to buy a whole box of new ones to replace it, but then I . . . didn't."

"It's the last night of your life, and you don't have a condom on you to have sex for the first time with your girlfriend?"

I make what I believe to be my most charming, adorable face. "No?"

"Denton," Taryn says, and I think she's about to grill me on where that condom actually has gone. "You are incredibly lucky that I happen to have acquired a couple of condoms in case of an emergency not unlike this one." She digs into her purse and pulls one out. "You're an idiot, but you're lucky."

"That's . . . amazing," I say. "Where did you get those?"

"The back of my dad's sock drawer."

"Ew."

"I know, let's not think about that."

"How did you know where your dad keeps his condoms?"

"Eh. Accidentally found them when I was little. Same spot ever since."

"Well."

"Well."

It takes me way too long to open the condom package, and even longer to figure out which side of the condom goes facedown (dickdown?), but four and a half minutes later, we have awkward, sloppy, stupid, extremely exciting (to me, at least) sex, me trying hard not to think about a lot of things, like the purple that consumes my entire right leg, down to and including my toes, and the fact that the prophylactic on my penis was intended to be used by Taryn's dad. Incidentally, I find that thinking about the latter is a wonderful antidote for those moments when I think the sex is on its way to ending too quickly.

It does end too quickly. But I think I've done better than most of the first-time teen dudes in every sex comedy ever, in that I've made it past the two-minute mark. Sweet.

Taryn and I sit side by side on the couch. Naked.

"Well."

"Well."

"That was pretty cool," I say. "Right?"

"Yeah. Really cool, definitely."

I want to ask if I was better than Phil, but that seems really stupid, and I think it would kill the mood.

"You wouldn't know that was your first time at all," Taryn says.

"Oh, cool. Yeah. First time."

SECOND TIME!

"You know, in French," I say, "they call an orgasm *la petite mort,* which is 'little death.' It'll be pretty great if my death feels like that."

I am realizing that when I feel guilty, I start talking nonsense.

"Yeah . . ." Taryn picks up her underwear from the floor and starts getting dressed. I was hoping we'd get to sit naked on the couch a little longer; it's fun. Though maybe gross for the couch.

"So, did you . . ."

"What?"

"Well, did you, like, have a *petite mort*?"

"Oh. No, but I never do." Taryn shrugs, and she slides her dress on over her head.

"What were all those noises you were making, then?"

"Noises?"

"No, I mean, the sounds you were making while we were doing it?"

"Oh, I dunno." Taryn turns slightly red. "I didn't realize they were annoying you."

"They weren't, they weren't. I just thought the sounds meant you were into it."

"I was feeling into it; I just didn't orgasm. It's not a big deal."

But it feels like a big deal, like we haven't done it properly.

"Let's try again," I say. "I can do better." If I really and truly satisfy her, maybe she'll never forget it. Maybe she'll never forget me.

"Denton, you did great, and you don't have time. You're supposed to meet up with Paolo."

"No, no, he can wait, it's fine, really. Wanna do this again?"

Taryn plops down onto the couch next to me, fully

clothed. "I'm not really in the mood, Dent. I love you, but I don't just want to be some sex object so you can feel like you did it correctly."

"That's not it at all. I wanna make you feel good."

Taryn puts her hands on my face. "Denton, you made me feel so good. And you make me feel so good. And I . . ." She starts to cry.

"I know, I know, I won't be able to come to prom, I'm sorry."

"Not that, you just . . ." Taryn wipes her nose with her hand. "You're . . . Oh."

"I'm 'oh'?"

But Taryn is looking at my lower half, transfixed. I want to believe it's because she's awed and astounded by my manhood, which has just rocked her world, but it's pretty clear that isn't the case.

The splotch is again spreading, across my waist, down my left leg, and even, yes, over my manhood.

"Aw, man, it's purpling my balls."

We watch as the ink stain comes to a halt, having given me a strange pair of purple-skin pants. Taryn is a combination of scared, delighted, and grossed out. "This is so weird."

"It's not a big deal. This always happens to me. It's this allergy thing I get in the springtime."

"Really?"

"No!"

I am hyperventilating a little because this creeping discoloration is really freaky. And I'm not ready for it to kill me. I lean back against the couch, feeling the rough stripes of the fabric against my back.

"Well, I don't know," Taryn says. "I thought you might have just put that together."

"No," I say. I'm starting to regain my normal breathing patterns when I look down and see something horrible. Once again, I find myself without words.

"What?" Taryn says, following my sight line down to her thigh.

She shrieks. And rightfully so. Because on her thigh is a reddish-bluish-purplish splotch just like mine.

13

I hide my nakedness behind the couch as Taryn talks up the basement stairs to her parents, who came to check on us when their only daughter started screaming like a lunatic.

"No, we're really okay. Denton played a joke on me, and it scared me more than he meant it to."

Yeah, funny joke, right? I gave Taryn the splotch! Hilarious!

"Denton's okay?" Taryn's mom asks. "He's not . . ."

"Dead? No, he's doing fine."

Attagirl, way to embrace the d-word.

"Don't be rude now, Taryn."

"I'm not being rude, Mom! I'm just being realistic."

But the basement door is already closed.

Taryn pops her head over the sofa, looking down on me in my naked crouch. "I don't know how I played it so cool, because this is really bad! What is this? Are we both dying?"

"No, I don't think so. I mean, you're not dying. Your deathdate isn't for decades—"

"SIX decades!"

"So there you go; you're not dying."

"But don't you think it's a little weird that we had sex and I immediately got this splotch thing that you have?"

Yes. Yes, I do. I think it's very weird. I'm freaking out. I STDed you. I think I STDed you. "No, it's not that weird."

"Do you think it's an STD?"

"No. I don't."

If I were half a man, now would be the time to tell Taryn about Veronica. But I can't. I just can't. It's scummy and embarrassing and hurtful and what the hell did Veronica give me?

Taryn is meticulously examining her splotch, and I notice something.

"You don't have the dots."

"What?" Taryn looks up, hair in her face.

"The little bright red dots that I have. You don't have those."

We sit side by side on the couch and compare our purple skin. My network of electric red dots is bigger than ever, and one touch anywhere on my legs shifts the whole lot of them, still in perfect formation. But Taryn's splotch looks more like an ordinary rash.

"So mine is kinda different," Taryn says.

"Yeah, definitely different."

"Maybe it's just an allergic reaction."

"I bet it is."

Taryn takes two deep breaths, wipes away some tears, and looks at me. "Why are you still naked?"

"It's around here somewhere," Paolo's mom mutters into the pantry.

I'm sitting at Paolo's kitchen table, feeling like I'm eight years old again, the morning after a Pow-Dent sleepover. I'd usually wake up first and pad out to the kitchen table to chat with Paolo's mom as she cooked mind-blowing chocolate chip pancakes.

Currently, though, she's sifting through shelves, looking for some anti-anxiety supplement thing she thinks might help me. (Apparently, I seem anxious. Who knew.) Paolo isn't home yet. He's off working on "a surprise" for me. A sweet gesture, but unless it's some kind of life-lengthening elixir, I don't think I'm interested.

"Aha!" she says. "Here it is."

"So, it's like Xanax, or something?"

"Gosh, no, I wouldn't give you that garbage. This is herbal, from my homeopath." Paolo's mom turns around, a proud smile on her face, unscrewing the lid on a white container. "Take two. They will absolutely make you feel better."

"Okay, thanks," I say, downing the pills with a swig of water. I do feel better, almost immediately.

"Right?" Paolo's mom says to me.

"Yeah, those are amazing."

"Picture?" she asks as she grabs her digital camera off the counter. She hardly goes anywhere without her camera.

"Oh, ha-ha, sure." I smile from my place at the kitchen table as the flash burns my retinas.

"It's a keeper," she says, looking down at the screen.

She stares at it intently, and I see her tear up a little bit, which catches me off guard. I feign a sudden interest in the plaque above the sink that says THE DIAZ FAMILY.

"Mom, didn't we talk about this?" Paolo says as he appears in the kitchen, a big plastic bag in his hand. "How we're gonna limit the number of cries per day?"

"I know, I know." Paolo's mom sniffles. "Just thinking about you two, how much fun you used to have . . . One quick picture, then I'll leave you boys alone." She snaps a shot of me and Paolo smiling uncomfortably. "Denton, you are a gem. I'll see you at your Sitting."

As she heads out of the kitchen, Veronica heads in, and my insides leap. Mother and daughter narrowly avoid bumping into each other before Veronica sees me in the kitchen and changes her direction.

"You can come in here," I call out to her, but I know she won't.

"Don't mind her," Paolo says, reaching down into his big bag. "She's been superweird since your funeral. I think she's gonna miss saying mean things to you."

"Yeah, maybe."

"That, or she's moping about being apart from her boyfriend."

"Wait, Veronica's got a boyfriend?"

"You know, some college thing. Okay, so I have in this bag a final parting gift for you. Ready?" He unfolds this huge rectangular cloth canvas, which he's covered with photos and images and his signature awesome cartoon drawings. When I look closely, I see that it's got references to all these different moments and events in my life, to movies I love, to inside jokes we've had.

"Wow. This is amazing."

"I know, right? It's for your coffin."

"Oh. That's why it's shaped like that."

"Yeah, yeah."

I don't like thinking about my body underground in a coffin, even with this amazing me-collage on top of it. It's still preferable to cremation, though. Body burned into nothingness? No thanks!

"Thanks, Pow."

"On to more important things: you and Taryn get nasty again?"

"We . . . did." Unlike Paolo, who's pretty graphic in describing his sexual adventures, I'm not much of a kiss-and-teller. It makes me uncomfortable, like I'm exposing my most vulnerable self in casual conversation. Not to mention that Veronica could be overhearing everything we're saying. I should at least throw Paolo something. "And it was good."

"Just good?"

"It was great, okay? But then . . ."

I tell Paolo about the splotch that was on Taryn, how freaked she was, and how—with an awkward kiss and a "See you at my Sitting"—I had to leave her mid-freak-out to come here.

"Holy crap, dude, that sucks."

"I know."

"She really did STD you!"

"Or maybe I gave something to her." I sigh. I walk to the fridge, all nervous energy, and take inventory, hoping for some kind of cranberry juice.

"No, man, I mean—just finished the cran-apple this

morning, sorry, hombre—maybe she gave it to you yester-day!"

"Right. Look . . . Taryn and I didn't sleep together yes-terday."

"You didn't?"

"We didn't."

"Did you have sex today?"

"We did."

"But not yesterday."

"Not yesterday."

Paolo has plopped down at the kitchen table, thinking really hard about all this.

"You said you had sex yesterday, though."

"Well . . . I did have sex yesterday."

Paolo is thoughtful, then astounded. "Dude . . ." He is speaking very quietly. "Are you telling me you got yourself a prostitute?" He mouths the word *prostitute*.

"No! What? No!"

"You said you had sex that wasn't with Taryn, so I don't know!"

"Okay, okay, look, I wasn't gonna tell you this, but I had sex with . . ." I shake my head toward the kitchen door twice.

"Why are you jerking your head around like that? I can't understand what you're saying."

"No, look at me, I had sex with . . ." And I again give my head two violent shakes toward the living room as I simultaneously point with my finger.

"No . . . ," Paolo mutters.

I shrug.

"You did it with my mom?" Paolo whispers.

I'm about to violently disagree when the door opens and Paolo's mom walks in.

"Sorry to interrupt again. Left some work stuff in here."

Paolo is completely still as she rifles through a stack of papers near the phone. "Oh," he says. "Cool. Yeah."

He stares at me with a mixture of discomfort, disgust, and awe.

"Got it," Paolo's mom says, holding a notebook. "So serious in here."

She walks out.

"Wow," Paolo says, shaking his head in wonder. "You could cut that sexual tension with a knife! Can't believe I never noticed it. I mean, it makes sense in a way. I could see myself doing it with your mom if she weren't married."

"Whoa, whoa, stop, stop. Ew, man."

"Oh, so you can do it with my mom"—Paolo realizes how loud he's being and reins it in—"but when I even *mention* returning the favor with yours, you get all squirmish."

"*Squirmish* is not a word, and I absolutely did NOT do it with your mom. Geez, dude, give me some credit here."

Question marks hover over Paolo's head. "You didn't do it with my mom?"

"No."

"Oh, so what was all the—" Paolo stops short, looking as if he's just seen someone rub feces on his bike. "Veronica."

I grimace.

"My pure sister, Veronica . . ."

"I'm sorry, dude."

"Tainted. By you."

"Okay, let's not—"

"Oh man . . ."

"Is this weird?"

"A little!" Paolo's eyes bug out for a second like a cartoon.

"Weirder than me doing your mom?"

"Uh, yeah. It's my sister!"

"Okay, well, your logic system is different than mine, but in any case, I'm sorry. To be completely honest, I don't even remember it happening."

Which, I have to say, is quickly becoming one of the great tragedies of my life. I'm harboring all the guilt and shame of being a cheater without any of the awesome memories of the sex itself.

"You don't even remember? Wait. I was with you the whole time Veronica was here, then my mom drove you home."

"What? No, man. I woke up in *your house* this morning."

"This house?"

"Yeah."

"Shame on you, dude!"

"I'm sorry!"

"So you came back?"

"I don't remember getting in your mom's car in the first place." Do I? There's a fuzzy memory trying to make itself known in my brain.

"Look, all I know is I said good night to you and my mom and went to sleep as you guys were heading out the front door. Right after you made those prank calls."

"Prank calls?"

"You gotta remember that! You called almost every pizza place in town, said you were a state official and that pizza was being banned? Enzo was really upset."

"Enzo of Enzo's Pizza?"

"Yeah, dude. It was amazing." Paolo takes out a pack of clove cigarettes, pops one in his mouth, and lights it up right there in the kitchen. It's a little startling, as it's a new habit.

"You're allowed to smoke in the house?"

"I guess so," he says, and I'm suddenly impressed that, considering how much his mom spoils him, Paolo didn't grow up to be more of a dick. "Just like you were allowed to stay here so you could bang my sister."

"Paolo, I'm sorry, really."

"And *then* you banged Taryn today! It's like, that's not right, you know?" He gestures frenetically with his clove. "Messing around with my sister's heart."

"She seems to be doing fine, Pow. She doesn't even wanna look at me."

"Yeah, 'cause her heart's been messed with!"

"But she's got some boyfriend, so who cares? I mean, what about my heart, you know? Which, may I add, won't be beating for much longer?"

Paolo exhales a stream of sweet-smelling clove smoke. "It's okay, D. I'm just joking around."

But I'm not sure if he is, and frankly, I don't think he knows either.

"I don't mean to get all worked up about this," Paolo says. "Maybe it's just because Veronica's always had a crush on you for, like, forever."

"Really?" Whoa. My heartbeat quickens.

"Nah, of course not really."

"Oh."

"I always thought she genuinely hated you, actually. That's why this is so shocking. You want one of these?"

"No thanks. Trying to stay substance-free for my last hours so I can die in a clear-minded state." Also, cloves give me a headache.

"I hear ya. Definitely not the way I'm gonna do it, though. I have the total opposite philosophy." He drops his voice to a conspiratorial whisper. "I might try to OD, bro."

"I hope you're kidding."

Paolo raises his eyebrows and shrugs while inhaling his clove. The multitasking throws him off, and he has a coughing fit.

"Anyone dying in there?" Paolo's mom shouts from the hall.

"Nope, all good," I say.

Paolo takes a sip of my water. "Hey," he says. "Are you supersure you wanna remain substance-free?"

"Yeah, no clove for me."

"I'm not talking about a clove. I'm talking about this little friend I brought." He says the last part in a high-pitched funny voice as he opens up the pack to reveal a joint nestled in cozily amongst the cloves. "You did my sister, dude, you owe me at least a hit."

I first smoked pot a few months ago. It's fine, but I don't think it works on me. I end up sitting there asking "Wait, so what did you say it should feel like?" way too many times.

"You're actually guilting me into doing this?"

"I dunno, you actually did my sister, so . . ."

"All right, all right, fine, one hit."

"Hooray!" he says in the high-pitched voice, pulling the joint out and making it soar over our heads like a rocket ship. "Wheeeeee!"

"But I've got some serious stuff I wanna talk to you about, so don't get too high. And I wanna get back to my house a bit before midnight so I can talk to my dad."

"Cooly, let's head out to W-Town. Lemme take a whiz and grab my bowl." W-Town is short for WoodsTown, the name we invented for this spot in the woods behind Paolo's house. (And, yes, I have a special hangout spot with both my girlfriend and my best friend. Joke away.)

"Why do you need your bowl? You have the joint."

"Extra for me. Hee hee! Could you be a dear and grab a paper clip from my mom's office? For bowl-cleaning purposes? Thank you forever!" Paolo says in a goofy voice as he closes the bathroom door behind him.

I walk down the hall to Paolo's mom's office. No one responds when I knock on the door, so I let myself in.

Before Paolo got his own computer, he and I used to spend hours in here playing on his mom's computer, random games and stupid instant-message conversations. It's pretty much how I remember it, except that it seems smaller now. There's a huge shelf of books, a desk with a computer, and a large filing cabinet next to that. Paolo's mom works as the librarian at Bridge Road Elementary, one of the two grade schools in our town, and when I was young, I never fully understood why an elementary school librarian needed a full office. Now I get that this is probably less of a work-related room and more of a place where Paolo's mom can be alone with her thoughts and pay bills or whatever it is adult people need to get done.

She's an impressive lady, having raised Paolo and Veronica totally on her own. No one talks about Paolo's dad much, but from the little information I've gathered, I know that he left Paolo's mom before Veronica had turned one and before Paolo was even born. Lame. Paolo's mom has had boyfriends over the years, but none of them have stuck around all that long. The sadness of the entire situation is hitting me for the first time.

My eye is drawn to a spot above her computer where a cat calendar is hanging from the wall. The month of May features a fuzzy black-and-white cat looking out from under a piano bench, but what really gets my attention are the two red circles around tomorrow's date. Paolo's mom has emphatically marked my deathdate, though she hasn't written anything inside the circles. Maybe she's being respectful, or maybe it was just too painful to write the words out.

I flip away from my red death circles and, sure enough, on the next month there's a circle in blue for Paolo's deathdate. Geez. Why my death gets two circles in red and Paolo's only one in blue is anybody's guess, but either way, color-coding our deathdates seems pretty morbid. Adjacent to the calendar, I see a framed picture of me and Paolo at age seven or eight. It's us in the front yard with our arms around each other's shoulders, looking really happy.

This office is bumming me out.

I refocus on my task of finding a paper clip. Seeing none on the desk, I pull out its wide metal drawer, which contains a meticulously arranged carnival of office supplies.

The rectangular container of paper clips is easy to find, smack-dab in the center of the festivities, and I grab one, then two to be safe, and start to head out of the office.

But, as I do, I see the filing cabinet, and I stop in my tracks.

The hefty bottom drawer is slightly ajar. This is unusual. Highly unusual.

That bottom drawer is a thing of legend for me and Paolo. Because it's always locked. As long as I've known Paolo, as many times as I've been in this office, that drawer, the Bottom Drawer, has been unbreachable without a key, which we've never had.

"Stuff for work," Paolo's mom would say in response to our daily interrogations about what she kept in there. "Boring grown-up stuff."

We, of course, had our own theories, which changed and evolved as we did:

"She's totally a spy. All her spy papers and maps are in there, including lists of people she's killed."

"I think there's a Komodo dragon in there. They're illegal to have as a pet because they're almost extinct. Remember that time we thought we heard a noise coming from inside it?"

"I bet she keeps pictures of my dad in there, and old letters from him, so when she's alone, she can read them and look at them and cry without me and V being around."

"Maybe it's where she keeps her supply of dildos and vibrators."

We were in high school for this last one. It was funny, but after we'd laughed about it for fifteen seconds, it dawned on both of us that it might be the most accurate theory of all. We haven't talked about that drawer much since.

And now it's open.

I have to look. Even if it is an invasion of privacy, it feels like the universe has given me this gift for a reason, helping me unravel one of life's Huge Mysteries before I'm gone.

I grab the drawer's front handle and pull it open. My heart starts beating a little faster, and a line of sweat drips down my temple. My body understands what a big deal this is.

But I'm instantly disappointed to see that, after all this time, all this anticipation, the drawer is filled with . . . file folders. Of course it is. I feel stupid that we ever thought otherwise.

I open the first one—why not?—and see a photocopied reader's guide for some kids' book called *Jumping Jimmy and the Bean Factory.*

My excitement has deflated like a sad balloon, and now I'm just going through the motions, looking through the second and third and fourth file folders, all filled with reader's guides for stupidly named kids' books. *Denton Little and the Disappointing Drawer.* Just as I decide to stop wasting valuable life minutes and shut the drawer, something decidedly non-reader's-guidey blurs past my vision. I realize I have hit a whole section of file folders with a new weight and heft to them.

It's an old photo of a baby in blue, presumably a little boy, asleep in his crib. Great, we've got reader's guides and baby pictures of Paolo, what an exciting revelation.

But as I take in the photo, I see that the baby's skin

is lighter than Paolo's. And I notice a familiar friend lying right next to him.

Blue Bronto. My old stuffed companion, adorably and unmistakably himself, only brand-new instead of worn-out and raggedy.

The baby in the picture isn't Paolo. It's me.

I flip to the next photo. It's a picture of my dad holding me when I was a baby.

Why are these in here?

I start rapidly flipping through the photos stacked behind this one. They're all photos of me, some as a baby, some not, many also featuring my dad.

"Hey, Dent, you need something?"

The interruption catches me by total surprise. I bang my wrist against the cold metal of the filing cabinet, dropping both of the previously procured paper clips as I do so.

"Ah no, no, sorry, I was just looking for a paper clip," I say as I slide the drawer shut, stand up, and turn around to face Paolo's mom. Part of me wants to ask why the hell she's got pics of me and my dad in her office, but a larger part feels embarrassed that I was snooping through her stuff in the first place and would prefer to let the whole thing slide by, passed gas that everyone tacitly agrees to ignore.

"Oh, well, you're not gonna find a paper clip in there. That's just boring work stuff, you know that."

Boring work stuff, right. I'm reading Paolo's mom's face like I'm looking for Waldo, trying to spot any hint of nervousness, weirdness, or discomfort, but she's as cool as ever, no red-and-white-striped nerd here.

"Of course, yeah, I wasn't even thinking. You know, my mind's in a zillion places right now."

"I know, honey, I know," she says, stepping quickly past me to her desk drawer, where she pulls out a paper clip. "Here you go."

"Thanks."

"You okay?"

"Yup!" I'm all smiles. "Thanks again for those pills."

"Anytime."

We stand there for a moment, staring at each other.

"Okay, well, I'm gonna get going. Me and Paolo are gonna take a drive before my Sitting."

"All righty, you boys be careful." She taps her fingers on the desk twice. "I'll see you later tonight, Denton."

"Sounds good," I say. As I leave the office, I try to distract myself from thinking about those baby pics by glancing at my phone. It's 10:13. One hour and forty-seven minutes before DeathTime commences. Better make 'em good.

There is no question that I am high right now.

Everything is hilarious. I can't stop smiling.

I was only planning on taking the one hit, but a sister-related guilt trip from your best friend can be a powerful thing, and somehow one spun into two and then five, and I really didn't think pot even worked on me, but now I'm holding Paolo's bowl and lighter, even though I don't remember him passing them.

"So, wait, this guy at the funeral knew your real mom?" Paolo asks, one hand on his hip and one sneaker resting on a gray tree, lodged in the V-shaped intersection where branch meets trunk.

"Yeah, that's what he— What are you doing?" I ask. The crook is kinda high off the ground, and Paolo's position looks uncomfortable.

"Relaxing, dude. Finish your story."

"Oh, so, yeah, this guy says he knew my mom and I should call him if anything strange happens."

"What the eff . . . You should call him and be like, 'So, something strange happened. I bumped into this weird guy at my funeral, dude. Oh, wait, it was YOU.'"

I'm cracking up, even though there's a small part of my brain that is scolding me for recklessly ditching my substance-free plan. I've got a lot to accomplish in the last hours of my life, but right now it all seems funny. "How long will I feel high for?"

"Eh, not too long. Two hours? Three?"

"Oh wow," I say. If I want to talk to my dad before midnight, I'm still gonna be high. I shift the bowl and lighter into one hand and take out my phone to check the exact time. I am greeted by two texts that I've missed during my highness.

The first is from Taryn: *Sorry I totally freaked. It'll be ok tho, right? Miss you. Hey to Pow. See ya soon.*

The second is from my stepmom: *Just ceking in to mak sore u r ok. Pleaase be Hume by 1145. If u go outside wear bug spry. Luv u too much. xxoxoox.*

The texts remind me that there are these other people in my life. People who love me and stuff. But their messages don't exactly feel real. What are text messages anyway? People push buttons on tiny machines to form words that are placed side by side to form sentences, which—

"Everything okay over there?"

I look up, startled. Paolo is now situated on a tree stump, meticulously repacking the colorful glass bowl. "What? Yeah."

"You've been standing there staring at your phone for at least ten minutes."

"Oh. Really?"

"Yeah," Paolo laughs. "I asked you to pass me the bowl, like, five times. I got up and got it myself."

"Sorry. My mom wanted to make sure I'm wearing bug spray."

Paolo passes me the newly packed bowl.

"Man, I can't get any higher," I say. "I need to talk to my dad, remember? To ask him about all this stuff with my mom."

"Whatever you need, bro. It's your deathdate," Paolo says.

I take out my phone and tap out quick *Thanks, I love you*s in response to both texts. It's trippy that the same message is a perfectly appropriate response for my stepmom and my girlfriend. How can that be? It seems like—

"Helloooo," Paolo says, followed by a quick whistle.

I've spaced again. I've lost all sense of time.

A glance at my phone reveals that it is now 11:17. We should head out in fifteen minutes or so.

"So," Paolo says. "I know you're gonna talk to your dad—he's such a sparkling conversationalist, I'm sure that'll go great—but for reals, how come you haven't called that guy from your funeral yet? Like, if he actually knew your real mom, wouldn't you wanna talk to him?"

"Ahhh man, no, I never got the number. My stepmom intercepted it." In the distance, we hear a police siren. "But, okay, check this out: he also said I shouldn't trust anybody, even government people, and then me and Taryn were at that spot we always park at, and this suspicious cop appeared and examined me and shit!"

"What? That's insane!"

"I know! And you know who the cop was?"

"Someone famous?"

"No. What? Why would . . . It was Phil's grandpa."

"Whoa."

"Yeah."

"That must have been the oldest cop you've ever seen."

"I mean, yeah, he's, like, in his sixties, but that wasn't really my point."

Paolo lights the bowl once more, inhales. "Phil sent his grandpa out to, like, check on you guys. That's so messed up."

"Yeah, that was my point. You think that's possible?"

Paolo exhales a thick cloud of gray. "No such thing as coincidence, bro." He loves to get all mystic spiritual. Especially when he's smoking.

"Hey, I did solve another mystery, though." It's out before I'm even aware of what I'm saying, as if my mouth has made the decision to speak before consulting my brain. "I saw what was in the Bottom Drawer."

"Ha. Yeah, right," says Paolo as he smacks a gnat on his forearm.

"No . . . really."

"You saw what was in the Bottom Drawer?"

"Yes."

"*The* Bottom Drawer? In my mom's office?"

"Yes."

"No, you didn't. That thing's been locked my whole life. When?"

"Just now, when I went to get a paper clip. It was open a little bit, so I looked. And then your mom walked in."

I have Paolo's full attention. "What? Do you know how much time I've invested in trying to see what's in that drawer? And now you just walk in and it's open? What the hell was in there?"

"There were some reader's guides for kids' books. And then also . . ."

"Porn, right? A crazy amount of power dildos, right? You can tell me, dude."

"No, no. What are power dildos? I only got to look for a second, but there were a bunch of baby pictures. Of me. In there. Also pics of my dad."

"Baby pictures of . . . What the hell?"

There is a sharp twig snap to my left, which momentarily freaks the hell out of me. It's Veronica, making her way to where we are in the woods, looking as wonderful as usual.

"Can I talk to you for a minute?" Veronica says to me, clearly displeased. (What else is new?)

"What are you doing out here, V-card?" Paolo says. "This is our last chill time. You and Denton should work out your drama later."

She shoots Paolo a sisterly death stare. "Why don't you smoke some more, kill off a few additional brain cells? This'll be quick."

"It doesn't actually kill brain cells; those studies are complete BS. And even if they're not, I only got a month of life left, so how many brain cells do I really need?"

"Apparently not many. Can we talk?" And Veronica is once again blazing her fiery brown orbs into mine.

"Yeah, sure, of course."

She motions for me to follow her and grab her hand, so I do, feeling excited that things are again good between us and all my stupid mistakes are water under the bridge.

"Be quick," Paolo shouts. "Denton needs to be back soon."

As Veronica wriggles out of my grip, I understand that she hadn't actually been gesturing for me to hold her hand. Whoops. But she extracts her hand in a subtle way, like she doesn't want to hurt my feelings, and it gives me an odd kind of hope.

I've never been one of those dudes who're always checking out girls' asses and stuff, but as I follow her deeper into the woods, it's practically impossible not to look. She's wearing these dark blue jeans and a bright yellow T-shirt that accentuate all the curves of her body. Unlike Taryn, who is an inch taller than me and fairly skinny—a pretty flamingo—Veronica is on the shorter side, with more meat on her bones. A sultry bunny.

"Stop looking at my butt," Veronica says without looking back.

"Oh, sorry. I mean, I wasn't."

"Sure."

I have trouble embracing my primal male instincts. Even now, with mere minutes of guaranteed life left, I'm simultaneously feeling guilty about betraying Taryn and like I could never be man enough for Veronica.

"Hey, I know you want some private time with the dude of the hour, but how far are you taking us?"

She stops short and turns toward me. "This'll do." We're at least one hundred feet away from Paolo, but I can still sorta see him if I look through the trees.

Veronica looks at me, unsmiling. "Take off your pants."

Well, that's not what I expected her to say. "Ah, look, I already cheated on Taryn once, and I feel like—"

"I'm serious. Take off your pants."

"Um, do you at least first wanna talk about what happened between us last night . . . ?"

"No. Now."

I look toward Paolo's section of the woods, thinking maybe I can use him as an excuse not to disrobe, but he's smoking his bowl and looking in the opposite direction.

"Come on," Veronica adds for good measure.

"Okay, okay. I didn't realize you were such a dominatrix."

I pull off my Pumas, chuck them to the side, undo my belt, and pull off the jeans I'd changed into after leaving Taryn's, exposing my blueberry legs to the world once more.

"Whoa." Veronica stares, transfixed. "Paolo told me it was only on one leg."

All of my sexual fantasies evaporate as I realize Veronica just wants to get a look at my splotch legs. I don't have time for this. Standing in front of her in only my boxers and a T-shirt is still pretty sexy, though.

"Yeah, well, it got worse. What do you care?"

"What do I care?" Before I can process what's happening, Veronica slides off her jeans, and it is so surprising and exciting that my body automatically reacts. I awkwardly adjust my boxers so it's less obvious.

But then I get it. This is not a sexual overture. Veronica's right leg is fully submerged in purple.

"Oh no no no, you too?"

"Yes, me too. What the hell is this?"

"I dunno. I kinda thought you gave it to me last night."

"You thought I gave this to you? No way. NO WAY."

"Okay, hold on, let me look at it." I move closer to inspect Veronica's leg. It isn't lost on me that this is the second pair of exposed lady legs I've stared at in the past few hours. I'm momentarily distracted by a small patch of scar tissue on her knee. Maybe she fell off her bike when she was little.

"Well?" Veronica asks from above me.

"Yeah, I mean, it's the same thing I have, but you don't have the red dots."

"What do you mean? Lemme see."

And then she's crouching down in her T-shirt and underwear and looking intently at my right leg. Even though the context is all wrong, this does approximate some fantasies I may or may not have had.

"Can I touch it?" Veronica asks.

Please! Yes! Touch me! "Sure, feel free."

Veronica strokes my leg with her index finger, and the brigade of red dots shifts as usual, but really, who cares about that. This is the sexiest moment of my life.

"Wow, they move."

"Yeah." There's been a subtle shift between us. It feels like we have some unspoken connection, and the air is thick with possibility.

"But I don't have them."

"No."

"Your legs are really hairy."

"I know."

"And the purple stuff is just on your legs?"

"Yeah, up to my waist."

This time, she doesn't even ask permission, she just delicately lifts my shirt up a little bit.

Best day ever. (Not really. I'm about to die.) (But sorta.)

"Um . . . ," Veronica says as she stares at my torso, and I again try to subtly shift my position so my erection is less blatant. "It's not just up to your waist."

"What?" I say, laughing because I think she might be flirting with me.

"It's higher than that."

I take my eyes off Veronica's dark hair and look at my body. Sure enough, the splotch has consumed all of my stomach and the top of it is hovering on my chest, right below my nipples.

"And so it is," I say. I feel oddly Zen about the whole thing, as if it's always been my destiny to slowly turn purple. Or maybe that's just the pot speaking.

Veronica looks up at me. "What do you think this is? Am I dying, too? And why do you have those red dots when I don't?"

"I really have no idea, but I don't think you're dying. It was the same with Taryn's."

Once again, the words are out of my mouth before I even realize I've said them.

"Wait, who? Taryn? She has one of these, too? Oh, now this is lame. This is so lame. You passed us this nasty purple thing by having sex with both of us. What the hell?"

"Honestly, wait, no, I don't know if that's actually what's happening."

"Well, it doesn't take some kind of rocket genius to figure it out!"

"Rocket genius?"

"Hey, deaf people," Paolo says as he emerges from between two trees. "We have to— Ohmigod. Oh geez!" He turns his head away from the sight of Veronica crouched down at my knees. "What the hell, Dent! Instead of hanging out with me, you're getting a beejer from my sister. Mad props, but also: so uncool!"

Veronica has snapped up out of her crouching position like some kind of attack cobra, the top of her skull whacking into my lower jaw. I bite my tongue, hard. It hurts.

"I was not giving this slut a beejer, okay?" Veronica says, quickly pulling up her jeans. "And next time, maybe you should give some kind of heads-up instead of barging in on us."

"You can't 'barge into' a patch of space in a forest, okay? You need a door to 'barge in.' "

"Shut up, Paolo."

"You shut up, V."

I grab my phone out of my pocket, hoping that we'll still be able to make it to the Sitting in time for me to talk to my dad. Once I click off the notification of nine missed calls, five texts, and four voice mails, however, I realize that we will definitely not be making it to the Sitting early. Or even on time.

I look to Paolo and Veronica, panic in my eyes. They're still midbicker.

"Hey!" I shout, my tongue throbbing. "Wer lay!"

"Huh?" Paolo says.

"Ith twell-oh-two."

"Oh shoot."

Paolo and Veronica stare at me as if I'm about to keel over and die any minute.

An owl hoots.

It's officially my deathdate.

15

"You sure you're good to drive?" Paolo asks.

We're in Danza (that's my car's name), Veronica in the front seat and a visibly antsy Paolo in back, his head popping Whac-a-Mole-style between ours.

"Yeah, no, I mean, I love to drive, and this is kinda my last chance, so yeah. I'm good."

"Oookay," Paolo says, "you the boss."

My driving is admittedly not at its best right now. I keep speeding up because I'm late for my own Sitting, but then I remember that (a) I could get pulled over (which may or may not involve another encounter with Horrible-GrandpaCop) or (b) I could get in an accident and die. So then I slow down.

Speed up.

Panic.

Slow down.

Panic.

Repeat.

I lean my head toward Veronica and look into the rear-view. "Hey, um, could you guys be keeping an eye out for things that could kill me?"

"Sure," Veronica says. "There's something on your legs. That might kill you. And then it might kill me."

"Right, right, again, really sorry. But that's not what I meant. Like, outside stuff. Since I'm officially able to die now."

"Oh, is it your deathdate or something? Gee, I had no idea."

"You got it, D," Paolo says, rotating back and forth from one car window to the other. "No killy stuff as of yet."

We pass Tensmore Shopping Center, and I see a few kids I know from school loitering in the parking lot near Harold's Bagels. I'm gonna miss those bagels.

"While I have you both here," Paolo says. "V, Dent has informed me of your intimate time together last night. Very interesting turn of events. When were you planning on bringing me up to speed on this?"

"Ohmigod," Veronica says, shaking her head. "I guess, P, I was thinking I'd tell you once you sprouted your first pube."

"Really?" Paolo asks. "Well, joke's on you, because I have tons of pubes!"

"Eugh," Veronica says, looking out the window in disgust. "Whoa. Cop."

I glance at the rearview.

A cop is indeed tailing us. Well, at least it's possible that he's tailing us. It's also possible the cop just happens to be driving behind us. In my ten months of licensed driving, this paradox has consistently caused me to lose my shit.

More than once, I've turned into a random driveway just so a cop car could pass me.

"Stay calm, Dent," Paolo says, his face near my ear.

"DUDE," I say. "Could you put your freakin' seat belt on?"

"Yeah, yeah, all right, all right," Paolo says, buckling up.

I try to see if it's HorribleGrandpaCop driving, but right at that moment the cop car switches lanes, passes us, and speeds away.

Phew.

I turn to Veronica, my whole being flooded with relief. "Whew, that got tense. And, of course, cops always spee—"

"D!" Paolo says. "KILLY STUFF! KILLY STUFF!"

Within a single second, my brain spins through a rapid series of thoughts that goes something like, *Why is he shouting nonsense oh maybe he's actually yelling about something in the road shoot I'm not looking at the road look at the road moron oh no this is it this is how I die this is it,* and I do look at the road, but it's too late. Something blurs across my field of vision, and I'm pushing on the brakes, but there's a dull thud as the car comes into contact with the tail end of the blur.

We screech to a halt.

"Holy shit," Veronica says.

"Are you guys okay?" I ask.

"I don't think it's us you should be worried about," Paolo answers.

"What was that? Did you guys see what that was? A deer?" I ask.

"I don't think so, dude."

"Oh man. Okay, okay."

"You want me to go out and look?" Veronica asks.

"Should we?"

"Nah, maybe the last big event of your life should be a hit-and-run; that's actually pretty fun."

"Okay, thank you for that, Veronica, I'll go look."

"I'm coming, too," says Paolo.

"We're kind of right in the middle of the road, so—"

I am out of the car before I hear the end of Veronica's sentence.

You know that feeling the moment after a glass slips out of your hand, when you're watching it fall, almost in slow motion, as you tell yourself you're an idiot and wait to see if it breaks or not? That is right now, and my eyes peer through the semidarkness to see if I've broken something. Or someone.

The night is warm, but there's a slight chill. Which might just be the chill of death. I wish I was joking. Sterrick Road is mainly residential, lots of trees and houses, and it's a road I know well because we're actually very close to my house. As I start to cross in front of Danza, a burst of air rockets at me from the left.

"DENTON, HEADS UP. MORE KILLY!" Paolo shouts.

I fall over to the right, landing on Danza's hood, as a sporty yellow car speeds by, barely missing me. I lie back and breathe deep.

That was almost it.

If my deathdate is going to be filled with a series of anxiety-provoking car crashes and narrow escapes from death, I may opt to end my life myself.

"HEY, DICKHEAD! THIS IS A THIRTY-FIVE-MILE-PER-HOUR ZONE! Thirty-five!" Paolo yells at the rapidly disappearing yellow car. "Dent, you okay?"

"Yeah, all good," I say. "Gettin' a little tired of you yelling warnings at me, but all good."

"I could *not* yell them if you want."

"You okay?" Veronica has popped open her door and is looking over it at us. "That guy was going crazy fast."

"All good," I say.

"Glad somebody is."

For a second, I'm indignant that Veronica has said this, but then I realize it wasn't her. The quiet female voice has come from the darkness to our right.

"Hello?" I say.

"Hello," the voice answers.

I slide off the hood and move with quick but cautious steps toward the source of these words, Paolo and Veronica backing me up. The first thing I see—in fact, nearly trip over—is a half-mangled purple bike lying on its side in the grass, its rear wheel jutting out unnaturally, its back reflector smashed.

The second thing I see is Millie Pfefferkorn.

She is wearing an American flag bicycle helmet and lying on her back, her arms stretched out way above her head, her legs extending forward in the grass as far as they can.

"I'm stretching," she says.

"Holy crap, Millie, you're what I hit?"

"I think *I'm* who *you hit* is the more accurate phrasing."

"Geez, I could have killed you! I'm so sorry."

"Maybe, yeah."

"Maybe? When's your deathdate?"

"Dunno."

"Ohmigod, that's right. You're undated." I feel silly having forgotten this, considering it was such a source of fascination to me when we were growing up. I couldn't believe she didn't know when she'd die. "Man, you gotta pay attention when you're on that thing. What are you doing biking around after midnight on a Thursday night anyway?"

"What are you doing driving around after midnight on your deathdate?" Millie grins, pulls out of the stretch, and sits up on her elbows. "You're late for your Sitting."

"Yes, thank you, I know. Are you okay?"

"Yeah, I'm fine. Hey, Paolo. Hey, Veronica."

"Uh, hi, Millie."

"Yeah, hey."

But Millie isn't entirely fine. There's a gash on her right leg, blood trickling down to her ankle. I guess I should be happy that it's a gash and not a splotch like every other girl around me seems to be developing, but still.

"Millie, you're bleeding."

"I'm fine." She stands up, adjusting her denim skirt and yellow T-shirt, which has a huge beagle's head on it. I've always thought Millie is one of those people who try a little too hard to be quirky, but this outfit kinda works. Minus the patriotic helmet, maybe.

"Look, I feel terrible. Come back to my house. My mom will be able to fix you up real good. Okay?"

"But it's your Sitting. And I'm not invited. I'm really fine. I landed in the grass. It's not a big deal."

"Your leg is kinda narsty, babe," Paolo says.

"Yes. Agreed. I officially invite you to my Sitting, Millie. Now get in the car. We'll throw your bike in the trunk."

So she does and we do, and now we are a party of four, driving the final minute or so to my house. By this point, it is 12:33 in the a.m., and we have officially crossed over from Pretty Late to Very Late. I stopped paying attention to the buzzing in my pocket many minutes ago, and I'm not looking forward to the moment we drive up. "I feel it might be awkward with me at your Sitting," Millie says from the backseat as she stares out her window.

"Seeing as we're gathering together to wait for my death, I think there will be plenty of other awkwardness to distract us. I wouldn't worry about it."

"Yeah, what he said," Paolo agrees.

"Okay. Any of you guys want some Gushers?"

We approach my house, me for the last time, and I pull alongside the curb into Danza's classic parking spot. Out of the corner of my eye, I can see a cluster of people waiting on the front steps for me, but my anxiety has fired back up, so I don't want to look at them yet.

I shift the car into park.

I turn the key in the ignition.

I breathe deep.

I look to my right, hoping to exchange one last dramatic look with Veronica, maybe one that nonverbally conveys everything that needs to be said. But she is halfway out the door. As is Paolo.

"She already left," Millie says from the backseat.

I look in the rearview. "Thanks, Millie. Very helpful."

I stare forward at the cul-de-sac that I know so well.

"You thinking about Fog?"

"No, not really. I'm just taking a moment here."

"Word."

Millie doesn't give any sign that she'll be leaving the car anytime soon.

"Your family is outside waiting for you, by the way. On the steps."

I ignore her.

"Also your girlfriend. What's her name again . . . Tara?"

Millie grins that grin of hers.

"Yeah. Exactly, Molly."

It appears Millie isn't budging, so I say a silent goodbye to Danza (*You have been a very awesome car. Thank you for everything, my friend*), open my door, and step outside.

My stepmom nearly tackles me. "Where have you been? Where have you been?" she says, her face buried in my shoulder. "I didn't know where you were, you weren't answering my texts, I thought you were gone, my Denton gone." She trails off into quiet sobs.

Well, I feel like a dick.

She pulls back, her hands on my shoulders, the usual drill.

"Don't you *ever* do that again." She is looking at me in a way she never has before, a combination of the strictest look she's ever given me, plus tears, plus so much love. It gets me right in the gut.

"Don't worry. I won't ever have the chance to do that again."

"Don't be a smart aleck, Denton." There she is. The mom I know and love. She kisses me on the cheek. "I'm glad you're home now." She closes Danza's door for me, puts an arm around my shoulder, and is about to walk me into the house when she stops. "What do you smell like? Look at your eyes. This morning, it's alcohol. Now you were smoking dope?"

"You call it *dope*?"

"Ugh, no wonder you were so late, come on."

"No, Mom, it has nothing to do with anything that was smoked. I accidentally hit Millie with the car."

Millie has been hovering just outside the car, five or so feet away from us, seeming unsure of the best place to stand.

"You *what*?"

"It was a total accident."

"Well, I should hope so! I don't see why you would intentionally hit her with your car. Probably because you were high on dope!"

"That wasn't why, it really wasn't."

"Everything okay over there, honey?" my dad says from the front steps, where he has been patiently waiting for the storm of my stepmom's emotions to pass. I love my dad, but he can be a real wuss sometimes.

"Oh, just peachy, sweetheart. Your son got high and crashed into Millicent, no big deal."

"Oh good," my dad says earnestly.

"Hi, Millicent, sorry about my son," my stepmom says. "Come inside, we'll get that leg cleaned up, get you an iced tea."

"It's okay. I can just go back to my parents' place. It's a quick walk. Almost a jump."

"A jump, that's very cute. But if you think I'm going to let you go back to your parents' with a leg that looks like that, you can . . ." My stepmom flounders with the end of the sentence. "You are wrong. You are just wrong."

Millie gives me a look, as if she's checking that it's really okay for her to crash my Sitting. I raise my eyebrows and shrug. "Okay," she says.

My stepmom ushers Millie into the house, and I head toward the clump of loved ones that includes my dad, Felix, and Taryn, who steps forward first. I'm touched to see she's wearing a sundress that she knows is my favorite; it's long and flowy and citrus-colored, and she looks amazing in it.

As she kisses me hello, I grow self-conscious that Veronica is standing right there, but then I see that she and Paolo have already gone inside. Why I'm still bothering to consider details like this when I could die at any second is beyond me; it's a built-in function of my software that I can't turn off.

Our lips come apart, and I taste Taryn's strawberry lip balm.

"You look pretty."

"You taste like pot."

"Yeah, Paolo got me to take one hit."

"I don't care," Taryn says, smiling. "I'm just glad you're not, you know, dead yet."

"Yeah. Me too."

"You look cute."

"Thanks. Maybe my purple splotch is making me handsomer."

Taryn takes a swig from the bottle of water she's holding.

"So, um, look . . ." She shuffles from one foot to the other. "My mom took me to the ER."

"What? Why?"

"Because of the . . ." She gestures to her thigh.

"Ohmigod, the splotch? You told her?"

"Yeah, I told her."

"About me, too? That you got it from me?"

"Yeah, I pretty much said that." Her parents will forever remember me as the guy who gave their daughter an STD and then died. "I'm sorry, Dent, but I'm glad I did. What if I'm dying, too, you know?"

"Right, right, sure." I feel an irrational stab of jealousy, like, *I wish I had time to go to the ER.* "So . . . Are you?"

"No, they said I'm not dying. The doctor couldn't figure out what it was, though. Probably some kind of rash or virus. She took some blood and stuff, and told me to get lots of rest and drink lots of water."

"Wow, okay. Are you good to be at my Sitting all night if you need rest?"

"I'm choosing to focus on the water part." She smiles and downs some more Poland Spring. "So . . . Maybe you just have a virus, too, right?"

"I guess. But mine has the dots. The red dots."

"Oh. Yeah." Taryn finishes off her water. The bottle crackles in her hand.

This conversation is the opposite of the word *turn-on*.

"Sorry I brought it up. I thought it would make you feel better."

"Thanks, Tar," I say, placing my hands on her hips.

"And don't worry, I wore this long dress to cover up my legs, so no one will see it."

"I thought you were wearing that dress because it's my favorite."

"Oh yeah. That, too."

"You could have worn pants to cover your legs."

"You think I'd wear pants to your Sitting?"

"I dunno. No?"

"You're funny." Taryn hands me a card in a lavender envelope. "This is for you."

"Oh, thanks, should I read it now?"

"Not now exactly, but nowish. When you have a sec."

"Nowish, got it." I slide the card into my back pocket.

"I really love you, Denton Little," Taryn says, looking at me meaningfully.

"I really love you, Taryn Brandt." It comes out sounding less sincere than I intended, and Taryn looks disappointed. "I mean it," I add, diminishing the power of the moment even more.

"I know," Taryn says, letting me off easy.

Felix swoops in. "Hey, hey," he says, patting me on the back. "You failed."

"Nice to see you, too."

"I know you were trying to give Raquel a heart attack by showing up way late to your Sitting, but she really held in there. Everything okay?"

This may be the first time Felix has asked me that and seemed to actually mean it. I'm half touched and half annoyed. He's been around my whole life, barely paying any attention to me, and *now* he cares? But then it occurs to me: Felix has been around my whole life. He's even been around since before I was born. So if that Brian Blum guy had any sort of relationship with my biological mom, maybe Felix might remember him.

"Yeah, all good. Just, you know, a little late, lost track of time, and whatnot."

"Sure, of course," Felix says, in a sweet but mildly sarcastic way that suggests I was late because I was doing a million inappropriate things. His tone is not lost on Taryn, who may be starting to wonder in more specific detail about why I was late. *Oh, no big deal, Tar, I was just hanging out in the woods pantsless with Veronica. Good times.*

"But, hey, I have a question for yo—"

"Oh shoot, I need to take this," he says, looking at his phone and backing away. "School stuff, won't take long."

There's the Felix I know. Never mind that I might die any minute. A phone call comes first.

"Yup. Sure. Nice," I say to no one in particular. Taryn sees the stricken look on my face. She kisses me on the cheek and whispers: "You're great." I put my arm around her and squeeze tight, which is my brilliant, nonverbal way of saying, *You're great, too.*

"Please forgive me," my dad says, startling us. "But I know your mother would like everyone to head inside at their, uh, earliest convenience."

"Sure, Dad. Hi, by the way," I say. I haven't seen him since the funeral, which feels like a long time ago.

"Hey, Dent. Having a good night?"

"Under the circumstances, yeah. I guess so. You?"

"Yeah, you know. It's been a little tense in these parts." My dad adjusts his glasses, uncomfortable with this death stuff, which is getting harder and harder to brush aside. Though acknowledging the tenseness is a minor breakthrough for him. He looks like he's about to say something important.

"Caught some of the Knicks game on TV. Great game."

Or not.

"Oh yeah, the play-offs started, right?"

"Sure did."

"They win?"

"Yup. In overtime."

"Great, great."

There's a million things we should be talking about right now, and none of them involve basketball. But this is how we communicate, this is our comfort zone, and it's going to take effort to steer us out of it.

"Dad . . . I actually really need to talk with you, if you have a second. About Brian Blum. And about my m—"

"I know, I know, that's . . . Uh, we will talk about it." My dad takes off his glasses and polishes the lenses on his shirt. "But for now let's just get inside so we don't keep your mother waiting." He pops his glasses back on. "Okay?"

"Yeah, sure, I guess," I say. "I just feel like the sooner—"

"Great. So come on in." My dad pats my shoulder and heads inside. Sometimes, I feel I know almost as little about him as I do about my biological mother.

"You'll get to talk, I know you will," Taryn says.

"Yo," Paolo says, popping his head out the front door. His eyes are pink. "You lovebugs wanna take this par-tay inside?"

I've been trying to delay the moment I have to walk through those doors and into the DeathRoom for as long as possible. I look up at the yellow moon—gray-cloud beard semi-covering its face—for what may be the last time and take a deep breath. "Good night, moon."

Taryn takes my hand.

"Okay," I say. "Let's get our Sit on."

16

Walking into the room where I will die doesn't feel the way I expected it to.

It feels kinda fun.

As I enter, everybody in the family room cheers and whoops and hollers in my direction. I release Taryn's hand and move my arms up and down like I'm raising the proverbial roof. I do this ironically, but—much like the party accessories at my funeral—I find myself questioning if maybe everyone who ever raised the roof thought they were doing it ironically.

There's lots of purple everywhere. (It's my favorite color.) Tablecloths, streamers, paper plates. And, of course, my purple body. It occurs to me that maybe I was genetically predisposed to love that color so my death by Purple Splotch would have a silver lining.

"Okay, everybody, your attention, please!" My stepmom stands in the center of the room and bangs on a plastic cup with a plastic spoon. It makes a pitiful pattering noise. "I have some sparkling cider here, and if we could just—"

"Sparkling cider?" Felix says. "Aw, Raquel, we can do better than that, can't we? It's Denton's last hurrah, at least give the guy a little champagne."

"No, no," my stepmom says, with the melodic lilt of a schoolmarm, "I think Denton's had enough fun with substance abuse for one day. Right?"

All eyes turn to me.

"Yeah, the cider is fine."

"I love sparkling cider," Paolo says.

"So, if you would all raise your glasses," my stepmom continues as Paolo's mom and Taryn jump into action like two of the seven dwarfs, pouring and passing cider around the room, "I would like to raise a toast to my son Denton. Such a smart, funny, handsome, brave boy." She's on the verge of breaking down. "And good. Such a good person." Am I? "Thank you for being you." She started the toast looking at me, but now she's having trouble making eye contact. "I'd say more, but I'll just lose it. So, please— everybody have a cup?" The big, dangly green sleeve of my stepmom's blouse billows as she raises her plastic goblet. "To Denton!"

"To Denton!"

"Denton!"

"Hear, hear!" my dad says.

And then: that brief moment of serenity and quiet as everyone drinks.

"Ah, every bit as good as champagne," Felix says, breaking the silence.

"Right?" Paolo says, genuinely marveling at its taste.

"Thanks, everybody," I say.

"And please, everyone, have something to eat." My stepmom gestures to the amazing snack table across the room. "We have way too much food here."

The chatter picks back up, and I step out of the spotlight. I scan the room for my dad but can't find him. I do, however, see my uncle Andre, aunt Deana, and ten-year-old cousin Tiffany sitting on the couch looking bored. They live in New York City, and they're not my favorites.

Uncle Andre—my stepmom's brother—is a large man of few words. And, yes, we often refer to him as Andre the Giant. Aunt Deana is thick, blond, and vaguely horse-like, with a way of talking about everything as if it has let her down. Tiffany is a stylish, round little girl who, despite being eight years younger than me, makes me feel über-defensive and judged every time we talk. I wave at them. That'll do for now.

On the far side of the room, Paolo is camped out near the snack table—dips, chips, nuts, veggies, cheese, cold cuts, and bread—eating a pretzel log with an unparalleled level of focus.

My eyes fall upon Grandpa Sid, whose small frame looks comical in our big brown recliner. "Hey, Grandpa," I say, realizing as I get closer that he may have been napping with his eyes open.

He blinks three times and smooths down the four or five hairs he has left on top of his head. "Hello."

"It's me, Denton."

"I know."

"Oh. Good. Well, it's great to see you."

"Would you mind getting me another club soda?"

"Uh. Sure, Grandpa."

"No ice!"

I take his purple plastic cup and head toward the beverages, which are on a little rolling cart next to the snack table.

I'm temporarily sidetracked by the framed pictures of me that are scattered all over the room:

Five-year-old Denton plays on the beach with a pail and shovel.

Thirteen-year-old Denton graduates from middle school, standing next to Paolo, both of them looking young and naive and dorky in graduation caps.

Ten-year-old Denton and Raquel and Denton's grandmother Eva (affectionately known as Mima), all dressed nicely, talk in a candid taken outside Mima's funeral.

Three-month-old Denton glares at the camera, the frame filled by his chubby, chubby cheeks.

Six-year-old Denton and fifteen-year-old Felix stand in front of the entrance to the Magic Kingdom, Denton excited and sparkly-eyed, Felix in sunglasses and barely smiling, still in his awkward phase.

My grandpa's husky voice cuts through my nostalgic reverie. "That club soda ain't gonna get itself!"

"Right, right," I say. "I'm on it, Grandpa!"

"No ice!"

I arrive at the beverage cart, where Paolo is now chomping on a celery stick.

"Hey," I say. "Hungry much?"

"Just wanted a little snack."

Reaching past a huge urn of coffee, I scoop some ice out of a plastic bucket and put it in my grandpa's cup.

"What are you doing?!" my grandpa shouts across the room, as if I've just set the house on fire.

"Whoops! Sorry, sorry!" I wish I could say I did that on purpose to mess with him, but I just forgot.

I pour him a new ice-free club soda, pour some Dr Pepper for myself, and pull up a folding chair right next to my grandpa's recliner.

"Here you go," I say, passing him his drink. "We missed you this afternoon at the funeral."

He sips his club soda. "I don't do those."

"Yeah, I know, Grandpa. You tell me that a lot."

"How can it be a funeral when the deceased is standing right there watching?"

"I know, it's a crazy thing."

Grandpa gives a big sniff and lightly rocks back and forth on the recliner a few times. "I'll celebrate your life once you're gone."

"Well, that's . . . sweet, I guess."

"Yes."

"But, you know, Grandpa, there won't be another funeral once I die."

"You won't get buried?"

"No, I will get buried, but—"

"And won't there be some kind of memorial ceremony when you're buried?"

"Sure, a small one, with just the immediate family, but—"

"That's where I'll do my mourning." He rocks back and forth a few more times, as if to punctuate the end of the thought.

"Okay."

"And for you, I'll mourn a lot. You're a good kid."

"Uh, well. Thanks, Grandpa."

We sit in silence as my grandfather continues his light rocking.

It's the first actual sitting I've done at my Sitting, and it's nice.

I breathe and look around the room, trying to identify potential causes of death.

Nothing calls out to me.

Carbon monoxide has no smell, right?

I take in the people around me.

Felix and Taryn talk about the AP chemistry teacher at our high school. They're both semi-convinced that he doesn't understand basic scientific concepts, and they wonder how he ever got tenure.

Aunt Deana rubs Uncle Andre's back while explaining why she's not going to say sorry to Anya (whoever that is) and that it should be Anya calling and apologizing to her.

My stepmom walks back in from the kitchen with a freshly bandaged Millie, who assures her that she doesn't need money for a new bike.

Paolo, still at the snack table, carefully guides a chip piled high with spinach dip into his mouth. Veronica watches, looking nauseated.

Life is happening. All these moments, these small, inconsequential conversations. We all have thousands of these every week and don't think twice about it. How many more will I have? Three? Six? Fourteen? One?

I don't have time for small and inconsequential.

I put down my Dr Pepper and bolt up out of my chair

into the kitchen, where my dad is standing by the stove, reading the *New York Times*.

"Are you seriously in here reading?"

"Oh, hi," my dad says, looking up from the Arts section. "No, uh, making tea." He gestures to a kettle on the stove. "Waiting for this to boil."

I do not understand what goes on in this man's brain.

"Okay, but . . . you've been in here awhile."

"Well, you know how I feel about crowds."

"There's, like, eleven people in there, Dad."

My dad clears his throat and folds up the newspaper.

"And I think this is sort of a unique circumstance."

"Of course, of course." He stares at the teakettle.

"I want you to tell me about my mother," I say.

For the first time in our conversation, my dad really sees me.

He stares at me for a long moment, hundreds of unspoken thoughts spinning in his eyes.

"All right," he says. He gestures to a chair at the kitchen table.

I sit.

He sits.

"What do you want to know?" he says from across the table.

I'm caught off guard by his sudden willingness to talk about this. I thought there would be some more hemming and hawing.

"I mean . . . Everything. Why didn't you tell me about Brian Blum? What haven't you forgiven him for?"

The kettle whistles.

My dad reaches out and turns off the stove without looking. Badass.

"Your mother, she was, well, she got involved with some bad characters."

"Like Brian?"

"Yeah, like Brian."

"Bad like criminals?"

"No, not exactly. Bad like they were inspiring her to make choices I didn't necessarily agree with. I started to feel like . . ." My dad stares at the table.

"Yes . . . ? Like what?"

"I felt like I was losing her."

"Right . . . You were. She was going to die."

"Of course, and that was so painful, but also . . . Well, there's lots of ways you can lose someone, Dent."

My dad looks at me like, *Now do you understand?* as if that explains everything.

"Okay," I say. "But what were her choices you didn't agree with?"

My dad rubs his neck. "Well, for starters, you."

"Me?"

"Yes, I, uh, didn't think we should have another child if your mom was going to die."

"I thought I was an accident."

"It was easier to tell you that, but really, your mother wanted another kid, and I didn't, and she, uh . . ."

"She what?"

"She went off, uh, birth control without telling me."

"What?" These words don't make sense. "What are you saying? That you didn't want me?"

"In a manner of speaking, yes, but—"

"That's so fucked up, Dad!" I feel like I've been smacked in the face.

"No, no, now don't misunderstand me. Once we had you, I loved you, I was so happy to have you in my life. I am so, so happy to . . . It was just the idea of you."

I can't believe it. This explains everything about our relationship. My dad's silence, his perpetual nonchalance about my life.

He never wanted me.

"Well, cool, Dad." I am up on my feet, though I don't remember deciding to stand. "So, guess it's great that I'm dying any minute, right?" My voice breaks as I fight back tears. "You'll finally get what you wanted."

My dad stands. "Dent, come on, you know it's not like that. Please, let me—"

"No, really, don't worry about it. All your information is too vague to mean anything anyway. Just read your paper."

I leave my dad alone in the middle of the kitchen.

Back in the family room, everyone's laughing about something.

"Hey, sweetie," my stepmom says. "Did you get to talk to Dad?"

When I first found out that my stepmom was not the woman who gave birth to me, I became obsessed with learning everything I could about the woman who did. Was she funny? Was she nice? What did she like to do? I was an eight-year-old on a mission. The problem was, my primary source of information was my father, and he gave me pretty much nothing. You'd think he would want my mom's legacy to live on, for her sons to know as much about her as possible. Not the case.

My stepmom, meanwhile, was as gracious about the subject as she could be, but she had her own blocks. I'm not sure if she was made uncomfortable by something in my dad's behavior, or worried I'd love her less if I knew more about my real mother, but however you want to slice it, neither of them was as helpful to me as I think they should have been.

Felix had spent nine years with our mom, so he threw

the occasional gem my way. It generally fell into one of two categories: Fun but Superficial ("She loved rocky road ice cream") or Revealing but Hyperbolic ("She was so funny, Dent. Like, actually funny. I remember us laughing together for hours." Hours? Whatever you say). I never stopped feeling like it was a betrayal that he'd been complicit in the plan to hide her existence from me until I was eight. I mean, come on! Brothers gotta stick together, right?

This is all to say that, after months of steadfast devotion to it, the mission seemed impossible, a series of brick walls. My efforts resulted in this paltry list, the sum total of everything I know about my biological mother:

Her name was Cheryl Quinn. Then Cheryl Little.

She had curly light brown hair.

She had the same smile as me. (Well, I guess I have the same smile as her.)

She was funny.

She met my dad at grad school, where he was one of her pharmaceutical science professors. Apparently, they both had instant crushes on each other. Way to be a creepy teacher, Dad.

On their first date, my dad took her to a night of beat poetry. One of the poets took her top off during her poem, and my dad got really embarrassed, even though my mom thought it was hilarious.

She prided herself on being the rare breed of scientist who enjoyed being around people as much as she enjoyed being in the lab (i.e., the opposite of my dad).

Her favorite flavor of ice cream was rocky road. (Already said that, but I want to make my list as long as possible.)

She cared a lot about making the world better, and she

was very passionate about doing things to help the environment.

The day I was born was the day she died.

And now, admittedly late in the game, I have two more bits of information to add:

Her doctor was a (weirdo) friend of hers named Brian Blum.

She wanted me, and my dad did not.

Consider my mission officially resumed.

There's so much more my dad could probably tell me, but right now I can't even look at him. He's followed me in from the kitchen and is hovering uncomfortably on the other side of the room.

It sucks that he never wanted me, but it sucks even more that he's withheld so much information from his dying son. His reticence used to be something that annoyed me, inspired a shake of the head and a roll of the eyes, but now I feel genuinely furious.

I need to talk with Brian Blum.

"You okay?" Taryn asks as I plop down next to her on the couch.

"Uh . . . Yeah." I force a smile. "I am. Thanks."

"It's your turn, Felix!" my stepmom says.

While I was in the kitchen, a game of tell-your-favorite-Denton-story seems to have spontaneously broken out. I don't think this will make me feel better; it's possible I might cringe myself to death.

Felix tells the story of a three-year-old me accidentally taking a bite out of his tuna fish sandwich, even though I had my own. I still remember that. Felix got up to go to the bathroom, and when I looked down at the table, I suddenly thought I'd been given two sandwiches. Sweet little idiot.

Most of what people share follows this general trend—Denton the well-intentioned doofus—except for my aunt Deana's story, which is about Felix.

"That wasn't Denton," my stepmom says.

"Oh," Aunt Deana says. "You sure?"

Veronica is next, so I can only half pay attention to Millie's story, which seems to involve spotting me singing a made-up song about snacks as I walked home by myself one day. It strikes me as a little creepy that Millie had secretly been watching me, but the thought is whooshed away by the flood of anticipation for Veronica's words.

She begins: "Uh . . . can I pass?"

Oh. Burn.

"Well . . . ," my stepmom says.

"I'm joking, I'm joking."

"Ha-ha, that's funny," I say, trying to quickly rearrange my facial expression from dejected to relaxed.

"My tale of Denton. Okay, so, when I was nine and Paolo was eight, I used to love messing with Paolo. I would hide his favorite toys, rearrange the furniture in his room, add facial hair to his posters, that sort of thing. He hated it."

"Yeah, I did," Paolo says.

"So one day, I borrowed some pink paint from Amanda Litensky's garage—she lived a few houses down from us—and I carried this huge can all the way back to Paolo's room." Oh, *this* story. "I have no idea how; it felt like I was carrying a small planet, but I was determined. When I got home, Paolo was in the backyard with Denton, of course, the two of them pretending they knew how to kick around a soccer ball."

"Hey! I'm really good at soccer," I say.

"No, you're not," Veronica says.

"I know."

"So, anyway, the coast was clear. I sat down on the floor of Paolo's room with his beloved box of action figures, and, one by one, I started—ha-ha—I started dipping them into the can of pink paint. Head to toe. And then I would leave them on a sheet of newspaper to dry."

"Such a mean person," Paolo says.

"I remember I'd just finished pinking Wolverine—"

"Poor Wolvy," Paolo whimpers.

"—and I looked out the window to make sure the Bonehead Boys were still playing nerd soccer, that I still had time left, but only Paolo was out there. Suddenly I hear the door open behind me."

I don't think I've ever heard Veronica talk this much at one time about anything, let alone about me. There's excitement pulsing beneath everything she says, her dimples bouncing around like fireflies, and I can't help but smile, in spite of the fact that I can feel Taryn looking at me, wondering why I'm grinning like an idiot.

"And there's Denton standing in the doorway, confused, while I crouched at the window, totally frozen. The can of pink paint was sitting there, big and obvious next to the pink action figures." I remember that image so clearly, how my first thought was that it looked like a tiny aboveground pool and a small squadron of pink men lying on their backs, tanning. "I was caught red-handed. Well . . . pink-handed. And Denton was like, 'I came to get us some shin guards.

Paolo says we don't need them, but I think we do.' Which was also hilarious."

"It was getting dangerous!"

"Sure it was, Denton." It was. "And I see Dent taking the whole scene in, putting two and two together, and I'm getting ready for him to sprint into the backyard to tell Paolo, but instead he gives me a sly look and says, 'Ninjas.' And I was like, 'What?' And he was like, 'You're making them all into pink ninjas. This is so cool.' Which made me confused for a few moments, like, *What? No, I'm painting my brother's action figures pink so I can ruin them.* And I was even more confused—like, shocked, even—when he got down on the floor and started helping me dip the action figures in the paint."

"You helped?" Paolo says, horrified.

"Wait, wait," Veronica says. "The point is, I could tell Denton obviously knew I wasn't making pink ninjas, and he was just trying to spin the whole situation in a cool light to help out his best friend."

Oh. Wow, no. I really thought we were making pink ninjas. Like, honestly, to this day, that's what I thought happened. Probably shouldn't say that aloud.

"Which, of course, was not a good enough spin to convince Paolo that I wasn't just trying to destroy things he loved, but it was a valiant effort." Out of my peripheral vision, I notice that Taryn is texting. "And that was the first time I thought Denton might have the hint of the slightest potential to be kinda cool." Though this can barely be considered a compliment, it's accompanied by a sweet look from Veronica. I smile back, a little goofily, and I feel Taryn's eyes on me.

"I didn't think he was cool," Paolo says. "I thought he was an idiot. They painted my shin guards pink, too."

"Ninja guards," I mutter. Once we started, I got really into the pink ninja thing.

"Anyway," Veronica says. "That's my story."

And she smiles at me once more.

I smile back.

And then I turn and smile at Taryn.

She gives me the ol' face-is-smiling-but-eyes-are-not.

"What?" I say.

She shifts her weight away from me on the couch. Everyone in the room is watching, including Veronica. "It was a fun story."

"Okay," I say. "Great, then."

"Yes, great," my stepmom interjects. "So next, and last—but not least!—is Grandpa Sid." He snores from his big chair. "Hon, you wanna wake your dad up?"

"No, hon, let's let him sleep," my dad says. "It's so late."

"I think he'd want to tell a story at his grandson's Sitting, don't you?"

"I'm not entirely sure that's true."

As my dad and stepmom debate the merits of waking up Grandpa Sid, Taryn and I detour from the main conversational highway onto a bumpy little side road, which, honestly, I would have preferred to avoid. Rocky patches of private conversation aren't my favorite.

"You said you love me."

"I do love you." I try to wrap my arm around Taryn, but she wriggles away.

"So why are you looking at Veronica over there with googly eyes?"

"I wasn't," I say, but even I'm unconvinced by my delivery.

"Why did you show up here with Paolo and Veronica? Were you guys all hanging out or something?"

I flash back to an image of Veronica at my knees in her underwear.

"No, no, not at all."

Half paying attention to the scene across the room, I see that my dad has won and Grandpa Sid has been granted permission to continue sleeping. The Denton story game thus concluded, people begin to shuffle around us, but we hold strong on the couch.

"It's okay if you were," Taryn says. "I'm just curious."

"Sorry to interrupt, hon," says a grating voice, "but we have to get going. Tiffany's tired." Aunt Deana gives me a quick, emphatic kiss on the cheek. "We love you, and we'll miss you." She speaks the Language of Obligatory Things to Say, with little detectable emotion underneath.

"Oh, sure, love you, too. I, uh . . ." I want to say something more meaningful. Instead, I look to Tiffany. "Probably never been up this late, huh?"

She rolls her eyes and heads to the front door. Sweet goodbye. So sad I won't get to see her grow up into a hideous lady-beast.

Uncle Andre looms up behind Aunt Deana and puts out his hand for a shake. "Bye, buddy," he says as I stand up, and his massive bear paw envelops my tiny hand. He gives me a wink that seems all out of context, more *You're gonna get laid tonight* than *Goodbye forever, nephew.*

"Bye, Uncle Andre. Take care."

"Yeah, yeah," he mumbles as he heads out. "Thanks, Rocky, bye, guys." He calls my stepmom Rocky.

As they leave, I'm reminded of what a unique little trio they are: they all have the same deathdate. It's not for another thirty-eight years, but still. Will all of them be in the same car accident? Same natural disaster? Victims of the same lethal virus spreading across the US? Or—and this is my favorite—a crazy shoot-out between those three during their Sitting, which ends with them (and maybe others) lying bloody on the family room floor? I realize that's not the kindest fate to imagine for family, but it'd also be pretty badass, the three of them in their family room, caught in a Tarantino-style web, Tiffany's gun trained on Deana, Deana's on Andre, and Andre's focused squarely on Tiffany. One of them moves to wipe a bead of sweat off an eyebrow, the others freak out, and *BLAM!*

"Goodbyes are hard," Taryn says, completely misreading the look on my face.

I nod.

"But," she continues, "so, you really weren't hanging out with Veronica?"

Damn. I thought I had been saved by Aunt Deana, but Taryn's persistent. If I'm gonna be interrogated, I decide to return the favor. "Who were you texting before?"

"What?" She squirms.

"You were texting. During Veronica's story."

"Oh, that, nobody, it . . . it wasn't a big deal."

"Nobody?"

"No, well . . . It was Phil, okay?"

Rage sneaks out from a trapdoor and floods my entire body. It's not rational, but Phil has that effect on me.

"You're texting that jerk-bag during my Sitting?"

"I see what you're doing, how you're flipping this away from your googly eyes to make this about me and Phil." She's smart. "There's nothing happening with me and Phil, Denton, and there never will be."

"So what'd he say?"

"Hey, my babies," Paolo says, appearing behind the couch, his arms around both of us. "Life is precious; let's not argue." He's always had a keen friend-in-distress radar.

"You're right," I say. I dive into the shiny magenta bag sitting at Taryn's feet and flail around in there until my hand finds the plastic rectangle it's looking for.

"Stop! Get out of my bag, Dent! Seriously!"

I keep her at bay with one arm as I check the messages on her phone. Paolo stands back with his hands up, trying to disengage.

There, at the top of Taryn's queue of texts, is what I'm looking for:

PHILLY 2:33 am

Is he dead yet?

Fucking Phil.

"Whoa," Paolo says, looking over my shoulder. "That dude is cold."

"Yes, he's a total jerk," Taryn says. "Which you'll notice is what I told him in my text back, that he's a jerk and that you're still totally alive."

"Oh wow, thank you for that bold display of loyalty. So glad you told *Philly* I'm alive."

"That's old. I just never got around to changing his

name back to Phil in my phone. Because I don't care about him!"

"Then why did you text back?"

"Aarrgh! I'm just trying to do the right thing here, okay? My boyfriend is dying, and I'm trying to do the right thing." Tears are streaming down Taryn's face, and I feel bad and angry and tired as she propels herself off the couch and out of the room.

"Taryn, wait . . . ," I say halfheartedly, even though I genuinely want to stop her. Millie sits across the room, having witnessed this whole scene, her eyes still focused in my direction, as if I'm a semi-engaging movie.

"Your neck is purple," she says.

I lean back on the couch and close my eyes.

"Are you dead yet?" Paolo asks.

18

I wake up to the sound of Phil shouting outside.

I hadn't wanted to fall asleep. Sleeping during your Sitting means you might die in slumberland, so *holy crap, don't do it!* But it turns out deathdates are kinda exhausting.

One moment, you're pissed at your girlfriend and your dad; the next, your eyelids are sandbags. I'd draped a throw blanket over most of myself—so my parents wouldn't see the small bit of ominous splotch that had made its first public appearance—and reluctantly fallen into a strange cycle of groggy wakefulness and short bursts of sleep.

I awoke at one point, still unsettled by the surprise appearance of Brian Blum at my funeral. Couldn't he have reached out first by phone? Or email? It occurred to me that maybe he *had* reached out via email. As my deathdate got nearer, I had cut myself off from everything Internet and put up a vacation responder (*Hey, hey, everybody! I'm done with email! Yes! It may have something to do with my upcoming deathdate. Or maybe I'm just one of those cool people who disassociate themselves from all technology to make some statement about society. No, it's the first thing. If you wanna tell me something, call me on my cell! And/or come to my funeral on Thursday! Love, Denton*) because, really, what's important in life? Whenever I hear of those rare cases where people died while checking their email—in spite of the fact that they knew it was their deathdate—it makes me incredibly sad. Your last time on earth, and you're staring at a little screen with words on it?

But in that moment, that was exactly what I felt I needed to do.

And there was indeed a message with an address I didn't recognize and a subject line that read *for denton— IMPORTANT.* I got excited, as one does when faced with an all-caps personalized message. But it was just spam encouraging me to use Viagra for *huger erections! !!* No thanks, happydinosaur@happydinosaur.com! My erections are perfectly huge already.

There was also an email from Dave Chu, a close friend of Paolo's and mine, who graduated last year and is now at NYU. He apologized for not being able to make it to my funeral. He had a final he couldn't miss.

But nothing from Blum. Otherwise, my in-box was filled with notifications from my Facebook wall, which was completely blowing up. That was nice. I know, a series of completely superficial messages (*Gonna miss you!* or *Love you, Dent!* or *RIP DENTON!!!*) ultimately means very little, but it made me feel like People Care.

Just as I was about to turn the screen off, I noticed— stuck amongst the nettles and thickets of homogeneous four-word goodbyes—an email from the government. The subject line read *Your deathdate,* and it was a standard form letter, apologizing for my upcoming loss (of life) and thanking me for my time as a US citizen.

Niceties out of the way, it proceeded to go into a checklist of things Uncle Sam wanted to make sure I'd handled before I took my leave: Had I handed over my ID, passport, birth and death certificates, etc., to a trusted loved one or stored them in easy-to-find places? Had I given permission to have my organs donated, if that was my preference? And then lots of questions about my will and my dependents and any student loan debts I might have, queries I could assume didn't apply to me based on my inability to understand them. (My parents always said that my bank account—$312.88—and my belongings—even with my extensive movie collection—didn't merit creating a will. I tried to write one up just for dramatic effect, but then I found myself thinking way too hard about who should get what, which was making me sad.) The email was signed by one Karen Corrigan, Secretary of the US Department of Life Conclusions (USDLC), and my last thought before I fell back into sorta sleep was that her closing (*Finest regards and thank you, Karen Corrigan*) was irritating.

The next time my eyelids raised—what could have been minutes, seconds, or hours later—Taryn had made her way under the crook of my right arm, snuggled up against my chest. I registered her presence like I do sunlight, aware of a pleasant, warm feeling without thinking too much about its source. My eyelids lowered.

And then: indecipherable, aggressive shouts from the front lawn.

And now: I am awake, my dreams have evaporated, and I am confused.

"Wha?" Taryn says as she stirs.

"Did you hear that?" I say.

"Hear what?" Her eyes have the look of someone who is only sixty percent awake.

"I don't know, it sounded like Phil shouting."

"You heard that, too?"

"Yes, that's what I'm saying."

"Oh. Yeah," she says. "Oh no."

My stepmom appears in the doorframe, looking concerned. She lifts the dimmer switch on the family room lights, which has, at some point in the past hours, been lowered. I can see Veronica and Millie just behind her in the kitchen, also seeming freshly awakened by the garbled ramblings outside.

"What is this, Denton?" my stepmom asks.

"I don't really know, Mom."

My dad, Paolo, Felix, and Grandpa Sid must still be asleep.

"You awake in there?" Phil slur-yells from outside. "Wait, no, I mean: you ALIVE in there?"

In her semi-alert state, Taryn slumps forward on the couch, face in hands. "Ohmigod," she says.

"If you aren't dead yet, come out here and face me," Phil yells. "Like a man!"

"I'm so sorry," Taryn says through her hands.

Is Phil actually outside challenging me to a duel? Maybe I'm still dreaming.

Something hard, maybe a rock, plings off one of the front windows of the living room. "COME AWN!"

I'm not dreaming.

"Do you know who that is?" my stepmom asks.

"I do, yeah. It's Phil, from my cross-country team."

"Ooh," my stepmom realizes. "He's the one you talked about during your eulogy, isn't he? The one you called a tooler?"

"A tool, yeah."

"And he used to be going with you, right, Taryn?"

"Well, yeah," Taryn says, letting her hands slide back down to her lap. "I guess you could say it like that."

"Okay," my stepmom says, decisive and sure as she strides across the family room toward the front door.

"Whoa, whoa." I'm up on my feet and blocking her path to the door. "Come on."

"I'm going to tell him to leave."

"Well, that's great, but . . ."

"But what?" my stepmom says.

"I dunno, it's a little, like, embarrassing that my mom has to go out and fight my battles for me."

"Denton. You're the one person in this house guaranteed to die in the next few hours. This is just common sense." I was gonna suggest that none of us should go out there, but now this feels like a challenge. "Please move, sweetheart," my stepmom says. "This'll be quick." But my adrenaline faucet is on, and I'm feeling fairly ferocious.

"No, Mom, sorry."

She looks at me with a brew of anger, defiance, and shock that I'm not instantly deferring to her.

We stand face to face, neither of us willing to budge.

"HEL-LOOOO?" Phil shouts. "Are you dead or just deaf?"

"I'll go talk to him," Taryn says, rising from the couch. "This is my fault anyway."

"Yeah, like I'm gonna let you go out there alone with him," I say. "We can both go."

"Dent—"

"Don't argue with me on this, Tar."

My stepmom, in a masterful feat of agility, wriggles behind me to block the front door. She bolts it shut as a new shower of rocks cascades against the house.

"More where that came from," Phil says, followed by some angry muttering, which, under other circumstances, would crack me up.

"No no no," my stepmom says. "None of us are going out there, 'kay? We're going to pick up the phone and call the police."

Yay, that's what I wanted to do in the first place! "Cool. Good idea, Mom," I say.

"That's not necessary, Mrs. Little. He's just drunk." I hate hearing Taryn talk that way, like she knows him so well. "Really, I can go out there."

"Nope. Sorry, Taryn." My stepmom smiles sympathetically as she slowly shakes her head side to side.

"I guess the *LITTLE* in your name is because you're a LITTLE PUSSY BOY!"

I'm officially outraged that this guy is even a small part of my last night in the world.

"Sorry, Mom," I say. "Come on, Taryn."

I lead the way toward the back door.

"Denton! No! No!" my stepmom calls after me as we pass through the kitchen, through the laundry nook, and out the door.

"Where's he going?" I hear my now-awake dad say.

"You are a coward, dude!" Phil yells from the front yard, his words getting louder as we curve around the side of the house. "Taryn! Are you still in there? Send your boy out! Unless he's DEAD!"

"I'm not dead, dude." We emerge from the shadows next to the house as the sun is just beginning to rise. I imagine it looks pretty cool. "Calm down."

Phil, however, is visibly jolted by my emergence from somewhere other than the front door. He staggers a couple of steps to regain his balance. He's about as drunk as I've ever seen another human being. Probably a pretty close approximation of where I was at two nights ago.

"Taryn, get back inside!" he yells. "This is about me and . . ." He points messily at me.

"Phil, you shouldn't be here," Taryn says in her sweetest voice.

"GET THE HELL INSIDE!" Phil says, bending over and awkwardly fumbling around in the grass. As Taryn and I exchange a confused look, Phil rises up, his hands gripping a rifle.

My stomach drops.

Whatthefuck.

"Yeah, okay?" Phil says, pointing the long neck of the big brown rifle at me. "See why you should go inside, baby?"

"Ohmigod, Phil," Taryn says, panic-breathing. "Don't, stop, don't."

"Go."

Taryn's eyes are drenched in apology as she slowly backs up.

"Yeah, go inside, Tar," I say, surprised I'm able to find words.

"Shut up, man!" Phil yells. "I'll use this!"

"Whoa!" My hands involuntarily fly up into the air. "Okay, okay, chill out, dude."

"Oh, Mr. Cool over here. 'Be chill, *man*.'" Phil's face is a sweaty mess. He looks mildly insane. "'I'm Denton, and I'm so chill, dude.'"

The front door swings open, and Taryn slides in.

"I don't want anybody else coming out here either!" Phil says.

It's just the two of us now. I can't believe this is how it's going to happen.

"I could kill you right now, you know," Phil says. "I could be the reason today is your deathdate."

I feel like we're playing a game of pretend, reenacting something we've seen in dozens of movies. We stand in the early-summer air on my front lawn, me with my hands up and him with his gun pointed at me, awkwardly tremoring as he tries to keep it steady. It's the first gun I've seen in real life. A subtle breeze grazes my scalp and the back of my neck. I hear Phil breathing.

I make a split-second decision to apologize for declaring Phil a tool during my eulogy.

"Look, Phil, I just want to—"

"You guys have sex?" Phil asks.

The question catches me off guard, and at first I think I've misheard him.

"What guys?"

"Did you and Taryn have sex? Do it? Have *intercourse*?"

So this isn't about being shamed in front of his class-mates. It's about Taryn.

Well. Which answer will get me the least shot?

"No, man, no."

"You did! I know you did!"

"Look, Phil, I'm gonna be dead one way or the other in the next eighteen hours, so I mean—"

"That's not the point!"

"Phil," my stepmom says from the front porch.

"I said for no one to come out!"

"I've called the police, and they'll be here any minute," she continues, her voice trembling.

I'm looking into Phil's eyes, and I think he's crying. It's hard to tell; they may just be bloodshot.

"I can't believe she had sex with you. I was with her for three years before we had sex. And with you guys it's, like, six months and then good to go."

"To be fair, we were working to a pretty strict deadline. So to speak."

Phil grunts. "Whatever."

"Please don't hurt him, Phil." Taryn has stepped outside now, with my stepmom lingering in the doorway behind her.

Phil springs back into shooting form. "Why shouldn't I? I can't believe you did it with him!"

"We broke up! I can do whatever I want. Look, Denton will be dead soon anyway. What's the point of you going to jail for it?"

Her phrasing almost makes it seem like she's on his side, but maybe that's the point. As Phil takes in what she says, a couple of things happen at once:

I see a cop car driving up the block behind Phil, out of his line of vision.

Paolo appears, also behind Phil, creeping out from the side of the house with a frying pan in his hand.

Both things are potentially good, but it's a delicate crucible of a situation, which could implode if handled poorly, the scene in the movie where just as the bad situation is defused, some idiot who isn't paying attention tries to help and inadvertently makes everything terrible again.

Not that Paolo's an idiot per se, but seeing him holding a frying pan flashes me back to our brief stint freshman year as a doubles pair on the tennis team. It ended tragically during a match against Haventown South when Paolo lost his grip on his racket, sending it soaring over the net into the forehead of one of our opponents (seventeen stitches).

Paolo, getting closer, makes a slow swinging motion with the frying pan and shrugs at me: *Should I hit him with this?*

I slightly raise my hand: *Not yet.*

The cop car's siren isn't on, but you can hear the sound of an automobile moving toward us. Phil is amply distracted by his conversation with Taryn and doesn't seem to notice.

"We have something special!" he says. "That's the point."

The cop car pulls up to the curb.

"I know, Phil, we did. But we're not together anymore."

Phil turns his head slightly toward Taryn, away from me, for the first time. Paolo is five or six steps away. I prepare to signal him or to charge at Phil myself.

"I know," Phil says, "but— What the hell happened to your chest?"

"What?" Taryn says, voice rising.

I wasn't expecting that, and I can't help turning to look at Taryn, illuminated by a beam of sunlight as she stares down at the uncovered patch of skin around her collarbone. Which is purple.

"Ohmigod, ohmigod," Taryn says, rushing back into the house.

Rising to a challenge during a crisis was never her strong suit.

"What the hell was that?" Phil says, laughing a little as he turns his head back to me, slackening his hold on the big rifle. I laugh a little, too. I might survive this yet.

But then Phil does a quick double take, as if he's caught a foreign body in his peripheral vision. Suddenly he's back in shooting form, his rifle sights set on Paolo.

"Whoa, whoa!" Phil shouts. "What the hell are you doing?"

Paolo stands still, a few feet from me and Phil, frying pan by his side. "I . . . thought maybe . . . I'd cook myself an omelet."

"Like hell you were. What the hell, man? Go stand over there by your gay lover." He gestures with his gun, violently and cinematically, to the spot where he wants Paolo to stand. "Go!"

I look to the police car, thinking that any second a cop will be emerging to save the day. Not sure what's taking so long.

Paolo shuffles over next to me, and now we are a pathetic twosome. With a gun trained on us. Though I do feel better with him here.

"So this one over here thinks he can sex up my girlfriend 'cause he's dying. And his little butt boy over here thinks he can hit me with a pan. I should shoot you both."

"Yeah, we know, you've made that very clear," I say. "And I got your death threat letter yesterday, so thanks for that, too."

"What death threat letter?" Phil says.

"Oh. Shoot, no, dude," Paolo says quietly. "I sent that to you."

"You?" I say. "What? Why?"

"I thought it would be obvious it was a joke! I put it in the dumbest font!"

"No, it completely freaked my shit out! Your deathdate is a very vulnerable time, you'll see."

"Aw, man, I was wondering why you hadn't mentioned it yet. I thought 'Watch ott' made it very clea—"

"SHUT THE FUCK UP!" Phil shouts.

We do.

"Sorry," I say, still feeling bold. "It's just, there are better ways I could be spending my last hours than standing here. Really."

"Easy there, D," Paolo says. "It's not all of our last hours."

And then I realize that, with Paolo dying in a month, both of us side by side on the execution line isn't so confidence-inducing after all. We are screwed. I will die instantly, while Paolo sticks it out through his injuries for a month before biting it.

What is that cop waiting for?

"Oh, better things you could be doing? Like my girlfriend? You're right, time's up." Phil cocks the gun and adjusts one last time, aiming squarely at me. "Denton Little, you're dead."

He fires.

All that stuff they say about your whole life flashing before your eyes in your final moments is such a cliché that I almost don't even want to go there.

But my life did flash. In the second between realizing that Phil was indeed going to pull the trigger and the actual pulling, stuff was flashing all over the place. Not events, just quick, vague snapshots.

FLASH: My stepmom in the kitchen.

FLASH: My dad reading in his favorite chair.

FLASH: Taryn holding my arm and laughing.

FLASH: Paolo on his bike.

FLASH: Veronica kneeling below me in the woods.

FLASH: Felix, in football gear, charging out of the house.

Hmm. That final flash seemed out of place. I couldn't think of a single time Felix and I had ever played football together.

Maybe it's because it wasn't a flash.

Felix barreled out of the front door wearing a football helmet, shoulder pads, and one of those fencing bodyguard things, and as I watched him full-on tackle Phil at the precise moment Phil's rifle fired, shoving the gun barrel toward the sky, I realized it wasn't a memory. It was actually happening. Right here and now. Holy shit.

My body tenses. My toes curl.

The bullet's new upward trajectory steers clear of me and Paolo, and the bullet blasts harmlessly into the sky.

I am still alive.

Because of Felix.

SQUAWK! A screeching noise erupts from the tree behind us.

Guess it wasn't entirely harmless.

The creature-squawk is followed by the sound of a gazillion birds dispersing throughout the sky. Felix has Phil pinned to the grass and is forcing him to hand over the rifle. Taryn and my stepmom and my dad and everyone else in the house are rushing out the front door toward us, shouting my name. I am surprised how happy I am not to be dead. I thought I was ready for it.

"Philip," an all-too-familiar voice says from my left.

I have a sinking feeling, and sure enough, when I turn to face him, I discover that it's my buddy from last night. Phil's grandfather. Aka HorribleGrandpaCop. Of course. He lumbers out of his police car toward us, finally deeming the moment appropriate to intervene.

"I was hoping you weren't gonna fire that gun off, son." He's holding his sunglasses, polishing them with part of his blue police shirt. "I was giving you the benefits of the doubt, 'cause you're my own flesh and blood, but—"

Phil, pinned below Felix, begins to bawl. "Oh no, don't tell Dad, Grandpa, please," he says, mush-mouthed and teary-eyed.

"That'll be Officer Corrigan, Phil-Phil. I'm on duty."

I'll stick with HorribleGrandpaCop, thank you very much. Maybe just HorribleCop for short.

"I didn't think it was loaded, I swear!" Phil bawls. "I just wanted to scare him! I just wanted to scare him. . . ."

"Well, that's all well and nice, but it was loaded, son, and I don't think your daddy's gonna like knowing you took his gun out the house to scare people with."

"I know, I know, I'm sorry, please, don't take me to jail."

"Absolutely take him to jail, Officer!" my stepmom shouts from her spot on the lawn, not too far from where we're standing.

"All right, all right, I have this handled, ma'am. No need for the peanut gallery to intervene."

"I think there is a need, Officer, seeing as I called you almost a half hour ago and you proceeded to sit in the car as my son and his friend were held at gunpoint by your *grandson*. Are you insane? We could have you fired for negligence!"

"I had it under control, ma'am."

"Did you? Seemed like the only thing under your control was your nepotism. If my older son hadn't gone out there to save him, my younger son would be dead! Is that what you wanted?"

"With all due respect, ma'am, isn't it this young man's deathdate today anyway?"

My stepmom is temporarily rendered speechless. I'm surprised, too. Was Phil's grandpa really going to let me die like that?

"Well . . . What?" my stepmom stammers. "How do you know that?"

HorribleCop looks like he's been caught off guard for a second. Then he regains his composure. "Oh, 'cause I encountered your son earlier today. Or yesterday, I should say. Isn't that right, Dinton?"

Something's weird about all this.

"It shouldn't matter that it's his deathdate; your job is to *protect* people. Now arrest this young man. I don't care whose grandson he is."

"Please don't!" Phil wails.

"All right, all right, hold on to your dignity, son." HorribleCop turns to Felix. "Young man, thanks for helping out here. You can rise up off Philip, if you don't mind."

Felix awkwardly scrambles up, still bearing the strange load of sports equipment. I can tell that he doesn't trust this man either. I've never loved Felix more.

HorribleCop squats down clumsily and picks up the rifle. "Evidence," he says, though he hasn't even bothered to put on a glove before grabbing it. "Now you get on up, too, Philip." Phil does a strange sort of push-up, slips on some morning dew, regains his footing, and rises. "Sorry for any inconvenience this fella has caused you all," HorribleCop says to the assembled mass of people on the front lawn, putting his arm around Phil as if it's a family picnic, "but you can be assured the issue will be handled."

"You're referring to attempted murder as an inconvenience?" my stepmom asks.

"Now, ma'am, don't worry. We will not be taking this lightly, and this boy will be taken to jail."

"Oh no," Phil says, barely audible through his messy emotions.

HorribleCop squeezes Phil's shoulder, which seems less stern reprimand and more *Play along.* Phil shuts up.

"Philip, why don't you apologize to Dinton?"

Phil looks down for a few seconds and sniffles. "I'm really sorry, dude. I didn't think it was loaded." He's not making eye contact, but he sounds sincere.

"Thanks," I say, almost in spite of myself. I wanted to stay silent, like a real badass, but the guy seems so pathetic.

"Don't hate me, Taryn," Phil says, and I'm surprised to see that she has reappeared on the front porch, now wearing one of my stepmom's fancy silk scarves, presumably to cover her purpleness. Taryn just stares at Phil, a well-calibrated blend of anger, disappointment, and sympathy playing on her face.

"All right, all right, come on now, Philip," Horrible-Cop says as he ushers him over to his HorribleCopMobile. "Don't worry, buddy. Grudges don't last forever. She'll come around."

HorribleCop throws the rifle into the trunk, then opens the front passenger door. He doesn't even have the decency to put my attacker in the backseat. As Phil gets in, he looks back at me, and for a moment I think I see a flash of a cocky *I'm getting away with it* expression in his eyes, but it's quickly replaced by the contrite little boy.

We all remain still as we watch HorribleCop get in the car, turn the key in the ignition, and drive away. He beeps the horn once as he passes. I'm not even kidding.

"Pretty cool dudes," Paolo says, breaking the silence.

I turn to Felix. He's not a big hugger, but I hug him

nevertheless, crushing all that random sports gear between us. "Thank you."

"That's why I'm here," he says into my ear, and, much to my surprise, I can hear that he's crying.

"I'm so glad you were," I say, astounded that he cares this much.

"I really didn't think he was gonna pull the trigger. . . ."

"Lemme get in on this," Paolo says, worming his way into our hug.

"I'm sorry I dragged you into that, Pow," I say. "That was terrible."

"You kidding? I just crossed four things off my bucket list."

The rest of the mob pounces, led, of course, by Stepmama Bear, who wraps her arms around me. "My brave, stupid son."

"I know," I say into her shoulder.

And then Taryn is hugging me and apologizing on a nonstop loop. "I'm so sorry Dent I ran away and I am the absolute worst I just was so overwhelmed because this was my fault that he was here it was all my fault and I thought he was gonna shoot you but I swear I didn't run in because of the splotch I mean it was partly that but mainly I couldn't watch him shoot you I just couldn't so I ran inside but that was terrible of me and I'm so so sorry. . . ."

"It's okay, Tar. It's okay."

"I'm not going to school today," she says. "My parents said it's all right."

"Oh. Right, yeah." I forgot that school was a thing that would still be happening for people. "Thanks."

"Kiss me."

I don't feel like kissing her. But I do.

I'm relieved to hear a commotion behind me, which

gives me a nice excuse to stop. "Wait, I just wanna see what's happening over there," I say, and she looks rejected, like she doesn't fully believe that's why I've pulled away.

Over by the tree, a small group is huddled, staring at something and talking in hushed voices. "I think I can heal it. I really do," Millie is saying as she sits cross-legged on the grass.

"Heal what?" I say.

"Oh," Millie says, startled by my sudden appearance and seemingly unsure whether or not I should be shielded from this information. "Well . . . This bird."

Next to Millie on the ground is a little bleeding blue-bird, its dark pebble eyes staring blankly up at the sky.

"Phil," I say, remembering the loud squawk after he fired his gun. "Aw, man."

The bluebird's beak is slowly opening and closing, like it's trying to tell us something really important, but no sound comes out. Its whole body quivers.

"Oh, poor birdie," Taryn says, having sidled up next to me. She's wrapped herself around my arm.

"Does anyone have a pen? Or keys?" Millie asks, looking up at us. "I wanna try to get the bullet out."

I reach into my pocket for my car keys, only half believing this is a helpful idea.

"Um . . . I think it's too late," Taryn says.

The bluebird's wing and beak movements slow to an almost imperceptible level, its life evaporating before our very eyes.

Then they stop altogether.

The bluebird's eyes remain open, and I'm tempted to push down its eyelids to help preserve its bird dignity.

"Poor guy," Taryn says.

Staring at the dead body of this little creature that was alive mere moments ago is a real trip. World's worst magic trick.

It must be a size thing. I've seen bugs die, and it's never seemed like a big deal. But when it's bird-size or larger, it's freaky.

And people-size? Man, I can't even imagine.

Well.

That's not entirely true.

There is a memory. One my brain and I have worked hard to bury deep down and far away.

But it surfaces. My grandma Mima at her Sitting.

She's on the couch, in mid-conversation. Then, all at once, she's clutching her chest and gasping for air. And her eyes. Vulnerable, pleading, desperate. Trapped.

A chaotic, panicky feeling descends as my brain reminds me in huge, bold, italicized, highlighted letters: *YOU ARE PEOPLE-SIZE. THIS WILL BE YOU. JUST LIKE MIMA.*

"Hey, hey, you okay?" Felix says into my ear as I crouch over, hyperventilating. I can be held up at gunpoint for fifteen minutes, no problem, but show me a dead bluebird, and I lose my shit.

"Yeah," I try to say, but I think it sounds more like a grunt. I don't know if I am okay. I might be very not okay.

"Dent, Dent, look at me," Felix says. My dad and stepmom are on either side of him, and it feels like everyone else has gathered, too. *Don't wanna miss the good stuff! This could be IT!*

"Whoa, what's on his neck?" my stepmom says.

I feel light-headed.

I feel nauseous.

I feel like I'm dying.

"I think . . . this might . . . be it . . . ," I am barely able to say.

"No, I think you're just having a panic attack," Felix says, his narrow brown eyes filled with fear. "Let's go back inside."

All the blades of grass combine into a blurry mass of green, a child's finger painting.

Bright white dots appear on the outer edge of my field of vision.

"I don't know, I don't know, he just saw that bluebird die and started breathing heavy," I hear Taryn saying to someone.

I've given up trying to control the roiling ocean that is my respiratory system. Instead, I try to focus on all the things in my life I love and am thankful for:

I love green grass.

. . .

. . .

I love

. . .

. . .

. . .

. . .

It's hard to think.

. . .

. . .

. . .

Then all is black.

The beeping is steady, reliable, almost comforting.

There is a machine next to my bed.

Beep. Beep. Beep.

The room is all white.

On the wall, there's a drawing of a cartoon bird.

I peer down at my arm, expecting to see an IV, some sort of hookup to the beeping machine. There is nothing.

"Hello?" I say.

Someone clears his throat from the corner of the room.

Mick, my death counselor, has, I guess, been sitting in a chair the whole time. As always, he's wearing a polka-dot tie.

"What's happening?" I ask.

He blinks and gives me a half smile.

I am uncomfortable.

I push off the covers and walk out into the hallway. It is strangely deserted. Fog the frog—Millie's and my old friend—hops by. I turn a corner and find myself in a pizzeria.

"Get a room, you two," Paolo says from behind me. I spin around. He's sitting in a booth with Veronica, Taryn, and Phil. There's one damp slice of pizza in the center of the table.

Phil has an arm around Taryn, his face nuzzling her neck. She's laughing.

"V, you don't do this, do you?" Paolo asks.

"What," Veronica says, "get all PDA with my hot college boyfriend from college? Sometimes. We do it everywhere."

"I'm right here," I say to them.

They all turn their heads and stare blankly.

"Who are you?" Paolo says.

"HEY!" a thick woman behind the counter shouts. "YOU." She points at me.

"Yeah?"

"Phone call." She holds out the receiver. I walk across the tiled floor to get it. "Hello?" I say.

"You wasted it." It's a low voice I don't recognize.

"Excuse me?"

"You wasted your life." Then a dial tone.

"What was that about?" Veronica says, appearing at my shoulder, her face close to mine.

"You're supposed to be dead," Phil says, appearing at my other shoulder.

"I'm not dead now?" I ask.

"Nah."

"You know what you need?" Veronica says, starting to crack up. "A haircut." She pulls out shiny silver scissors.

"Yeah!" Phil shouts. "Haircut! Haircut!" All the customers start chanting along with him. "Haircut! Haircut!" I do not want a haircut.

Veronica runs one hand through my hair, her fingers lightly grazing my scalp.

"This is how we cut the hair," she sings as she starts snipping, her body close to mine.

"That actually feels good," I say.

I smile at Veronica.

She smiles back.

"Not for long," she says.

She grabs a handful of my hair and pulls.

I scream.

21

I gasp as I open my eyes. Paolo's mom is looking at me.

"It's okay, shh. It was just a dream," she says.

I blink and look around, trying to orient myself. I'm in my bed. Paolo's mom is in my desk chair near the bed, her bag and her camera at her feet.

My stepmom bounds through the door. "Ohmigod, thank you, thank you, you're alive! You're still alive!"

My dad and Felix and Taryn and Millie and Paolo and Veronica follow closely on her heels. My stepmom's arms wrap around me tightly once again. If I had a nickel for every tearful goodbye/reunion we've had in the past twenty-four hours, well . . . I'd have fifteen or twenty cents. But it seems like it's all we do lately.

"I sit here for hours and nothing, but I go out to pee for three minutes," my stepmom says, "and of course you wake up."

I'm still shaking off the grog and confusion. "Hours? What time is it?"

My stepmom joggles her sleeve to get a look at her watch. "Two-forty-seven."

Those numbers take four seconds to mean something.

"Wait, two-forty-seven in the afternoon?"

"Yeah, you've been sleeping awhile. At least eight hours," my stepmom says. "How do you feel?"

"Oh man, I guess okay . . . I was having strange dreams. I thought maybe I was dead."

"I know, sweetheart, I know." And my stepmom's got me in another tight hug. "Not yet, not yet."

"You're okay, bud," my dad says unhelpfully.

"How could you not tell us about this purple rash?" my stepmom asks, leaning back to look me in the eyes. "This could be very serious. You need to share these things with us."

"I didn't want to worry you."

"You're way too late for that, sweetie."

"Well, it doesn't hurt or anything. And it's not spreading too fast. . . ." I look down at my hands. They're purple. With red dots. "Oh no," I say. I roll up each hoodie sleeve in quick succession. Purple arm. Second purple arm. "When did this happen?"

"While you were sleeping," Taryn says, her first words since I've woken up.

"Starring Sandra Bullock," I say. Even in a distressing moment, I can't help myself.

"And Bill Pullman," Taryn responds. This is a little game I make her play, which she usually doesn't enjoy, but today she's willing to indulge me.

"Nice one, I didn't think you'd know his name. Hi, Tar."
She smiles.

"Also Peter Gallagher," Millie says. "My favorite actor."

"Um. Right," I say. "Him, too."

"Your face is purple also," Millie says.

"Aw, seriously?" I rub my hand down my cheek, as if I'd be able to feel it. "My face?"

The room nods.

I sigh. "Super."

"So," my stepmom says. "We'll give you a few minutes to get yourself together, and then your father and I will take you to the hospital."

No.

"We wanted to take you as soon as you passed out, but Felix said it seemed like a panic attack, and the best thing we could do was just let you sleep."

"And I still think the hospital is unnecessary," Felix says. "No one wants to spend the last hours of their life like that if they don't have to."

"Felix," my stepmom says, "he's purple, for God's sake! And Taryn has it, too. I mean, come on! We have to be responsible here."

"The doctor thought it was just a twenty-four-hour virus," Taryn says quietly.

"Yeah," I say, "Taryn went to the ER yesterday, Mom."

"It seems like," Felix says, "whatever this virus is, it's not harmful if there are no red dots. Like, in those cases, I think it might be dormant. Benign."

"Suddenly you're a doctor over here?" my stepmom says.

"No, no," Felix says, shrugging and shaking his head.

"But I know how to use the Internet. I was reading up on how viruses usually operate. Just a theory."

"Super theory, really, but Denton *does* have the red dots. So what about him? What about your brother?"

"Mom," I say. "I completely understand why you'd want me to go to the hospital, but honestly, I already wasted so many hours of my last day sleeping."

Wasted.

The word slaps my face like ice water.

"You wasted it," the voice on the phone in my dream said.

All at once I understand.

I haven't just wasted these hours by sleeping.

I've had a golden ticket since I was five, since I learned of my premature deathdate, and I've been trying to "just live a normal life."

If that doesn't qualify as wasting, I don't know what does.

"Denton, do you hear what I'm saying? DENTON!" my stepmom shouts into my ear.

"Whoa, yes, yes, I'm fine. Sorry, zoned out for a second."

"Don't apologize, please don't apologize."

I should have died this morning—murdered by Phil on the front lawn—but I didn't.

I've been given a gift.

Maybe I've only got an hour, maybe six, but whatever I have, I can't squander it away trying to do the right thing, worrying about what people think.

"Okay, sure, no problem, I'll go," I say to my stepmom.

There's no way I'm going to the hospital.

I need to find Brian Blum.

Not sure how, but I will.

I'm more awake now, and as I look at Paolo's mom, I think about the way she was staring at me when I woke up, just the two of us alone in a room. Kinda creepy. I shift slightly in the bed, and my hand grazes Blue Bronto, tangled up in the covers. I'm reminded of an even bigger question.

I deserve answers.

"Cynthia," I say, too forcefully for the casual tone I was hoping to strike, "can I ask you something?"

I want her to look nervous at this, but she looks as sweet and composed as ever, maybe even a little flattered that I've singled her out for questioning. "Sure."

"Well," I say, inserting a healthy, dramatic pause, "why do you have baby pictures of me with my dad locked up in your office drawer?"

Paolo's mom's expression doesn't change as she takes in my question. A quick scan across the room, though, shows me that everyone else's expression has, their collective interest piqued. I feel kinda bad that I've put Paolo's mom on the spot like this, but whatever. I'm tired of feeling bad.

She looks down and sighs. "Yeah, I thought maybe you'd found those when you were in my office yesterday."

"I did."

"Oh gosh, I know that must have been weird for you. This is . . . a little embarrassing."

"Cynthia . . . ," my stepmom says. "What is this?"

Paolo's mom takes a deep breath. "Well, we all know that Veronica and Paolo's father left me a long time ago, before I met any of you. And being a single mom got lonely at times. . . . Oh, this feels so silly. . . . But when I first met Lyle, I . . ."

"Oh," my stepmom says.

"I had a tiny crush, that's all." Paolo's mom looks down and covers her eyes.

There's a silence as we all process what she's just said.

"Wait, on my *dad*?" I say.

She nods.

My dad is confused and blushing.

"Ah, I must seem pathetic," Paolo's mom says.

"Pretty much," Paolo says.

"It was only for a few years—"

"*Years?*" my stepmom says.

"But I just left the photos in my photo drawer. As a reminder. Of . . . what one day I could maybe find with someone. You're so lucky, Raquel."

Lucky to be with my dad? Has she ever tried to carry on a conversation with him?

"Well," my stepmom says, looking supremely uncomfortable. "Thank you. But, Cynthia . . . you didn't even meet Denton until the boys were in kindergarten."

A seed of something sprouts in my mind.

"Right, no, obviously," Paolo's mom says. "So, those baby photos . . ."

"Oh no," Paolo says.

"Denton, do you remember in elementary school when you and Paolo worked on that family history photo project?"

Paolo's mom had a crush on my dad.

"Uh-huh," I say, only half listening.

"Well, when you guys were over, I . . . I made copies of some of the photos that had you and Lyle in them." Paolo's mom looks lost. "I'm not proud, I don't know what I was thinking. Please forgive me, Raquel. Lyle, too."

"Excuse me," Veronica says as she weaves through the people in the bedroom and walks out the door.

If my mom were a stalker, I'd be uncomfortable, too.

"Ron, wait," Paolo's mom says. She seems like the loneliest lady in the world.

But hold on a second: those photos weren't just of my dad. They were photos of me, too. In fact, the first photo I saw featured me by myself.

Not to mention that Paolo's mom has been taking photos of me—with or without my dad—the whole time she's known me. I can even remember one of my soccer games in third or fourth grade: I was waiting around on defense, daydreaming, when I noticed Paolo's mom and her camera way behind the sideline. I thought it was strange because Paolo wasn't on either team. I was about to wave at her, but then the ball soared past me, and the coach shouted, "Wake up, Little!" I sprang into my pretending-to-play-defense stance, and when I looked again later, she was gone.

Paolo's mom once had a thing for my dad. She's been taking photos of me since I was a kid. I know close to nothing about my biological mom, whose name may or may not be Cheryl.

Ohmigod. What if . . . what if Paolo's mom *is* my mom?

I stand up out of bed.

"I, uh, I'm gonna go pee," I say.

"I'm truly sorry," Paolo's mom says.

"You're aggravating him," my stepmom says. "Just give it a rest."

"No," I say. "It's . . ."

I have no idea how to finish that sentence.

I pad out the door and down the hall.

I stare into the bathroom mirror at my purple face.

Paolo's mom might also be my mom. No. It makes no sense. And yet it makes all too much sense.

"Ever heard of knocking?"

Veronica is sitting on the toilet.

I pretty much jump out of my skin.

"Ohmigodyouscaredthecrapouttame," I say. "I'm so sorry, I'll go."

"I'm not taking a dump or anything. You'll notice I'm fully clothed."

"Oh good."

We're quiet for a moment.

I want to share my theory with her, but then I realize:

If it's true, then I had sex with my half sister. Oh holy crap. I push it out of my mind. I focus on Veronica. She's wearing jeans and a dark green turtleneck sweater.

"A turtleneck in May?" I ask, trying to be cute.

"No, dick, I'm not wearing this because it got cold." She slides down the turtleneck part to show me her now-purple neck.

"Oh," I say, taking a seat on the edge of the bathtub.

"Dent, how's it going in there?" my stepmom says through the door. "You okay?"

"Totally fine, Mom. Just need to take a few minutes." I look at Veronica, and she has one hand over her mouth, like she's about to start laughing.

"Let's just give him some time in there," my stepmom says, away from the door.

Veronica, meanwhile, is cracking up.

"What's so funny?"

"You said you're 'totally fine,'" she says through giggles. "Just seems kinda hilarious, considering you could die literally any minute. This day is so weird."

You can say that again, sis!

Her laughing triggers memories of the creepy Veronica from my dream, and I'm momentarily unsettled.

"Yeah, it kinda is."

"Kinda? I'm on the toilet having a chat with you, Denton. And we're both purple." She says that last word in an emphatic way that makes me smile. "Not only that, but no one has any idea *why* we're purple; my mom is telling your parents she's crushing on your dad; you're gonna die at any moment—"

"I know," I say, starting to laugh a little myself. "It's like, *What the HELL is happening?* And Phil was here this morning with a gun! Trying to kill me. That actually happened!" I've never seen Veronica laugh this much. "And we had sex! You and me! We sexed it up!"

She stops laughing.

The silence hangs in the air between us, a stranded balloon.

"Too soon?" I ask. Maybe she also figured out we're related.

"Yep." She doesn't seem mad, exactly. More annoyed. She stares past me, absentmindedly rubbing her index finger back and forth along her lip.

I remind myself that I could die in a matter of minutes.

"I gave you my virginity, you know? And it really sucks that I can't remember a single. Freaking. Detail."

"You seriously don't remember a single thing? You were that drunk?"

"Apparently."

"Hey, speaking of which, did you throw up on my bed?"

"Um . . . Oh, you know, I do remember one thing from that night: you telling me 'It's just because I feel bad for you' before kissing me."

"Oh. Right. I did feel bad for you." Veronica readjusts the way she's sitting on the toilet. "This isn't very comfortable." She stands up and stretches, both arms lifting into the air. As she does, her sweater lifts and I get a peek of midriff. I know she might be my sister, but it's still crazy attractive. Even if she is purple. She moves past me to the other side of the bathroom.

"Wait, don't leave," I say.

"I'm not," she says.

Oh. Good. The television is on downstairs, and I strain my ears to figure out what's being watched. Some sort of daytime talk show.

"I felt bad for you," Veronica blurts out as she abruptly

turns around, "because you manipulated me into feeling bad for you. You were all sad because Taryn had dumped you, milking it and milking it. And she hadn't!"

"Well . . . I was confused!"

"And why were you even still at our house? My mom was supposed to drive you home!"

"I have no idea!"

"Huh." Veronica narrows her eyes.

"What do you think?" I say. "That I, like, told your mom not to drive me home so I could hook up with you?"

"All I know is me and Pow said goodbye and you guys were heading to the car. Then five minutes later, I'm sitting on the couch watching TV, and you and my mom walk back into the room. She says you've decided to sleep over because you're so tired. And then you, like, sat down on the couch next to me and said you were 'so bummed.'"

"Okay, okay, back it up a second. Were you hanging out with me and Paolo before I left? Or, whatever, fake-left?"

"Yeah, a little bit. You were making prank calls. It was pretty funny."

"Man, I wish I remembered doing that. . . . So during that time, Taryn was gone, right?"

"Yeah, she left before I got there."

"Right, okay, so was I sad about being dumped then? Did I mention it at all?"

Veronica bites on her thumb and looks at the ceiling. "Maybe not."

"Aha! Right? If I thought I'd been dumped, I would have been talking about it. So why did I think that later? Did Taryn text something as I walked to your mom's car that I mistook for a dumping? Or call me?" I rip my phone out of my pocket and scroll through the history from two nights ago. Nothing.

"So what, then? My mom randomly decided to convince you that Taryn had dumped you?"

And with a shock of electricity, I remember something else from that night. Paolo's mom stands on the front porch of Paolo's house: "You sure you want me to drive you home? You're very welcome to stay here, you know."

I tell her I'd like to go home but thanks.

"Of course, sweetie. I just thought with Taryn having broken up with you like that, you might want to be around other people your own age."

I tell her that Taryn didn't break up with me.

"Oh no . . . I thought maybe you hadn't understood that. That's why she left early. She said it's over, Denton."

I don't remember what happened after that, but I remember the feelings. Heartbroken. Confused. Lost.

"Yeah. I think maybe she did," I say to Veronica.

"'Cause that makes so much sense."

It's certainly not outside the realm of Bizarre Crap Paolo's Mom Has Been Doing in the Past Day. Though I'm not sure how this would relate to her being my mom. Maybe she isn't. Right now I have to assume that. Because I'm too attracted to Veronica to think of her as my sister.

Veronica looks in the mirror and brushes her hair back with her hand. "We should probably stop hiding in here. At least you should."

She walks toward the door.

Don't waste it, Denton.

"Wait wait wait," I say as I stand up from the bathtub.

Veronica sighs and turns around.

"Just . . ." I take the leap. "You're a phenomenal person."

"Funny."

"I'm serious."

She looks down at her sneakers. "For what it's worth, Dent, I think you're pretty cool, too."

Dynamite explodes in my chest.

"Really?" I say.

"I guess, yeah."

"So, wait," I say, encouraged by this tiny victory. "Can I just ask how it was? When we . . . I mean, was I awesome or what?"

"Well, you made me purple. That wasn't awesome."

"Again, can't apologize enough about that."

"But, otherwise, it was fine. You were just . . . touching my boobs a lot."

"What? That sounds like a good thing to me."

"No, like, a lot a lot."

"Oh my God, okay, never mind."

"I mean, for your first time, it was pretty good," Veronica says.

"Geez. Thank you? I guess."

I try to slide by Veronica in the narrow space of the bathroom so I can leave—I've gotten bored of feeling inferior—but she puts her arms around me.

"I really should get out there," I say as I hug her back, feeling her body pressed against mine, my face in her hair, inhaling the same peachy, minty, soapy smell that I remember from her bed. I don't actually want to leave. I would be fine to finish out my life right here.

"I'm really gonna miss you," Veronica says into my ear. A chill goes down my spine.

Before my brain can even form the thought *If not now, when?* I've gone in for the kiss.

Veronica kisses me back.

Our tongues are full-on invading each other's mouths, deep, hungry kisses. I know how potentially wrong this is, but I don't care. This is happening.

I slide my hands down her back and onto her butt. (Definitely not going for her chest.) She doesn't remove them. I am invincible. Maybe I've died. Maybe this bathroom is heaven.

There is a knock at the door. We freeze.

"Dent, you still in there?" Paolo says. "We're all trying to give you your space and alone time, but . . . Just making sure you're okay."

Veronica's mouth pulls away from mine, but our bodies and faces are still very close. I'm not sure if I should speak.

"'Cause you've already had more than enough time to rub one out, if that's what's going on. I don't know, you might take more time with it than I do."

"Oh, nasty," Veronica whispers, more to herself than to me.

"I could have probably jerked it twice by now, actually. Two and a half, if we're gonna be real."

I should speak.

"Hey, Pow, I'm all good. I'll be out in a second."

"Hold up, hold up," Paolo says. "Can I come in there?"

Veronica slinks out of my arms and rolls her eyes as she crosses past me back to the toilet.

"Uh . . . Just give me, like, two minutes, and then we can talk out there."

"No, dude, we can't do it out here."

I look to Veronica like, *Oh, Paolo, up to his zany tricks again.*

She shrugs like, *Might as well let him in, because I know you're going to either way.*

"All right, come on in," I say, opening the door just enough for him to get inside. "But—"

"What the hell is she doing in here?" Paolo says as I carefully close the door behind him. "Oh man, you guys were . . . Oh, barf-a-tron." Paolo spins around, trying to shield his eyes.

"No, it's not like that," I say.

"Dude, this is hard-core. You guys are doing it in the bathroom? With everybody right outside?"

"Shhhh!" Veronica and I say.

"Pow. We were talking in here. That's all. I really did come in here to pee, but she was in here already."

Paolo looks back and forth from me to Veronica to me, not fully trusting my story. "You guys did get dressed pretty quickly for two peeps who were bumping uglies."

"Ugh, stop talking," Veronica says.

Paolo sizes us up some more. "Look, you guys are both practically my siblings, so—"

"I am your actual sibling," Veronica says.

I might be, too.

"Right, yeah, I messed that up. You are my sibling, and Denton is practically my sibling, so I love you both like brothers. No. I'm the brother, and you guys . . . What

I mean is, whether you guys were doin' it up or not, I love you and I support this union."

"Thanks," I say. "What did you need to talk about?"

Paolo looks momentarily confused by my question, caught up as he is in his TV cop routine. "Oh right." He turns on the sink and splashes water on his face. "This is kinda serious, and if you want me to be honest, I'm freaking out a little." Paolo turns off the faucet and grabs a maroon towel off the rack.

"Okay, sorry. FYI, that's the towel I use to dry off my balls."

Paolo rips the towel off his face and throws it to the ground. "Aw, man! Geez!"

Veronica laughs, which I like.

"Dude, you can tell us."

"No, I can't," Paolo says, "because it's not something I have to tell. It's something I have to show." He unbuckles his belt and begins to unzip his fly.

"Whoa there," I say.

"P, stop!" Veronica hides her eyes.

"You're gonna think this is hilarious," Paolo says. "You, too, V. A regular chuckle fest."

He pulls down his pants.

On his right thigh, just below his Daffy Duck boxers, is the splotch.

"You've got to be kidding me," I say.

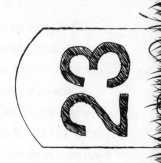

23

"You STDed me!"

"Okay, hold on a sec here, hold on." I'm trying to think, to get a handle on this, but my head is spinning.

"You guys had sex?" Veronica asks. "Ohmigodohmigod." She lifts the toilet seat up and kneels down in front of the bowl.

"No! Of course we didn't have sex!" I shout.

"At least not that we know of . . . ," Paolo says.

"What? Dude, can you get my back on this?"

"Well, we don't know what's happening! We were both pretty wasted two nights ago!" Paolo says. "Though, Ron, you wanting to throw up at the thought of two dudes doing it is very un-PC. Get with the times, babe."

"I don't care about two guys doing it," Veronica says, hovering over the toilet. "It's you guys doing it. It's me and my brother doing the same guy on the same night." She dry-heaves.

Though I'm 99.99 percent sure it didn't happen, I suddenly feel nauseated, too. "Move over," I say as I crouch above the toilet next to Veronica.

I am dry-heaving and taking deep breaths. What if I die right now? What if I start vomiting and can't stop and I throw up all of my insides? *It's so sad,* people will say. *He pictured himself and his best friend doing it and got a case of Unstoppable Vomit.*

I look at Paolo's splotch. "You have no red dots on yours, right?"

"Nah," he says. "I wish I had those; they're sick."

We watch him poke at his splotchy thigh.

"You can probably pull your pants up now, dude," I say.

"Now that they're down, it's kinda freeing."

"Pull up your goddamn pants!" Veronica says.

"Geez, what's up your butt?" Paolo says, shuffling his jeans back up.

"Veronica's got it, too," I say.

"What? The Purple Plague?"

"Let's not call it a plague."

"Wow," Paolo says, ignoring me. "Well, of course she does, because you guys did it. A lot. I bet she's got it all over."

"We only did it that one time," I say.

"When you caught us in the woods, I was looking at Denton's rash thing. Not giving him a beejer, dumb ass," Veronica says.

"Whatever," he says, picking up a white container of spearmint floss. "Can I use this?"

"Now?" I say.

"I forgot to bring my teeth stuff last night."

I shrug. We are all silent for a minute, the staccato of Paolo's flossing the room's only sound. I slowly get to my feet. I guess my next step is to leave the bathroom and figure out how to get in touch with Brian Blum. There's no way Veronica's gonna make out with me again now.

I remember what's outside this room, and guilt rains down upon me. "You guys think Taryn could hear us in here?"

"Man up, dude!" Paolo has stopped flossing.

"What?"

"You know what." Paolo is not someone who scolds, so it's startling. "This is the end of your life. You gotta own that shit." He takes a dramatic step toward me. "You are Denton Little, dammit, and I won't let you go to the grave worried that people are angry at you. Who cares, dude."

"Yeah, I completely agree," I say. "I've—"

"I get it. You care about Taryn. You guys have developed this thing between you, these little jokes—'Ooh, Denton, I very want to kiss you very much times.'"

"That's not what we say."

"It's all very sweet, and in a perfect world you'd both go to college, take some time off to explore other short, exciting-but-ultimately-empty relationships, then realize you are meant to be, get married, have eighty kids, and live in a huge shoe on the edge of town."

"A shoe?"

"But in a perfect world, you wouldn't be dying today. And I wouldn't be dying in less than a month. This is not a perfect world, make no mistakes about it, and we don't have the gift of time that everyone else has. And it's scary, and it's confusing, and so maybe we mess up a little bit.

Maybe we try to use butter to masturbate and it works out really bad. But you gotta own that shit."

Paolo goes back to flossing. "I only say it because I love you, dude. You know that."

"Yeah. Thanks, Pow." I should own that shit. "You okay, Veronica?" I ask. "Paolo and I . . . That never happened. He probably just rubbed his face on my ball towel yesterday or something."

She continues focusing on the toilet water and says nothing.

"Own that shit," Paolo says in a melodic singsong, reaching far back into his mouth.

"I'm not gonna own it if it didn't happen."

"Yes! I just dislodged a piece of corned beef from my sandwich last night. That'll hold me over till my next meal."

"Okay. I'm gonna leave this room now."

I walk out into the hallway as Paolo asks Veronica, "You want me to put my finger down your throat? Might help." I close the door behind me.

I feel inspired.

I stand on the second-floor landing above the stairs and watch sunlight filter through the big foyer window, making dust particles glorious.

I construct a plan for whatever time I have left:

1. *Find Brian Blum. Ask about my mom.*
   And if she is Paolo's mom.
2. *Be real with Taryn.*
3. *Be real with everyone (i.e., be the opposite of*
   my father).

4. Do something awesome and memorable.

5. Make out with—

"Yo," Felix says from behind me, leaning out of his old bedroom, wearing glasses and a faded oversize T-shirt from some 5K race he ran for charity. "How you doing? Having fun in that bathroom, eh?" He grins like an idiot.

"What? No. Did it sound like we were having fun?"

"I don't know what it sounded like. I was trying to take a nap, and then I was listening to you guys shouting at each other about sex."

"Denton!" my stepmom calls from downstairs. "Your father and I are ready to head to the hospital whenever you are."

Yeah, I won't be doing that.

"Cool," I shout back. "I just have to pee first."

"Isn't that what you were just doing for the past fifteen minutes?" my stepmom asks.

Oops. Good point. I never actually went when I was in there.

"Right," I shout, "but I have to go again. My stomach is being really weird."

"Nice cover," Felix says.

"Okay," my stepmom says, "we'll have the hospital check that out, too. Come down when you're ready."

"Oh, Raquel," Felix says under his breath, smirking and shaking his head.

We stand in silence for a moment. I wish I had more to say to him.

Own that shit.

"How come you never want to really talk to me?" I ask.

"What?" Felix says, a look on his face like that's the last thing he expected me to say. "We talk."

"Yeah, I mean, we joke around and stuff, but you don't really know me. You don't ask how I am."

"Of course I ask how you are. I'm always keeping tabs on how you are."

"Keeping tabs? That's what I mean. I'm talking about having a conversation."

Felix looks at me for a moment, then takes a few steps down the hallway and motions for me to follow. We walk into the shadows, away from the bright foyer.

"Hey, I know I haven't always been the best brother," he says, looking the most serious I've ever seen him. "And I'm sorry about that. I probably could have been around for you more."

"No, I mean . . . Well, yeah, actually, you could have, but it's okay. You saved my life this morning. That counts for something."

Felix puts a hand on my shoulder. "I'll always have your back. You know that, right?" He looks into my eyes, that same odd intensity from yesterday.

"I think so."

"Good." He pats my shoulder, then retracts his hand and heads back down the hall into his room. "I'm gonna go change."

Not the most satisfying brotherly moment, but it's something.

"Oh," he says, leaning back out. "Almost forgot." He reaches into the pocket of his shorts and hands me a business card.

"Thought you might want this." He smiles and shuts the door.

I look at the card.

BRIAN BLUM, M.D.

Obstetrics & Gynecology
908.473.5689

"Wha—?"

I knock on Felix's door.

"Hey," I shout-whisper. "Feel, how did you get this? Do you know him?"

I hear him moving around, but he doesn't respond.

"Felix, please," I say.

His door opens again. He's now wearing a button-down shirt over running shorts.

"You should call him." Felix buttons as he talks. "Screw that hospital shit. It's your life."

"But—"

"Love you, Dent." He shuts the door.

"What's going on up there, sweetie?" my step-mom says.

I'm unsure how I can possibly put off this hospital visit for much longer, but I have to try.

"Oh, I'm, uh, I'm gonna lie down for a sec; I don't feel

great. But not in a death way. Just, like, a need-to-lie-down way."

"But that's *why* we need to take you to the hospital!"

I scamper down the hall and into my room, which is thankfully now empty.

I close the door and sit on the bed.

I stare at the card.

Felix knows Brian.

Felix has my back.

Felix isn't telling me things.

I don't have the mental energy to untangle more cryptic knots.

I take out my phone.

I push Brian's number into my keypad.

I press call.

24

Brian picks up on the second ring. There's jazz playing in the background.

"Hi," I say. "Is this, um, Brian?"

"Denton," he says. "You got my number." He sounds genuinely relieved. "You okay? Feeling all right? Has anyone strange been following you?"

The barrage of questions throws me off. I'm reminded that I don't even know this man.

"Yeah, uh, feeling fine, more or less," I say. "But . . . Well, I would love to ask you some questions about my mother. If that's okay."

"Yes, of course. Of course. We shouldn't stay on this line too long, though. Can we talk in person?"

"Oh," I say.

"Obviously wouldn't work for me to come over there," Brian says. "I don't think your parents would be too happy about that."

"No. You sure we can't talk real quick on the phone?"
Who does he think might be listening in?

"No, no. I mean, look, totally up to you, but I could . . .
Well, I could swing by and pick you up? We could go somewhere to talk. If you feel all right with that."

I'm not sure how I feel. I was thinking this would be
a brief but enlightening phone conversation. Instead, this
paranoid man, who I have no actual reason to trust, wants
me to leave my Sitting to meet up with him.

"You still there? Denton?"

But if I don't go, where does that leave me? Headed to
the hospital with my parents and as ignorant as ever about
my mother?

"Um," I say.

I summon all of my untapped stealth skills as I creep down
the steps.

Leaving the house on my deathdate to get into a strang-
er's car probably qualifies as reaching the reckless life-
endangering stage. But I need to do something.

I hear my stepmom, my dad, and Paolo's mom chatting
in the kitchen, so I swerve quietly into the laundry nook.
I have a view of the family room, where Taryn and Millie
are sitting on the couch watching some romantic comedy.
Grandpa Sid is still in the big chair, now awake. "No, you
shouldn't, because you're an ass!" he shouts at the screen.

Sit tight, Taryn. BRB. Maybe.

I crack open the back door and step outside. The day
is still beautiful, almost tauntingly so. The smell of grass,

flowers, and sun. I sneeze. Loud. I'm only three steps away from the house. I don't think anyone heard. Please let my death not be a result of seasonal allergies.

I duck and run through the yard and out to the sidewalk. I'm meeting Brian two blocks from my house so that we won't be seen. I keep a close eye on the power lines above me. If one of them falls or sparks, I am ready to weave and dodge.

You know, just a purple teenager stealth-running down the street, nothing unusual here.

A brazen squirrel skitters right into my path. I make a quick move so it'll run away, but it doesn't. It stares me down.

"Oh, fuck you, squirrel," I say. "I'm not gonna die of rabies, all right?"

It steps closer.

"ALL RIGHT?" I shout. The squirrel bounds away.

Yeah, that's right. I'm not so nice anymore, am I?

My moment of pride fades when I realize I've just yelled at a squirrel.

There's a green Honda Civic parked curbside that matches the description Brian gave me. I get in.

"Hi," I say.

"Pistachio?" Brian asks, holding out a handful of them. He's wearing a scratchy brown-and-green-striped handwoven shirt.

"Um, no thanks."

"Okay." He cracks one between his teeth. "Also got half a turkey sandwich here, if you want it. Didn't know how hungry you'd be."

"Oh, thanks." I am pretty hungry, actually, but first I'll

take a few minutes to gauge if Brian's the kind of guy who would poison a teenager.

"No prob. Seat belt?"

"Yup." I buckle up.

We drive.

The car smells like salad.

"Thanks again for getting in touch," he says. "You did the right thing."

"Sure. Um, where are we going?"

"I was gonna ask you, actually. I don't know this town too well. Anywhere under the radar we can park to talk?"

I'm about to mention me and Taryn's spot, but that's a little too off the beaten path to feel comfortable. Instead, I direct us toward Tensmore Shopping Center. We can park in the back, with the skaters and the druggies.

"So, let's talk," Brian says. "What's up?"

"Um, well." Where to begin? "A cop stopped me the other night for no reason."

Brian's head turns fast. "You serious? Like, a local cop?" He looks alarmed. "Why'd he say he was stopping you?"

"Said something about a deathdate statute to make sure I'm not planning on committing any end-of-life crimes. Then made me get out of the car and asked if I had a fever or, like, a virus or something."

"Huh."

"I mean, I wasn't purple yet then, so he couldn't have been referring to that."

"Oh right, right." Brian takes a quick glance at me. He's not thrown at all by how I look. "The purple."

"Do you know what this is?"

"Do I know? I mean . . . It's probably, you know . . . Maybe it is some kind of virus."

We pass HealthBuzz Gym, its muscular bee smirking at us from the sign.

"Do you think it's fatal?"

"Look," Brian says. "At the end of the day, I'm primarily a gynecologist. If you don't have a vagina, there's gonna be a limit to what I can do."

"Sure, of course."

"That was a joke," Brian says. "Kind of."

"Oh right."

We pass Kool Kones Ice Cream.

"So you were stopped by a cop," Brian says. "Any other unusual government types around?"

"Um . . . I don't think so. But, like, what exactly makes you think the government would be following me around in the first place?"

"Oh." Brian turns his head to look at me, then stares back at the road. "Well, I could tell you that, but then I'd have to kill you."

I freeze in my seat. I shouldn't be here.

"Ohmigod, that was totally a joke," Brian says, seeing how freaked out I am. "I'm sorry, I . . . Under the circumstances, I could see how that would be the wrong thing to say."

"Maybe," I say.

"I promise I'm only trying to look out for you. But I'm in a tricky situation because there's . . . Well, there's some things I just can't tell you."

Brian seems like he's being honest, but I'm still questioning my decision to be here. I need to get what I came for and then get home.

"You can tell me about my mom, though, right?"

"Her, yes." Brian smiles nervously. "Absolutely. What do you want to know?"

"Oh, a lot." I start big. "Like, did she have other kids?"

Brian chuckles. "What do you mean, like, besides you and Felix? Not that I know of."

"Right, but . . . I mean, is it possible that my mom didn't actually die and she's, like, my best friend's mom? Like, you guys made up this other woman Cheryl to, like . . . cover up . . . the fact that . . . this other lady . . ." I trail off. Now that I try to articulate it, this theory makes close to zero sense. Negative sense, maybe.

"Hmm," Brian says, looking concerned. "No, Cheryl's your biological mother. I'm very sure of this. Seeing as I delivered you. Out of her."

My sense of self deflates. Brian must think I'm very stupid.

"Yeah, no, that does make sense."

We slow-stop at a traffic light. Brian is a careful driver.

"I know it's probably been hard," he says, turning to look at me, "to have your actual mother gone your whole life, so of course it'd be easier to imagine that the woman who gave birth to you is someone you've always known."

That *was* nice to imagine.

"I really get it, man," Brian says. "It's just not the case here."

"Okay," I say. I feel like crying, and I don't even know why.

At least I didn't have sex with my sister.

"But I think the real problem here is, it sounds like no one's been telling you a thing about Cheryl. Now's your chance."

A car honks behind us. The light is green.

Brian drives.

"Um . . ." I finally have what I want, and I can't think of a thing to ask. "So, like, you were my mom's best friend but also her gynecologist? Wasn't that a little weird? Checking out all her . . . lady business?"

I'm ashamed that this is my first question; I don't even know why I asked it.

Brian laughs. "Well, we were close, and that's my job. It was nothing I hadn't seen before."

"You mean on other ladies?" A motorcycle passes us. It startles me.

"Yes, that, but also, well . . . Before I figured myself out, your mother and I were together for a little while."

"You were . . ."

"We were a couple. During our freshman year of college. I was confused, and we got along really well, so, for six months, we convinced ourselves we could be a couple." He clears his throat. "It didn't work out. Obviously. Your mom's not my type." He chuckles again as he stops at another light.

"My mom was your girlfriend?" In all my thinking about my biological mother, I usually focused on the years after she had met my dad. So her relationship with Brian Blum is surprising in and of itself, but also because it makes me realize there are huge chunks of my mom's life I never even bothered to consider. It's embarrassing.

"Yep, she was."

I think about my mom and Brian back then, as college freshmen, more or less the same age as I am now. "How did you meet?"

"We lived in the same dorm. Actually, your mother was the first person I met when I got to school. I was moving all my stuff into my room, my parents awkwardly standing around helping—God, I haven't thought about any of this in years—and your mom popped her head in, this ball of energy with huge, springy brown hair. 'Hey, I'm Cheryl! I'm trying to meet everybody today so I can get it over with.' I liked her right away." Talking about my mother has relaxed Brian considerably, which relaxes me, too. I can almost forget that he jokingly threatened to kill me a few minutes ago.

Green light. We drive.

"You know, I think your mother knew I was gay before I did," he says, almost to himself.

Okay. Guess Brian's gay.

"And even once she knew, we stayed together for five more months. She later told me she liked the challenge, that she really thought she could make me fall in love with her, in spite of the fact that I was attracted to men. I have to say, she sort of succeeded."

"What, like, you were in love with her?" I ask as we pull into the Tensmore parking lot.

"In some ways, sure."

"Wait, you're not gonna drop some crazy bomb on me right now, like you're my actual father or something?"

Brian laughs. "Lyle is one hundred percent your father."

We pass Mike Tarrance walking out of Sanjay Tuxedo with a huge bag, and I'm reminded that prom is tonight.

"Your mother and I hadn't, uh, interacted in any way remotely close to that since that first year of school."

"You can go around there." I point, trying to simultaneously give directions and change the subject.

"And even then we probably only slept together a dozen or so times." *Only* a dozen? "She's actually the only woman I ever had sex with. Wait, no, there was another one my senior year of college. But that was an accident. Well, not an accident, but it happened because of a bet. Like, a funny bet."

"Eh, okay." Brian's picked a strange time to start TMI-ing, what with me about to die any minute. Actually, maybe that's what makes me the perfect person to tell this stuff to. I've got nowhere to take it but the grave.

"I think I've lost the thread here," Brian says. No shit, dude!

He parks the car. There's no one else back here except one twelve-year-old-looking skater kid kicking his board up over and over again near the brick wall.

We're both silent. I unwrap the half of turkey sandwich and take a bite. I'm starving.

"So why is my dad so mad at you?" I ask as I chew. The questions are now flowing free and easy.

Brian sighs. "The day your mother died was . . . a hard day. For everyone involved."

"Is he angry because you were the doctor who let her die?"

"Well . . . That's part of it. It's complicated. I didn't

actually want to be the doctor to deliver you. Just like your dad, I was a little shocked that your mother had gotten pregnant so close to her deathdate. It was . . . irresponsible. Selfish."

"So you're in the wish-I-never-existed camp."

"No! Oh God, no, and I'm sure your dad doesn't feel that way either. It's just that bringing a child into the world, knowing it was going to be motherless, seemed unfair. Not to mention that the baby would likely be the thing that killed her."

I have to remind myself that the baby he's referring to is me.

"But she knew all that. She just wanted to . . . to make sure the baby made it out alive. I told her there was no way I was going to deliver her child, no way I would be the doctor who lost her. But she was a very persuasive lady."

"How was she persuasive?" The kid's skateboard ricochets against the wall.

Brian smiles. "When your mother got her mind set on something, you knew she was going to get what she wanted. If you tried to convince her otherwise, you'd just be wasting time fighting the inevitable. That's how."

"Was she intimidating?"

"Nah, not really. She was more charming and funny and determined. And weird."

"Weird?"

"There was one semester where she decided she only wanted to wear shorts. No pants, no dresses, no skirts. Just shorts. So September through December, that's what she did."

"That's a little crazy."

"That was your mom."

I came from a woman who insisted on wearing shorts in December?

"And she was determined to have me as her doctor. So, after much time wasted fighting the inevitable, I agreed." Brian rubs his brow with his index finger. "Which I never should have done . . ."

"Why not?" I say.

Brian looks up, and I'm startled to see tears forming in the corners of his eyes. "I thought I was doing the right thing, you have to understand that."

"Sure, of course you were. But . . . what are you talking about exactly?"

"It doesn't matter now." Brian joins the ever-growing ranks of Adults Losing Their Shit in Front of Me.

"Brian . . . I mean, it was her deathdate, right? I'm sure you did everything you could. . . ."

"You're a sweet kid, Denton," Brian says, wiping his face with the scratchy fabric of his shirt. "I see so much of the old Cheryl in you."

"Oh. Thanks, I guess."

There's the sound of rolling wheels as the kid skates away. Just us back here.

Brian cracks another pistachio. I wonder if my parents have realized yet I'm not at home.

"So how . . . how did my mom actually die?" I ask.

The question floats in the air for many seconds.

Brian adds his shell to an existing pile on the dashboard. "When she was giving birth to you, you were in breech— flipped the wrong way—so we had to do a C-section. And . . . it didn't go as planned."

"So she died because of me."

"Whoa." Brian turns and leans toward me. "No," he says. "Absolutely not."

"But just on a technical level, if I hadn't been flipped the wrong way, then—"

"Denton." He's focused on me in a way that makes him look like he's trying to balance a stack of books on his head. "If anything, you are the victim here, so please, *please* assure me you know it's not your fault. We did the C-section, and then . . . your mother was gone. No one's fault. That's life."

"Okay."

"Good." Brian leans back. He takes a deep breath.

"Did she know I wasn't going to live long?"

"What?" Brian says, for some reason caught off guard.

"When you took blood and hair and found out my deathdate? Doesn't that happen soon after the baby comes out? Was she conscious for that?"

"Oh," Brian says. "Uh, no, I don't think so. No, she didn't know how long you would live."

"That's good; it might have bummed her out." I absentmindedly pick up a pistachio. "Did she get to hold me?"

"She didn't," Brian says. "But she wanted to."

My nose is filled with tear snot.

"Get down!" Brian says.

"What?" I say, dropping my pistachio.

"Down," he repeats, and this time he physically demonstrates with an arm on my back.

"What's happening?" I say, awkwardly squished next to the glove compartment.

"That cop who stopped you," Brian says, looking into the rearview. "What did he look like?"

"Why?"

"There's a cop parked behind us."

I adjust myself just enough so I can glance into the side mirror.

Ohmigod. "It's him," I say. HorribleCop. Again.

"All right, just stay down," Brian says.

He calmly starts the car and slowly drives forward.

"Is he following us?" I ask.

"Not yet, no."

We keep moving. My whole body is tense.

"Now is he?" I ask.

I should never have left the house. I'm such an idiot.

"No."

I close my eyes. I feel the car turn.

"Is he following us yet?"

I don't want to spend the rest of my time in jail. I don't.

"Okay. You can get up," Brian says, breathing out, visibly shaken. "He never followed."

I slowly come back up, the muscles of my body screaming at me. HorribleCop is nowhere to be seen.

We drive the rest of the way in silence.

When we're once again curbside, a couple of blocks from my house, I unbuckle my seat belt and turn to Brian. "Thanks for, you know, telling me things about my mom that I never would have known. It really means a lot." I extend my hand to shake.

Brian takes it, leans across, and hugs me.

"It's been so amazing to meet you, man. Your mother

would be proud." I hope that's true. "Just . . ." Brian stares at me, trying to choose the right words. "You should know that if . . . Well, just trust your instincts. You know?"

I don't really know, but I nod anyway. "Sure, of course, yeah." I open the car door, and the spring air touches my face. I look back. "Bye, Brian."

He smiles. A few of his bottom teeth are crooked. "Bye, Denton."

I jog down the block toward home.

I figure if I enter through the back door, then maybe—just maybe—there's a chance no one will have ever realized I was gone.

I step in and click the door shut behind me.

The dryer's loud thumps muffle my entrance. Nice.

I take a few cautious steps toward the family room. I can hear my stepmom talking to Felix upstairs.

"But what I'm saying is, if he's not feeling well, I should go in his room and see if I can help."

"I know," Felix says, "but he said he wants to be alone in there. That he needs some time."

"Yes, but what if he's . . ."

"He's not, Raquel, I promise."

Wow. Felix must be trying to make up for eighteen years of subpar brothering in this one day. I'll take it.

The sound of the TV gets louder as I inch farther into the house.

There's no time to waste. With step one accomplished, it's time to move down the list.

Having a clearer picture of who my mother is gives me strength and comfort, like a second beating heart that's sprouted up next to the first.

I will talk with Taryn. I will be charming and funny and determined, just like my mom.

And I will be real. Because life is too short.

I am a powerful, benevolent truth teller.

"Taryn," I say, starting to speak before I'm even in the room, "I need to talk to you." Once the words are out of my mouth, I see that I'm staring at Millie and a sleeping Grandpa Sid.

No Taryn.

"She walked out," Millie says, looking up from some knitting she's doing. "She was crying. I'm assuming because of you."

"Are you serious?" I say.

"Do I look serious?"

"I have no idea."

"Exactly."

"Aarrgh," I say. Maybe I can still catch Taryn. I run to the front door and fling it open, the voice of my stepmom echoing in my wake. ("Denton! You're downstairs? How did you— No, do NOT walk out that door, DO YOU HEAR ME?") I stand on the front porch, scanning left and right for my girlfriend. She's down the street a little ways, getting into the old blue car that used to be her dad's. "TARYN!" I shout. She stops and looks. Then she continues getting into the car. She turns the engine on.

"Taryn, wait, wait, wait, PLEASE!" I shout as I run

across the lawn, trying to get there in time to stop her. She can't leave. I need closure.

Taryn seems to respect the effort I'm making on her behalf, because now she's shouting back at me through the windshield, "Denton! DENTON!" Strange, but, okay, at least she's acknowledging me.

As I run into the street, I start to get the feeling that maybe she's shouting my name not out of love but to warn me about something. I read her lips: "DENTON!! CAR!! CAR!!!"

Car?

In the next second, these things happen:

My right foot lands on the pavement weirdly.

I twist my ankle.

I hop up and down in pain.

A horn blares in my ear.

A yellow car blasts past me, so close I am sure this is my death.

Taryn shrieks my name from inside her car.

My stepmom shrieks my name from inside the house.

The car does not hit me, but the force of air as it passes knocks me backward, and my elbows slam into the curb.

In a bizarre delayed reaction, the yellow car, already past me, swerves to the opposite side of the street and knocks down the Werner family's mailbox. It stops, half on the curb, half on the street.

I look down at my feet and wiggle my toes inside my sneakers. My ankle is throbbing. My elbows hurt. They're covered with gravel and blood.

Taryn rushes across the street. I can hear my stepmom

and dad and the whole crew rushing over from the house. And someone is emerging from the sporty yellow car that almost killed me.

Holy shit.

That's the same sporty yellow car that almost ran me over last night. I'm sure of it. The person driving this car has been trying to kill me.

"Dent, ohmigod, ohmigod, I thought that was it," Taryn says, crouching down in front of me, crying. She leans in and kisses me. Apparently, the best way to end a fight with your girlfriend is to almost get killed in front of her.

"DENTON!" my stepmom yells as she runs up. "Are you okay? ARE YOU OKAY?"

"Yeah, Mom, I'm okay," I say, my eyes locked on the person getting out of the yellow car, ready to identify my assassin. It's gonna be Phil, I know it.

"How dare you leave this house? And who runs across a street on their deathdate without looking?" my stepmom says. She's crying, of course, as she leans in and kisses me repeatedly on the forehead, blocking my view of Yellow Car Driver. "Oh, you're bleeding, my baby's bleeding, okay, we need to clean you up. Felix! Run in and get some bandages and disinfectant."

"Oh shit, you okay, man?" says Yellow Car Driver, who has walked up to us during my stepmom's fawning.

It's Willis Ellis, that pothead who was at my funeral. I've gone to school with him since first grade, and he is, quite literally, the last person I would peg as a potential assassin. "You gotta watch where you're driving, Willis," I say.

"Dude, I am so sorry. And sorry about your mailbox, too."

"That's not ours," my stepmom says, disdain in her voice. "You'll have to go across the street and apologize to Fran and Hank. You should be ashamed of yourself, driving like that."

Here I am again, out on my front lawn, watching as my stepmom scolds one of my peers for almost killing me.

Willis runs his fingers through his dreadlocks. "Aw, man, I know, man." His eyes are red; he's a walking stoner stereotype. "Dude, I'm sorry I almost hit you," he says to me. "Jeannie keeps texting that I have to go pick up this corsage thing and then texting how come I'm not responding and I'm, like, texting back: *I'm driving!* You know?"

"You were texting while you were driving?" my stepmom asks, steam shooting out her nostrils. No texting while driving is one of her platform issues.

"Well, yeah, but only to say that I couldn't text because I was driving. And then I look up and this dude is almost right in the middle of the street. Hey, wait," Willis says, his face lighting up with a brilliant realization. "Ohmigod, you're dying today! WHOA. I could have killed you, man!" Gee, that hadn't occurred to me. "I would've felt extremely bad about that."

"You would have felt extremely bad when you went to jail for involuntary manslaughter," my stepmom says.

"Easy, Raquel," my dad says.

"Fun funeral, by the way," Willis says.

"Uh, thanks," I say.

"So is that why you're purple?" He gestures to my skin

and inadvertently touches my arm. The red dots shift. "Whoa." He touches my arm again. The dots shift. "It's beautiful." He reaches for me again.

"Okay, stop," I say, pulling my arm away.

"Your arm, man . . ."

"I know, I know."

I'm ninety-nine percent certain that Willis wasn't trying to hit me. Just a crazy coincidence, then, that he almost hit me twice. A really crazy coincidence.

"Willis," I say, "I think you almost hit me last night, too."

"Last night? No, dude, I didn't get in any accidents last night."

"Yeah, were you driving on Sterrick Road, a little bit after midnight?"

"Uh, which is Sterrick Road again? The long, woodsy road?"

"Yeah. I mean, I guess it's long and woodsy."

"I might have been driving home from Derek's house. He lives down a long, woodsy road. But I definitely didn't get in any accidents." Of course he has a friend named Derek who lives off Sterrick.

"I'm pretty sure it was you. It was the same yellow car. You narrowly missed hitting me."

"This car over here?" Willis asks, pointing to his car.

"Yeah, your car."

"This is actually my mom's car."

"Okay, so your mom's car."

"Maybe she was the one who almost hit you," Willis says. "She's pretty much an awful driver. Heh heh."

He is from another planet.

"Well, was your mom driving the car last night or were you?"

Willis looks down and thinks hard.

"Me!" he says. "It was me driving, I'm sure of it! Wow, can't believe I remembered that."

I can actually feel some of my brain cells dying just talking to him.

"Anyways, Jeannie's really on my back to pick this thing up, so I better get going," Willis says.

"You shouldn't be driving while . . . under the influence of anything," my stepmom says. "And I hope you're planning on paying for that mailbox you destroyed."

"Yeah, absolutamente. I'll bring the money back and drop it off in their mailbox. Heh heh heh. I'm just kiddin'."

My stepmom is not amused.

"Whoa, PaoloMan, didn't see you standing there. Hey, hey."

Paolo has been standing over me in a protective stance, with his hands on his hips.

"Yo, ChillisWillis, good to see you. Try not to kill my best friend on your way outta here."

My stepmom is disgusted to see that Willis and Paolo have some kind of friendship. I'm a little disgusted, too. Paolo looks at me and shrugs while making a subtle joint-smoking gesture: *Yeah, he's an idiot, but where do you think I get my pot from?*

"I most certainly will," Willis says. "Sorry again about the car situation. And, whoa, guess I'll be seeing you soon at prom. I don't even wanna go. Heh heh."

"Noyouwon'tI'llbedead," I say quietly to his turned back as he walks back to his car. He gets in and drives away, Dave Matthews blaring out the window.

"If this wasn't your deathdate," my stepmom says, "I would have torn his head off. Your head off, too."

"Understandable," I say.

"With those dreads, Willis's head would make a good sponge," Millie says.

We all look at her.

"For cleaning," she adds.

"Denton," my stepmom says. "You shouldn't have left the house without telling us. That was very dangerous."

"I know," I say.

"I'm just glad you're all right. We're not going to the hospital, okay? You got your wish. In fact, we won't be going anywhere. You're not allowed outside anymore. Okay? Not up for debate."

It sucks, but where the hell was I gonna go anyway?

"Got some bandages. Let's fix you up, Purple," Felix says, appearing at my right side.

"Wait, wait, wait. Can we get Denton out of the street before you do this?" my stepmom asks. "This is a major thoroughfare. We need to get away from here."

"It's a residential street in a suburban neighborhood," Felix says, "but message received. Dent, you good to stand up?"

"Sure," I say, but as Felix helps me to my feet, pain shoots up from my ankle, which I'd temporarily forgotten about. "Ow."

"What, your foot?" Felix asks.

"What's wrong, what's wrong?" my stepmom asks.

"My ankle, I ran on it wrong and twisted it. Right before the car came."

"Really?" Felix asks.

"Yes, really," I say. "What's so crazy about me twisting my ankle?"

"Nothing, just . . . It saved you."

"What did?"

"You twisted your ankle, and it saved you from getting hit by the car."

"Oh." I guess that's true. "Well, great, but it still hurts."

"Yeah, yeah, let's walk you over here." Felix assists me as I limp away from the street and helps me sit down on our front steps. He becomes surprisingly nurselike as he cleans out my elbow wounds and covers them with bandages.

"Such a good older brother," Paolo's mom says.

Everyone who was in the house is crowded around me, except for Grandpa Sid and Veronica. Taryn is next to me, rubbing my back. "Let's check out this ankle," Felix says. I fully extend my right leg and roll up my jeans. "Huh," he says.

"Huh what?" I say.

"Look."

I do, and I see that the red dots on my ankle are moving around uninstigated by anyone's touch, rapidly reconfiguring themselves in a grid pattern. "Huh," I say.

"Does it hurt?" Felix asks.

"It does. My ankle is kinda throbbing."

"The injury might have triggered something with this rash."

"Triggered something?"

"Well, I don't know, but let's keep tabs on it."

"Felix," I say, "what do you think I've been doing all day?"

He silently wraps my ankle with an Ace bandage.

For once, Felix is actually being an attentive, caring brother, so I don't know why I'm getting all irritated with him.

"I don't think Denton should be near cars anymore," Millie says.

"Thank you, Millicent," my stepmom says. "I agree."

"Me too," Taryn says.

"You hit me, then almost got hit, then almost got hit again," Millie says.

"I'll stay away from cars, everyone." With the danger having passed—at least for now—I see a restless look on Taryn's face, like she's remembered she's supposed to be mad at me. "Look, now that I'm okay and still alive, would you guys mind leaving me and Taryn alone out here for a little bit?"

"RUDE," Paolo says. He's kidding.

"I don't disagree, Paolo," my stepmom says, but she's not kidding. She and everyone else shuffle into the house.

Taryn and I sit on the porch step in silence. It really is beautiful out, one of those breezy, not-a-care-in-the-world spring days. The sun feels good. It's nice not to have to worry about sunscreen anymore.

"I'm so glad you're still alive," Taryn says.

I take her hand. "Me too."

"I was all set to leave and never see you again."

"Yeah, I got that. That's why I was inspired to run into the street without looking. To stop you."

"Because you care or because you hate having people angry at you?"

Can it be both?

She absentmindedly plays with a bundle of her hair as she stares at the ground. "Look, I get that today is your deathdate, and the last thing I wanna do is make this about me. I'm trying so hard not to, Dent. Really."

"I know that," I say. For her, this is trying hard.

"But I couldn't sit there any longer, waiting and hoping you would want to hang out with me."

"I do want to hang out with you," I say.

She looks up at me, then back at the ground, tears entering her voice. "I heard you laughing with her."

Oh man. I thought she was angry because I left the house and ditched her, but maybe she never even realized I was gone. She just heard me with Veronica. Well, this is cutting to the chase faster than I wanted to, but so be it.

"I got worried," Taryn continues, "so I went up to check on you, but before I could knock . . . I heard you laughing with her. In the bathroom."

"Yeah . . ."

"Why would you do that?" Taryn looks up at me, her eyes pink and glossy.

"I . . ." I hadn't anticipated just how much the truth would make me feel like a shithead, but I must press onward. "Taryn, you're completely right. It was wrong of me. I didn't plan it. Veronica was in there when I went to pee."

"So then why didn't you leave? Or tell her to leave?"

"I guess because . . ." Own that shit. "I was enjoying

talking to her. I've known Veronica for, like, ever, and we were laughing about how weird it was that I'm gonna die."

"But I wanna be the one laughing with you on your deathdate, Dent. . . ."

"Yeah, I know. You can laugh with me, too. Let's laugh about something right now."

"Don't patronize me," Taryn says, picking at the nail polish on her index finger.

I don't say anything.

"If this is some weird punishment for me spending time with Phil at your funeral, please, Dent, you have to forgive me. Please."

"Yeah, I forgive you, of course I do. Tar—and I mean this in the best way—just like you said, this really isn't about you. I'm going to die soon. Any minute, really, so—"

"And if you're blaming me for Phil and his gun, I'm so sorry, Dent. I'm so sorry. I wouldn't have ever forgiven myself if he . . ." She begins to sob—big, contorted-face bawling.

I put my arms around her. "Tar, it's okay, it's okay."

"I know you think I ran back into the house because I was freaked that I was all splotchy. I feel so bad about that."

I'd forgotten that happened.

Taryn looks up at me, a few stray strands of light brown hair covering her face. "Me running away doesn't mean I don't love you. I love you so much. Too much. It makes me angry at you."

I kiss her, and it's like one of the electric kisses from the beginning of our relationship. I remember making out at a party Max Reinhold threw when his parents went away for the weekend. It was a November night, and we were some of the only people in the backyard, but we didn't notice the cold at all.

We pull out of the kiss, still close.

I look at her and wonder: if I were going to live to old age, would she actually be someone I would marry? I try to picture us in a house somewhere, playing a board game with our kids, the family dog bounding over and hilariously messing up all the game pieces.

Who am I kidding? I have no idea what being married would be like. Or if Taryn would be that person.

"I want you to know how insanely important you are to me," I say. "Being with you these seven months has been one of the best things in my life. I mean that."

Taryn is drinking up my words, her hazel eyes brimming, so moved that it's making me think twice about leading with this section instead of the part where I confess what I did with Veronica.

"You're so pretty and so crazy talented and so funny. Your smile kills me every time. And you're smart. You think you're not, but you are. Seriously."

Taryn just stares, tears racing each other down her cheeks.

Behind us, the front door opens up. Taryn wipes her cheeks dry. It's Veronica—naturally—wearing a big black hooded sweatshirt that I recognize as Felix's. She navigates around us and bounds down the steps.

"Ron, wait!" Paolo's mom says, leaning out the front door.

"No," Veronica says, continuing to speed-walk away.

"You don't understand. Please!"

"Bye, guys," Veronica says, without turning around or taking down her hood.

I'm confused by what's happening. I know I don't want Veronica to leave, though.

"Veronica!" Paolo's mom says. "How are you gonna get home? I have the car keys."

"Guess I'll just have to walk," Veronica says.

"You're overreacting!" Paolo's mom says.

Veronica strides away down the sidewalk.

"Uh, bye!" I call out.

"Yeah, night," Taryn says.

I turn back to Paolo's mom, who's still suspended in the doorway, trailing Veronica with her eyes.

"Everything okay?" I say.

"What?" Paolo's mom says, as if breaking from a trance. "Oh yeah, nothing for you to worry about, certainly. Sorry to interrupt." She steps back in and closes the front door.

"Weirdest exit ever," Taryn says.

"I know," I say.

"And it's, like, a beautiful day. Why was Veronica wearing a hoodie?"

That's as good of a segue as any.

"Hey, so you know how before I was saying all this really isn't about you?"

"Yeah . . . ," Taryn says, already looking alarmed.

"No, don't worry, I'm just . . . Okay, so I'm going to die, right? My life is going to end. And I love you so much. I know that now, I really love you—"

"Are you breaking up with me?" Taryn says, eyes wide.

"Well, no, I mean, I'm about to die, so—"

"Did you cheat on me? Is that what this is?"

"Oh wow, whoa, easy, easy." I wanted to approach this with tact and integrity. Instead, this thing is rocketing out of my control.

"Did you?"

"I . . . Well, lemme get to that part."

Taryn gasps like she's in some kind of old-timey horror movie. She looks like she's in shock. "Get to that part? Ohmigod. You cheated on me. With Veronica."

"Well, sorta. I mean, yes, essentially, but I don't think of it as cheating—"

"What?" Taryn is very pale.

"I think of it as exploring. I'm a dying dude who needed to explore, and it has nothing to do with you. You get that, right?"

"I can't believe you," she says. An army of tears rises up and hangs on to the cliffs of her eyeballs, ready to jump.

"I'm sorry," I say. "I've never died before. I don't think I'm very good at it. But I still love you."

"Don't you say those words to me." As if in response to her anger, Taryn's splotch slowly snakes above her scarf and up her neck, blossoming outward to cover her entire chin.

"What are you looking at?" Taryn asks.

"Oh, it's . . . Don't worry, it's just your chin. . . ."

Taryn's hand shoots up to her face, and her brain-gears begin spinning. She looks at me, incredulous. "Veronica has this, too, doesn't she? Ohmigod. OhmiGOD." Taryn begins to straight-up weep into her hands. Which is even more devastating than her earlier sobs.

"Oh, Tar . . ."

I don't know why, but when I imagined the way this would play out, it wasn't nearly this painful.

"I'm sorry," I say. "I was so drunk I don't even remember it. At least the—" I stop before saying the words *first time*. There's no need to reference our bathroom make-out. Even being real has its limits.

Taryn's sobs peter out. She stares at me. It's brutal. Her mouth is moving, but she can't make words. "What . . . what did you do with her?"

"Taryn, please. It takes nothing away from what we have, it—"

"What did you do with her?" she says again, with a surprising amount of power.

I can't lie. "I guess . . . We did it."

Taryn puts her hand to her mouth like she's going to throw up, and it suddenly seems overdramatic. I mean, come on, I'm the one dying.

"I know it seems horrible, I do," I say. "But I got drunk for the first time, and it happened. And honestly, I'm glad it happened." Words are pouring out. "This—today—is about my life, and me, and I was never trying to hurt you. So I understand if you hate me, but I hope, I really hope, you can forgive me one day."

Taryn is crying and staring forward into nothing. She slowly stands and starts to walk away.

"I can't," she says quietly.

I watch as she gets into her car again, but this time I don't chase after her.

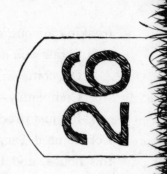

"No way. Screw you."

Paolo's not on board with my idea.

"Why not?" I ask.

"WHY NOT? I'm not gonna even answer that, I just won't."

"It could be fun. We could get creative with it!"

Paolo stares at me like I'm crazy. Maybe I am. "I'm sorry, are we talking about the same thing? Did you seriously just say we could 'get creative' with ways for you to kill yourself?"

"Yeah, you know, something legendary. Like with pills *and* a gun. You love Kurt Cobain; I thought you'd be into this."

Paolo puts the palms of his hands onto his eyes and breathes loudly. He's sitting in my desk chair; I'm on the edge of my bed. "Okay, I don't even . . . You are actually freaking me out, dude. Do we have to bring in a suicide expert to talk you down off the ledge? We can call a hotline."

"Oh, come on, I'm completely clearheaded right now—"

"Completely—"

"I'm just tired of waiting around for bad shit to happen! I obliterated Taryn's heart, your sister's gone, I'm stuck in this house, and I've got a dickhead cop hovering around waiting to do God knows what to me. What's the point of waiting it out another five hours? Why shouldn't I control the one thing I have control over and just do it myself? Didn't you tell me I should 'own that shit'?"

"That was about being a cool dude who bangs chicks and doesn't care, not about putting a bullet through your head while simultaneously chewing on pills!"

"I don't think the pills would be chewable."

"Whatever! Bottom line: you should've done this on your own, because now that I'm involved, it ain't happening."

He's right. I should have done it on my own. But I wussed out.

After Taryn drove off, I remembered to open the lavender envelope she'd given me, which had been sitting unread in my back pocket for hours.

It was one of those standard Hallmark deathdate cards—a picture of a pretty flower on the front under the words YOU WILL BE MISSED—but the note inside was a minor masterpiece.

It was a love letter, plain and simple. Long and pure and surprisingly eloquent.

She said that knowing a genuinely good guy like me was such a gift. Especially because her parents could be really cold to each other, and her dad had actually cheated on her mom when she was ten, and her parents didn't know that she knew that, but she had overheard once or something like that (I skimmed that section once I saw it wasn't about me), and it sorta messed her up. But the point was, I had shown her that there are guys out there with integrity and class, who are loyal and respectful and great. I'd shown her that it is okay to trust men.

I know.

As I sat holding the note, my mind drifted back to my list of things to accomplish before death, and suddenly number four (*Do something awesome and memorable*) took on a dark meaning.

I limped inside and up to my bedroom ("Dent, everything okay?" my stepmom asked. "Did Taryn leave?"), where I began to contemplate the ways I could do it.

I ruled out slitting my wrists: too clichéd and too awful for my parents to find. I thought I could hang myself, but how? The one time I'd tried to hang a picture, it took me two hours. I thought to myself that maybe it would have been easier if Phil had shot me this morning.

And then Paolo was knocking on my door, which I interpreted as the universe sending me an ally for this last mission.

Not so much.

Paolo rolls the desk chair over to the bed and puts his hand on my shoulder.

"Hey. How about we just watch a movie?"

"I'm down to single-digit possible hours left. Why would I want to sit and watch other people experiencing things?"

"Because you love movies," Paolo says quietly, spinning away from me on his chair.

"Sorry, I'm not trying to be a jerk. I'm just scared."

Paolo grabs my Magic Eight Ball off my dresser and starts absentmindedly shaking it. "We don't have to watch a horror movie," he says. "We could watch something funny."

"I'm not saying I'm scared of movies. I'm saying I'm scared to die, Pow."

"Oh. Right. I'm scared, too."

"Yeah." We both get quiet.

Paolo stops shaking the eight ball and looks at it. He slowly raises his eyes to mine. " 'As I see it, yes,' " he says.

"What?"

"I just asked the eight ball if you were going to live through today, and it said, 'As I see it, yes.' Holy shit, dude."

I can tell he's not joking. He actually believes in the power of this plastic toy.

"D, you could be like Harry Potter. Or Darth Vader or something. So cool."

I suddenly remember how lucky I am to have a friend like Paolo. And just like that, I'm not ready to die yet.

"Thank you," I say.

"Don't thank me," Paolo says, dumbfounded. "Thank this amazing contraption here. What great news."

"No, Pow," I say, taking the eight ball out of his hands and putting it on the floor. "Thanks for being my best friend."

"Oh," Paolo says. "You kidding? If I'd never met you, my life would have sucked."

I need to look away, and Paolo does, too. If I don't steer us back to familiar ground, this vulnerable moment may wreck me. "My life would have been fine if I'd never met you, but I still think you're an okay person."

"Thanks very much," Paolo says. "What's one level below 'okay person'? A 'sort of okay' person? Yeah, that's what you are. I hope I've been a helpful role model as you strive to get beyond 'sort of' status."

"Oh no, you've been terrible. Hanging out with you, I think I actually slid from 'sort of okay' to 'sort of not okay.'"

Paolo laughs. "Okay." There's still some sadness in his voice.

"Okay." I can't decide if it's comforting or awful when I think that Paolo will be going through all this in one month. Without me there to comfort him. I imagine what it would be like for me now if Paolo would be living until his eighties. Maybe I'd be happy knowing there would be someone around in sixty years who could tell people what my stupid jokes were like, what kind of a friend I was, what a nerd I was about smoking pot. Or maybe I'd just be insanely jealous.

"So, dude," Paolo says. "You freakin' left the house?" There's awe in his voice.

"I did," I say.

"That is so baller."

"Thanks, man." I tell him about my time with Brian Blum.

"Wow, he sounds like such a gentleman."

"I guess," I say. Classic Paolo, saying something that falls just a hair short of making any sense.

"Hey," Paolo says, "not to make you wanna kill yourself again, but what happened with Taryn out there anyway?"

I sigh. "Not good."

"She found out about you and me maybe having sex, huh?"

I laugh. "Yeah, exactly. Actually, could you hand me my laptop? It's on the desk."

"I thought you were done being online."

"Yeah, but screw that. I'm gonna die. I just wanna check Facebook real quick."

Paolo grabs my laptop and gives it to me. "Okaaaaay, but in my experience, Facebook is a surefire way to become more depressed."

As I bring Paolo up to speed on what actually happened with Taryn, I turn on my computer and go to her Facebook page. It's stupid, but I can't resist.

She hasn't updated her status since I saw her, but at the top of her Timeline, there's a post from Phil from this afternoon: no text, just an image of a little bear with sad eyes, holding a heart that says SORRY on it. So much for Phil being in jail. Unless you can Facebook from there. You get one phone call and ten minutes on the social network of your choice.

I hope he put a bear on my page, too, seeing as I'm the one he tried to murder. I scroll down Taryn's page and see a photo of jelly beans that I posted a few months ago. Taryn loves jelly beans.

I notice my in-box icon shows one new message, so I click on it.

Its subject line is *for denton—this is actually IMPOR-TANT,* and it's from Happy Dinosaur, a name that feels familiar, but I'm not sure why. I open the message and immediately feel like an idiot. It's another Viagra-type sales pitch. Damn you, Happy Dinosaur! Are you seriously following me from email to Facebook?

"What?" Paolo says.

"Aw, nothing. I just thought I had an important message, but it was another ad for boner pills."

"Oh, I love those! Read it out loud." Paolo closes his eyes, like I'm about to take him through a guided meditation.

"Really? Okay . . . 'Happy Dinosaur says—' "

"Ooh, Happy Dinosaur, very cool name, that's important."

"Yeah. 'Happy Dinosaur says: Come to Bloom!!!' "

"Whoa, nice imagery there, like your penis is a flower. . . ."

" '4 huge erections you can buy 120 pills for only $129.95!! !!' "

"That's a pretty decent price, actually."

"And then it's followed by a link to some website and a phone number. It says, 'Click/call to find the address.' What the hell does that mean?"

"Probably just a bad translation into English. That's why I love these ads so much. Is that it?"

"Yeah."

"Ah, nice. That was a good one." Paolo paces around the room, looking at my posters and my bookshelves, like he's done a million times before.

Since I'm already online, I decide to give my page a quick look. Even though dying while in the midst of checking one's own Facebook page is arguably worse than dying while checking email.

"Sorry about my mom, bee-tee-dubs," Paolo says. "Real letdown about the drawer, right? Just Cynthia crushing on your dad. Kinda weird. It'd be cool if they got together, though. We'd be brothers!"

My Timeline is jam-packed with posts. The first one I see says, *I will miss you, Denton Little!* It's from Gina Yarrow, this girl I had a crush on in fourth grade. Man, how come I never told her how I felt?

I comment: *Gina! Thanks! I had a huge crush on you in 4th grade. I used to write about you in my journal all the time.*

It feels good to write that.

Rick Jackson, this beloved dude from the football team, wrote: *You're the funniest guy I know. Much respect.* That's really nice. I don't think I've talked to Rick more than ten times, and we've been going to school together since first grade. I'm just that funny.

I comment: *Much respect to you too, Rick. You're crazy good at football. You bring a genuine grace to the game.*

A lot of messages just say *I'll miss ya!* or *Luv ya* or *You're the best!* but I'm still moved that all these people have written to me.

"What're you looking at now?" Paolo says.

"My page," I say. "I'm feeling really inspired."

A new comment pops up from Gina: *OMG I had a huge crush on you too!!! Aw man we should have hooked up hahaha. I won't forget you, Denton!*

"Oh man," I say, sparks in my veins.

"What?"

"This is amazing," I say. "Do you remember Gina Ya—"

A new comment pops up from Rick: *Thanks dude. That actually means a lot.*

"Gina who? Yarrow?" Paolo asks.

"Rick Jackson was just moved by something I wrote."

"Football Rick Jackson?" Paolo says. "What are you talking about?"

"This is it, Paolo. This is what I have to do before I die."

I see a post from Melissa Schoenberg: *The world is going to be way worse off without you. Much love.*

I comment: *Our Houdini project for Mrs. Blatt's English class is still one of my favorite school experiences ever. You're great, Melissa. Thank you.*

"What is what you have to do before you die?" Paolo asks.

"Be open with people. Do what my dad never did for me. Tell them something honest about themselves that will make them feel good. And help them understand themselves better."

Ashley Gupta from summer camp wrote: *I'm so sad.*

I comment: *Don't be sad, Ashley. I'm so happy for my life, and I'm incredibly happy that you were my first kiss. Awkward as it may have been.*

There is something magical happening, and I know, for the first time all day, that I am exactly where I'm supposed to be.

"So . . . ," Paolo says. "You're gonna stay on Facebook for the rest of your life, just, like, commenting?"

"Pretty much," I say.

I comment: *Your blue eyes are incredible, I've always thought that.*

I comment: *You're a natural leader, and that's gonna take you far.*

I comment: *Being around you always made me feel*

more comfortable, I don't even know why. You have some-
thing special.

A new comment comes up from Melissa Schoenberg:
Wow, I tota—

Paolo slams shut my laptop.

"Nope," he says.

"What the hell, dude?" I say. "This is why I'm here!" I
try to open my laptop back up, but he won't let me.

"I will NOT let my best friend die on Facebook. That's
almost worse than helping you end your life."

"You don't understand—"

"I do, actually. And I have a better idea."

"You have a better idea for conveying love and honesty
to all these people at once?"

"What's wrong with you? *Yes,* I have a better idea. But
here's the thing: it involves leaving the house."

"My stepmom made it quite clear that there will be no
more of that."

"Hey, what happened to the baller dude from this afternoon? Look, death is happening one way or the other.
This house isn't some kind of death-proof sanctuary."

"Well, where would we be going?" I figure he'll tell me,
I'll shoot it down, and then I can get back to business.

"Where would we be going? Oh, I'll tell you where we'd
be going. You want to make people feel good about themselves, right? Connect with people?" Paolo looks so proud
of what he's about to say.

"I told you, Pow, I don't wanna go to a strip club."

"Man, give me a little credit here!"

"Okay."

"Now you ruined the moment by assuming I'm a sleaze who only wants to go to the strip club."

"I'm sorry, but in the past you have often wanted to go to a strip club. Please continue."

Paolo cracks his neck. "Wait, gotta reboot. Get back in the zone." He jumps up and down in place. "Okay. Where would we be going? I'll tell you." He flips his collar up. "*P* to the *Rom,* dude."

I stare at Paolo.

"Prom! We should go to prom!"

Prom. Of course. "Together?"

"No, not together, man. Geez, you sleep together once, this guy wants to go to prom. Think about it. Practically everyone in our grade will be there. You can tell everyone anything you want."

"Well . . ."

"And, hey, since you and Taryn are on the splits, maybe you can have one more superhot fling before you kick it. What's more romantic than high school prom?"

"A lot of things, I think."

"Love will be in the air! People are gonna break out into fully choreographed dance numbers without ever having rehearsed! And everybody gets laid afterward!"

"I don't think you're correct about the dance numbers. And also, I don't have a ticket."

Paolo crouches down and puts his hands on my shoulders. "I want to slap you right now. But I won't, because I'm scared I'd accidentally kill you. You're not gonna have a life in a few hours! And you're thinking of not going to your own prom because you *didn't buy a ticket*? Come on, D, let's go down in a blaze of glory, man! *Thelma and Louise—* style! Freeze-frame car in the sky!"

"I only kinda get your reference. I've never seen *Thelma and Louise*."

Paolo's eyebrows shoot up in surprise. "You've never seen it? Why not? 'Cause you think it's a chick flick?"

"No, I don't know. I just never got around to watching an old movie about crazy ladies."

"It's so much more than that, dude."

"But, okay, assuming I'm on board for this blaze-of-glory, going-to-prom-ticketless idea, you think my step-mom would ever, in a gajillion years, let me go?"

Paolo puts his hand on his chin and does some intense contemplating. "I can be very persuasive," he says.

"Absolutely not," my stepmom says.

"Okay, gotcha," Paolo says. "No prob, Raquel."

I look to Paolo: *That's you being very persuasive?* He shrugs.

We're downstairs in the family room, a motley crew of Sitting survivors spread out across the couch, the recliner, and the floor: me, Paolo, my stepmom, my dad, Paolo's mom, Felix, Millie, and Grandpa Sid. It's 7:48 p.m. Prom started at seven.

"Um, Mom?" I say.

"Dent, darling, I very much understand what Paolo and now you are trying to say, but, sweetie, how can we possibly let you go to prom? You go three feet outside the front door, and you're almost killed. And you want to drive

246

fifteen minutes to the prom, where you'll stay for three hours, during which time any number of awful things could happen to you?"

"If I could just jump in here for a second," Felix says.

"Felix," my stepmom says. "Not now."

"But—"

"I said, NOT NOW!" my stepmom shrieks, standing up from the couch. I've heard her yell many times, but never anything like this warped banshee cry.

"Sorry," she says, taking in our shocked expressions. "Hey, how about I run out and get us some champagne and we can have our own prom here? I know I wouldn't let you have champagne last night, Denton, but I think everyone here would agree you've earned it."

My heart breaks for my stepmom.

"Mom, that is so sweet," I say, "but . . . I really don't want champagne. I want to go to my actual prom. I have something important to do there."

I watch my stepmom's features crumple into the human equivalent of a sad-face emoticon. The room is silent.

"Let the kid go to his dance!" Grandpa Sid shouts from the reclining chair, startling everyone. "I don't see what the big kerfuffle is."

"Well, Sid," my stepmom says, collecting herself, "the big kerfuffle is that today is Denton's last day, so if he goes to the dance, he may very well die there."

"Don't condescend to me, Raquel. I'm old, not a moron. I know it's his goddamn deathdate. You've all certainly made a big enough deal of it. I think the whole state knows." Grandpa Sid adjusts his body in the chair, grimacing. "Denton's a good kid, always does everything you've asked of him, always has a good attitude. I don't see why you can't let him have his dying wish, to go to this promenade."

I can't believe Grandpa Sid's going to bat for me.

And is that really what *prom* is short for?

"Yes, Sid," my stepmom says. "Of course Denton is a good kid; he's the greatest kid, which is why we want to be with him when he dies. You can understand that?"

"Then go with him."

My stepmom laughs. "Well, Sid, we can't just . . ." She trails off in midsentence, and I realize that she's actually considering it.

"No, that's okay," I say. "I'd rather not go to prom at all than have to go with my parents."

"You know what?" my stepmom says. "Yes, if we come along, I don't see why Denton shouldn't be allowed to go to prom."

"Yeah, Grandpa Sid!" Paolo hoots.

"Who?" Grandpa Sid says.

"Wait, wait, wait," I say. "I don't even know if parents are allowed in. And you guys don't have tickets."

"Again with the tickets, this guy!" Paolo says, gesturing at me with his thumb like a Marx Brother.

"Can I come along, too?" Paolo's mom asks.

"Hell no, Mom!" Paolo says.

I silently agree. You know what they say: *Never trust a lady who crushes on your dad.* No one actually says that. But they probably should.

"I'm sure we can get you in, too, Cynthia," my stepmom says. "Wow, now I'm thinking this might be a lot of fun!" Somebody punch me.

"Mom," Paolo says, "if you go, people are gonna think I brought my mom to prom."

"Sounds to me like good material for one of those funny raps you make up," Paolo's mom says. " 'I brought my mom to the prom and I think she's da bomb. . . .' " She's making terrible attempts at rap gestures and cracking herself up, and my stepmom joins in, the two of them giggling together in that annoying way moms do.

"This isn't helping your case," Paolo says.

"Fine," Paolo's mom says. "Then why don't you take someone else as your date? Since it's so offensive to bring me."

"Did you skip high school or something?" Paolo says. "It's beyond offensive. It's the absolute worst. And I can't take someone else. Seeing as prom started almost an hour ago, I think most people probably have dates already."

"I don't," Millie says from the end of the couch.

"Oh," Paolo says. "Well, yeah," he stammers, suddenly nervous. "Would you want to go to prom with me?"

"Sure. I brought something to wear just in case." She takes a yellow-and-purple-striped dress out of her denim purse and places it on her lap.

"Wow, okay." Paolo nods repeatedly to no one in particular. "Okay."

"I, for one," says Felix, "am very much not into this idea. Already did the prom thing nine years ago, and it wasn't even that fun then."

"Wait," I say. "We're seriously doing this?"

"Sweetie, it was your idea," my stepmom says. "If you'd rather we all stay home, that's fine, too."

"No, I mean, I want to go, but without . . . Like, Dad, this doesn't sound fun to you, right?"

My dad squirms and adjusts his glasses. "Whatever your mother thinks is best is what we should do." Damn you, Dad!

All eyes in the room are on me. I think about staying at home, clicking around on Facebook, eating chips and salsa with my parents.

"All right. Let's go to prom."

"Blaze of glory, baby!" Paolo says.

If you'd told me yesterday that the evening portion of my deathdate would involve me, my parents, and four others driving to prom together in the family minivan, I would have asked you what you were smoking.

It's a little humiliating that my stepmom refused to let me drive my own car. Pulling up to the prom in Danza sounds way cooler than arriving in our red minivan, but no one is gonna see us show up anyway, seeing as it's almost nine and prom started two hours ago.

"Please slow down, Lyle," my stepmom says.

"Okay, sorry about that," my dad says, understandably a little befuddled, as he hasn't gone faster than twenty miles an hour the whole ride and every other car is passing us.

I'm wearing an old, light blue suit of my dad's. When I realized I had already worn the only nice outfit I own to my funeral, my dad took me to his closet and told me I could wear this. It's a little big on me but fits way better than I would have expected.

"It's, uh, actually what I was wearing when I married your mother," my dad said.

"Oh wow. Wait, Mom or Cheryl?"

"Cheryl. Last time I wore it was a long time ago."

"That's crazy. You sure I can wear it tonight? I mean, if you'd rather—"

"I'm sure."

"Thanks, Dad."

"Sure." I started to leave the room when he stopped me. "And, Denton . . ."

"Yeah?"

My dad just stood there, staring at me.

"You okay?"

He cleared his throat. "Before your mother left us, she, uh, gave me a, uh, letter, which was written for you, that she—"

"What?"

"She'd written you a letter."

"I heard what you said. You're saying my biological mother, who I've spent my whole life, not to mention the past twenty-four hours, wanting to know more about, wrote me a letter and you never told me?"

"I know, I know, I realized I should give it to you, that you might need it."

"Need it?"

"Well. Want to see it. So, lemme just . . ." He reached up to the top of his closet, shifted some things around, and pulled down a shoe box, which he began rummaging through. "I think I know where it is."

I wanted to be angry at my dad, but he's a tough guy to stay mad at. He always seems like he's barely keeping up. "Is this whole box filled with letters from Cheryl?"

"This? No, these are old pay stubs. I can probably get rid of them now. Need a shredder. Ah, here it is." He was holding an old envelope, staring at it. It looked like tears were forming behind his glasses, but I couldn't tell for sure. He passed the letter to me. My name was scrawled on the envelope in my mother's happy, ladylike hand. "She wrote that to you at the beginning of her Sitting, the same day you were born."

"You already knew my name?"

"We did. But if you had been a girl, you would have been Dentona."

"Really?"

"No. Not really." My dad smiled. "We knew you'd be a boy."

"Oh. Dentona. That's funny, Dad."

"I'm sorry I never gave you that letter. It was shitty of me." Let the record show that was the first time I had ever heard my dad curse. It was pretty cool.

"We're leaving in five!" my stepmom shouted from downstairs.

"Woo!" Paolo shouted from another part of the house.

"I guess I should go get ready," I said to my dad, the unopened letter still in my hand.

"Dent," my dad said, massaging the knuckles of one hand with the other. "You've made me so proud."

It was like pushing a button that instantly made my eyes tear up.

"I can't imagine my life without you," he said.

"Thanks, Dad," I choked out. It was almost strange how much his words meant to me, like not realizing how thirsty you are until you've had a sip of water. "I . . ." Opening your heart is harder in person than it is online, so this was a good warm-up for the prom. "I can't imagine having a better father. Really. I love you."

My dad looked down, then away, then back to me. "I love you, too, Denton." I gave him a hug. It felt like a goodbye.

The letter's in my pocket now, still unread. My hand is resting on the rumpled paper of the envelope, which is oddly comforting. I should have read it when I was alone, but it seemed too important to rush through. I barely had time to change and say bye to Grandpa Sid ("You did good, Denton. Now pass me the clicker") and the house ("Good-bye, house. I've loved living in you") before my stepmom was rushing all of us into the minivan.

"Lyle, red light, red light, slow down!" my stepmom says, referring to the traffic light at least a hundred yards away from us.

"Yup, I see it," my dad says. "Don't worry, Raquel, you can relax."

"I really can't," my stepmom says.

"Driving too slowly is also a hazard, you know," Felix calls out from the way back. "We don't want someone rear-ending us."

"That's what she said," Paolo says.

"Fine," my stepmom says, leaning around her seat and looking back to Felix. "Lyle, maybe you should at least drive the speed limit." The car speeds up to a blistering twenty-five miles per hour.

Millie's in the bucket seat next to me, wearing her yellow-and-purple-striped dress. It's got a big purple bow on the front of it. She's also wearing a bracelet of purple and yellow beads, and she's got her ponytail up in this bun thing. She looks surprisingly attractive.

"You can touch my bow if you want," Millie says to me.

"I'm good, thanks," I say, realizing I was staring at her. I find some lint to brush off my pant leg.

I'm starting to have second thoughts about tonight. I've more or less signed up for being forever known as "the purple kid who died at prom." I guess there are worse ways to be remembered.

I peer outside the window and realize we are pulling into the parking lot of Haventown Gardens.

"Okay, nobody take your seat belts off until the car has come to a complete stop, please," my stepmom says.

We slowly crawl into a parking spot. We come to a complete stop. We take off our seat belts. We get out of the car. We walk toward the entrance. As we get closer, we hear the faint sound of music coming from the building, the thumping bass line of some wonderfully crappy pop song.

And then I know.

I can feel it: this is my destiny.

The decor in the lobby of Haventown Gardens is what I would classify as trying to be fancy but only barely succeeding. The carpet features pictures of flowers in ornate vases, and the walls have oddly shaped mirrors in random spots.

Two girls, who I quickly identify as Rhonda Davis and Jackie Krieger, talk in hushed tones right inside the front entrance. Jackie's fired up about something—I think that her prom date is missing.

"*He* asked *me* to come to this thing!" Jackie says, her eyes wide. "I didn't even wanna say yes, but I felt bad!"

"I know, it's not right," Rhonda says.

This is as good a place to start as any.

"I agree," I say.

Jackie and Rhonda both jump a little, startled.

"What? Who're you?" Jackie says. Her blue dress crinkles as she takes a step away from me.

"I'm Denton Little. We go to school together."

"Oh yeah. I didn't recognize you. Wasn't that your funeral yesterday?"

"Pretty much."

"That why your skin's all messed up?" Rhonda asks.

"Yep. Most likely."

"That sucks," Jackie says.

"Tell me about it."

"That your family?"

"Yeah." Everyone nods a hello to Rhonda and Jackie.

"Cool that you brought them to prom," Rhonda says.

"Yeah. Look, Jackie, I don't even know who your prom date is, but you shouldn't worry about it, you know? Who cares?"

"What?"

"You're such a funny, self-possessed person, you probably don't need a guy at this thing to have fun."

Jackie gives me the stink eye. "How d'you know how I am?"

"Oh, 'cause we were on the same volleyball team in our freshman-year tournament. Remember that?"

A smile slowly creeps over her face. "Aw, man, you're that goofy white dude, I remember you! You said some funny shit."

"Wow, thanks. Well, I should get going, but really, enjoy tonight, you guys. Life is short."

"Yeah," Rhonda says, either touched or confused.

We walk down a long hallway that appears to lead to the main party room. I feel great. My ankle isn't hurting anymore, so I've stopped limping.

"That was so sweet," my stepmom says. "What you said to those girls."

"Thanks, Mom," I say.

"Yeah, man, you weren't kidding about this spreading-the-love thing," Paolo says. "That was borderline insane, and I loved it."

We reach the end of the hallway, where a long table is set up in front of two closed doors, behind which lies the prom. Loud music is barely muffled by the doors, one of which opens as a crying girl in a pink dress exits the party and shuffles quickly by us. Before the door closes behind her, we get a glimpse of a dark room with flashes of neon.

With the distracting peek into the party room, I only belatedly take note of the two teachers manning the ticket table: Mrs. Lucevich, the tiny art teacher, and . . . Oh no.

It's Mrs. Donovan, the AP calculus teacher who I publicly insulted during my eulogy. I never thought in a million years I would have to come face to face with these people again. This presents something of a challenge.

"Well, hello there, Denton," Mrs. Lucevich says, sounding pleased and slightly taken aback.

"Hi, Mrs. Lucevich. Um, hi, Mrs. Donovan."

"Hello," Mrs. Donovan says, not raising her scary skeleton face up from the exams in front of her.

"Denton," Mrs. Lucevich says, her voice a little quavery, "how are you doing? What a nice surprise to see you here." I can tell she's choosing her words carefully, skirting any question of *Why are you purple?* or *Why are you not dead yet?* "And is this your family?"

"Yes, hi there," my stepmom says. "I'm Raquel Little, Denton's mom. And this is my husband, Lyle."

"Hi," my dad says, shaking Mrs. Lucevich's hand.

"I taught Denton art a few years back." Her eyes are

glassy as she looks at me. "He's a wonderful artist." That's a stretch. "So, I'll just need tickets, and you folks can head on in."

"Even from the parents?" my stepmom says.

"Well, I suppose we could make an exception for you four adults," Mrs. Lucevich says, winking at my stepmom. "Just tickets from the three kids, then." I give Paolo a *Told ya so* look.

"Yeah, about that," I say, laying it on as thick as I can. "We sorta thought, you know, that I would be, you know . . . by now. So none of us bought tickets. I'm so sorry."

"Oh right, of course, I completely understand," Mrs. Lucevich says, absentmindedly twiddling her fingers on the table. "Well. I think we should be able to—"

"No," Mrs. Donovan says, still not looking up from grading papers. "We can't let anyone in who doesn't have a prepurchased ticket." She points to a placard next to her, which reads: NO STUDENT WILL BE ADMITTED WITHOUT A PREPURCHASED TICKET.

"Well, surely you can make an exception in such an extreme situation," my stepmom says.

Mrs. Donovan looks up at last and locks her eyes on me. My insides crunch, like a *Jetsons* car contracting into a suitcase. "No, I don't think we can." She returns to her papers.

"Are you kidding me?" my stepmom says. "Please don't look away. Maybe you don't entirely understand what our situation is."

"Oh, I understand," Mrs. Donovan says, head up once again, giving us all a long look at the dark bags under her eyes. "You think because it's your son's deathdate, you should get some sort of special privileges."

My stepmom looks stunned, at a loss for words.

"Much like your son thinks I should consider therapy." Damn right, lady. "Unfortunately, he didn't buy a ticket in advance. Not only that, but admitting your son would essentially be an invitation to die on school property. It would be irresponsible of me, considering the liability issues."

"Are you insane?" my stepmom asks. "We're not going to sue the school. We just want our son to be able to enjoy the prom."

"And this . . ." She gestures to my skin. "What if it's contagious? Have you had a doctor examine it?"

I actually see the steam shoot out of my stepmom's ears and nostrils. "Yes. We have, in fact, and he said it's not contagious," she lies.

"Hmm. Well, be that as it may, there's nothing to be done here. Please step away from the table. Enjoy the rest of your evening."

"Mrs. Donovan," I say. "Could you look at me for a second?"

She does not.

"Okay," I continue, "I did say some terrible things, and I'm sorry, but I know you have good qualities, too—"

"Don't you dare apologize!" my stepmom says, a woman possessed. "Don't you dare apologize to this wretch of a person."

"Mom, I got this—"

My stepmom leans in and says, "Mrs. Lucevich, is it? Would you please be able to sell our group some tickets?"

"No, Candy," Mrs. Donovan says.

"Um, well, gosh, I just don't know if I should," Mrs. Lucevich says.

"Okay, then I'd like to see the principal, or whoever is higher up than you two."

"That won't be necessary," my dad says, stepping out in front of my stepmom. I can't believe he's giving up so easily.

"Dad," I say, "just let me talk to her—"

"No," he says, turning to our little group. "If you guys, uh, wouldn't mind, I'd like to have a quick word alone with Mrs. Donovan."

Well, this is interesting.

"Lyle?" my stepmom says, confused.

There's a look in my dad's eyes I've never seen before.

"Please, just back it up down the hallway. This won't take long," he says, lightly shooing us away.

"What's happening?" Millie whispers to me. "Is this something he always does?"

"No," I say.

"Exciting."

We all take backward steps down the hallway as my dad says, "Uh, Mrs. Lucevich. Candy. If you wouldn't mind taking a quick breather as well, I'd appreciate it."

"You shouldn't leave your post," Mrs. Donovan says, seeming possibly the slightest bit nervous.

Mrs. Lucevich is confused. Even from our vantage point thirty or so feet away, I can see the turmoil inside her brain. "Um. I . . . Well . . . I suppose I could use a quick bathroom break." She stands up, looks quickly to Mrs. Donovan, then down the hall to us, and walks through the doors behind her. Mrs. Donovan has gone back to her paper grading.

My dad looks up to the ceiling and takes a deep,

calming breath. He takes off his glasses and puts them on the table. I am mesmerized.

"Please put that aside for a second," my dad says to Mrs. Donovan. She continues grading. My dad slowly leans down to the table and places his hands on either side of Mrs. Donovan. "Put it away," he says, in a voice I've never heard before.

Mrs. Donovan looks up. My dad is angled in such a way that we can't see his face, but we can see Mrs. Donovan's, and she looks terrified. He continues speaking, now very close to her ear, in strong, hushed tones. We can't make out what he's saying, but it seems intense. Mrs. Donovan subtly nods throughout.

"Holy shit," Paolo says. "I think your dad is pulling a *Teen Wolf* on Mrs. Donovan."

"I was thinking the same thing!"

My dad says a few more things, then looks to Mrs. Donovan, who gives one final nod. He slowly rises from the table, popping his glasses back on his face. I'm not sure what just happened or what my dad said to Mrs. Donovan, but it seems like it might have been something along the lines of *I'll kill your entire family*. She is trying to hold her head high, but her expression reeks of defeat. I almost feel bad for her.

My dad turns back to us. "Well, we can go in now."

I want my dad to explain where that badassery came from, but it seems awkward to talk about it in front of Mrs. Donovan.

My stepmom reaches into her purse. "Should we pay for the—"

"Nope, nope," my dad says. "We can just go in."

My stepmom is shocked but impressed. "Well, okay, then."

We slowly walk past the table as Mrs. Lucevich re-emerges from behind the prom doors. "Ah, you figured something out, then. So glad to see that!" She holds the door for us as we walk through, Paolo and Millie leading the way, followed by Paolo's mom, then me and Felix, then my parents. Before I walk into the landscape of neon and darkness, I turn to Mrs. Donovan. "Thanks," I say.

She doesn't respond.

At first, I'm overwhelmed by the music, the people, the bouncing lights. But just as suddenly, the feeling melts away, replaced by a powerful sense of purpose.

Of course I was supposed to come here.

"I love you, Dent, but I do not want to be here right now," Felix says, staring at the writhing mass of bodies on the dance floor.

"You can leave if you want," I say, feeling the beats thump around me, inside me.

"No, I really can't," Felix says.

"This is fun," Paolo's mom says, doing tiny, controlled salsa moves.

"Please don't dance like that, babe," Paolo says. He looks to me and Millie and gestures to the dance floor. "Shall we?"

"Absolutely. Wait," I say, turning to my father. "Dad."

Pink and green spots reflect off his glasses. "Thanks for what you did out there. That was really amazing."

"Oh," my dad says, looking down. "That was . . . It was nothing."

"I agree, it was amazing," my stepmom says, giving my dad a kiss. "We'll be over here on the side." She adjusts the belt on her long green dress. "Be careful, please."

"We will," I say, walking away. I turn back once more. They look to me expectantly. "You guys are incredible parents." I turn away before I can see them react.

Paolo leads us toward the crowd. "This room is amazing!" I shout over the music. The theme of this year's prom is Livin' It Up! The irony is not lost on me, but they've done a beautiful job. Streamers in bright, rich colors, magnificent palm trees, luscious bunches of bananas, and—on the wall behind us—a big, sparkling papier-mâché mermaid.

"Dude," Paolo says, "I mean this in the best way, but are you on drugs?"

"If friendship is a drug, then yes!" I pull Paolo and Millie in for a hug. They laugh. "Okay," I say, looking them both in the eyes. "I'm gonna go connect with some people now."

"Do your thing, bro," Paolo says. "Give us a holler if you're getting your ass kicked."

"Best wishes," Millie says.

They walk off. I close my eyes, taking a moment to soak in the room and the moment. I remember how soon I will die and how little I have left to lose.

When I open my eyes, Anuj Mehta pops into view, shimmying to the music. Bingo.

I approach casually, say hello, and open my heart to him.

"What?" Anuj leans in closer as his prom date, a stick-thin girl I don't recognize, stares at me warily.

"I just said," I repeat, "you were really fantastic in *Damn Yankees* last month. You brought so much humor to the role."

"Oh," Anuj says, all sheepish. "Thanks."

"Do you think you'll give acting a shot?" I ask. "Like, as a career?"

"Uh." He looks to his date—who still isn't feeling my purple vibe—as if she knows his dreams better than he does. "No, my parents would hate that."

"But it's your life, Anuj. And you're always, like, mind-blowingly good in all the plays and stuff. I'm not just saying that."

"Oh cool, thanks." Anuj grins and combs his hand through his hair. "But I had to beg my parents to even let me do those shows."

"Just think about it. That's all I'm saying."

"All right," he says, in a way that suggests maybe he actually will. "Hey, you're Denton Little, right?"

"I am."

"No offense, but aren't you supposed to die today?"

"Any minute, man," I say as I walk away. "Any minute!"

I scan the room for who's next, and it becomes clear that my presence is no longer under the radar. Heads turn in my direction, talking to each other confusedly, checking the time on their cell phones and doing the math, trying to understand how I could be here. A huge chunk of people visibly steps away from me. But others make a beeline for me, and I'm soon in a messy whirlwind of high fives, hugs, and pats on the back.

"Dude!"

"Denton Little's here! Awesome!"

"What happened to your skin?"

"I can't believe it, you came!"

"When do you think you're gonna die?"

"Are you coming to Wildwood this weekend?"

"Yes, yes, thank you, thank you," I say, projecting my voice as I clear some space for myself. "I feel very fortunate to still be alive. But I'm going to die literally any minute, so I'm trying to be really efficient with my time. I have things to say to each and every one of you, important things, so continue with your dancing, and I will find you."

"What is he talking about?" Ben Goldstein says.

"Liza Rondinaro!" I say, spotting her a few people deep into the crowd. "I'm so sorry about what happened with us freshman year." We dated for two months, then I dumped her in an email.

"Oh . . . It's okay," Liza says, pushing a ringlet of hair behind her ear and looking awkwardly at Scott Landman, who I assume is her date tonight. "You don't have to—"

"No, you need to know that you are not unattractive, and you have a really unique sense of style; we just didn't have that much to talk about."

"Yeah, I know," Liza says as Scott starts to pull her away. "Please, I get it—"

"But that was no excuse for me to end it the way I did," I call out. Liza and Scott are far off on the dance floor now, so I let it go.

I tell Miller Bendon that his artwork is comic-book-level good.

I tell Ratina Jacobs that she's the only person I know who can pull off wearing overalls.

I tell Shu-wen Tsao that I've always enjoyed her dry sense of humor.

I tell DeShaun Robinson that I love his playful energy. I don't know him that well, but one time I saw him throw a football through the window of the teachers' lounge, and it cracked me up.

I tell Ed Powers that he's the most optimistic person I know and he should never lose that. Also that he has a badass superhero name.

"Wow, seems like it's going well," Paolo says over my shoulder. He's still with Millie.

"Oh, hey," I say. "It is."

"Can we talk to you for a sec, though?"

"Okay," I say, raising one finger to Shaina Lester, our conversation about her wonderful ability to clean lab beakers—seriously, she makes them shine—temporarily put on hold.

"What's up?" I ask, walking a few steps to the side with them.

"Well—" I notice Paolo's splotch has made its first public appearance, creeping up over his shirt collar. "Oh yeah," he says. "It's gotten bigger. So now Millie knows."

"Probably transferred to Paolo through saliva," Millie says. "Like mono."

Paolo and I stare at each other, realizing we're morons.

"Saliva!" I say. "Yes, of course! Millie, you're a genius."

"So you think we just made out but didn't have sex?" Paolo asks.

I stare at him. "No, man, neither. I think we shared a bowl last night. And the same glass of water."

"Ohhhh . . . Saliva," Paolo says. "Anyways, we wanted to let you know Phil is here."

"All right," I say. "It's a free country, I guess."

"Yeah, but he's been . . . saying some weird stuff. About you."

"Sticks and stones," I say. "Right?"

"Not exactly," Paolo says. "He's been—"

"Is everything going okay?" my stepmom says, appearing beside us. "You have so many friends, Denton. I'm so impressed."

"Oh yeah, it's going great, Mom. Thanks for coming to this and being so cool about everything. I love you."

"I love you, too," my stepmom says, teary-eyed.

"I think we may do some dancing now, right, guys?" I say, looking to Paolo and Millie, needing to get them alone again because, I'll admit, I'm a little curious to hear what Phil said.

"You know it!" Paolo says.

"Oh, we'll come, too!" my stepmom says. My dad puts a hand on her shoulder and gives her a look. "Okay, okay," she says. "Maybe we'll join you in a bit." Second Awesome Dad Maneuver of the night.

I step onto the dance floor, and lots of people cheer. It startles me.

"Yeah, Denton!"

"Denton's gonna dance!"

"Way to be real!"

The three of us start to dance, each doing a poor approximation of the robot.

"So what has Phil been saying?" I ask.

"Millie was the one who overheard it, right?" Paolo says.

"Yeah . . . He was saying that, you know, you're a pussy, and you stole his girlfriend, and—"

"Yeah, yeah, yeah, he knows all this stuff, Mills, get to the—"

"Right, okay, right, so then he was, like, saying his grandfather was a cop—which we know—and had it in for you or something. And maybe I misheard, but he started saying something about the government?"

"What?" I say.

"Yeah, so weird, right?" Paolo says.

"Sounds like he's just talking smack."

"Only one way to find out, though." Paolo's eyes gleam.

"Ah, look, I've got a lot of work left to do. I haven't even talked to Danny Delfino yet, and he needs to know how good he is at saxophone."

"I thought he was a drummer."

"He's *both,* dude, that's my point."

"Oh wow, that is impressive. But, okay, how about you talk to Phil first and find out why he's saying all this crap about you."

Phil is low on my list of predeath priorities. He's a mosquito buzzing at my ear.

I look to Millie. She shrugs. Guess it could be fun to swat a mosquito.

"All right, fine, but let's make it quick."

"Yeahhhhh!" Paolo says. We move through a mass of bodies vigorously bobbing along to the music. On a couple of occasions, I catch people staring at me with full-on pity, and maybe also disgust, like I'm some kind of leper they don't want near them. We keep walking.

Though I thought my right ankle was fully healed, I may be wrong, as it feels a little stiff. Actually, my ankle up through my calf has a numb, sort of rigid feeling to it. Mildly concerning.

The jungle of people around us starts to rise and fall faster, in time with some frenetic beats. I get a glimpse of Phil across the dance floor in a green bow tie and black fedora, talking animatedly to two other dudes, just as a huge body slams into me and knocks me to the floor.

I land on one of my scraped-up elbows, and it stings. A lot.

"Dude!" Paolo says.

"Wipeout," Willis Ellis says from where he's lying inches away. He smells like cologne and weed. "Sorry, dude. I was really feelin' it."

"You again," I say.

Someone spastically sashays by and almost steps on my fingers.

"Oh, heh heh, yeah. Me again." He springs back up, surprisingly lithe for his size. "Help you up, brother?" He towers over me, this friendly ogre in a mismatched suit, his huge dreads hugged by a blue bandana.

"Uh, sure," I say. He's pretty much proven himself to be my bad-luck charm, but I grab his hand. He yanks me to my feet. "Whoa."

"Dude can fly!" Willis says. "Heh heh." He's looking

down at my hand and the shifting red dots. "So cool that you're here, man. Really admirable. When my time comes, I'm just gonna sit at home, totally baked." I extract my hand.

"You okay?" Paolo asks.

"Yeah, I think so. My elbow burns, but otherwise . . ." My right leg is very stiff, and I'm starting to feel some numbness in my left, too. "All good."

"How many times can you crash into the same person?" Millie asks Willis.

"I guess a bunch," he says.

"I mean in terms of statistical odds. Just thinking aloud."

"Oh." Willis scratches his ear. "Anyway, sorry, dude."

"It's okay," I say. "Did you ever think about maybe not smoking so much pot?"

"Why, you want some?" He reaches into the inside pocket of his brown blazer.

"No, no . . . Never mind."

"I'll take some," Paolo says.

"All right, evvvverybody," a voice says through the sound system. I glance over at the DJ stand, and, sure enough, it's the same chubby DJ who did my funeral yesterday. Big week for this guy. "We're gonna slow things down a bit now, so, everybody, find your prom date and hold 'em close. I wanna see all you couples on the dance floor."

In some alternate reality, I'd be interlacing my fingers with Taryn's and leading the way to the center of the room. We'd stare into each other's eyes, our bodies close, feeling the beautiful void of our entire lives ahead of us.

"Pow, Millie, let's go," I say. I limp forward on my bad leg, looking down to make sure I tread carefully.

"What the—" Paolo says.

I look up.

Veronica.

She's walking toward us in the same jeans and black hoodie she was wearing earlier. Decidedly un-prom-like.

"Hey," she says. She's drunk.

"You okay?" I say. "What are you . . . How did you get in here without a ticket?"

She flops one arm in the direction of the back of the room. "I banged on that door. Then someone opened it."

"You are wastereeno, sis," Paolo says, awe and confusion in his voice. I don't know if he's ever seen Veronica like this. I certainly haven't.

"You don't know me!" Veronica says, slightly swaying back and forth. "Denton . . ." She leans in close, and our lips are almost touching. The alcohol smell is pretty potent. "I came here because of you."

I might love this girl. I kiss her.

"Whoa!" she says, jerking her head back. "I mean . . . That's not what I meant."

"Oh. Okay."

"Harsh," Paolo says.

"Dent." Veronica puts a hand on my shoulder and looks around. "You can't be here. You have to leave here."

"What? Why?"

She exerts what seems like considerable effort to steady her gaze onto mine.

"My mom."

Liza Rondinaro and Scott Landman slow-dance next to us. He whispers something into her ear and she laughs.

"Uh, what does that mean?"

"She's a liar."

"All right, easy there, V," Paolo says.

"She's been lying to me!" Veronica shouts. "And she's been lying to you," she says to Paolo. "And especially to you," she says to me.

"How about to me?" Millie asks.

"You think this is funny?" Veronica asks, turning sharply toward Millie, stone-faced. "This isn't funny."

"All right, it's okay, no one thinks it's funny," I say, getting an arm between her and Millie. "What do you mean, lying?"

And then the pieces click together.

I had it all wrong.

Paolo's mom never could have been my mom. But maybe her crush on my dad meant something else. What if she's been lying to Paolo and Veronica their whole lives about the identity of the biological father who abandoned them so long ago? What if their father is actually someone they've known for years . . . ?

"Ohmigod," I say. "It's my dad, right?"

"What?" Veronica says.

"She told you that my dad is your actual father. I can't believe this. Is that right?"

Veronica and Paolo look at me like I just confessed to seventeen murders.

"What the hell is this guy talking about?" Veronica says. "Our dad is our dad. Why would your dad be our dad?"

"We've talked with our dad on the phone," Paolo says. "His voice sounds nothing like your dad's."

"Oh," I say.

"And there's, like, videos of him holding V when she was a baby. He's totally Hispanic. With a mustache."

Eh, it was worth a shot. I'm oh for two.

"Still," I say, "isn't it possible that my dad—"

"Just shut up," Veronica says, a rarely heard layer of emotion creeping into her voice. "I heard her, okay? At your house, I heard my mom on the phone, and she . . . she actually works for some secret government thing."

Come again?

"Dent," Veronica says. "She's been, like, watching you. Your whole life."

30

"You on mushrooms or something, babe?" Paolo says.

"This is serious shit, Pow!" Veronica says. "Stop with the jokes and listen to me, okay?"

"I'm all ears," Paolo says. "It just sounds insane. And you're blasted."

"Okay, okay." Veronica moves her head back and forth as if to establish credibility. "I know I'm in poor form right now. I got freaked out, and I started throwing back liquids in an attempt to self-soothe. But you have to believe me, okay?"

The slow song ends, and the dance floor bounces back to life with a pop song about the club being ours tonight.

"Dent," Veronica says, putting her hands on my face. "You cannot stay here." What she's just told us is so crazy that I know it's probably true. I don't know what to do with the information, though. "You cannot . . . Oh . . ." Veronica moves her hands to my shoulders and takes a deep breath.

"You all right?" I say.

She vomits onto the dance floor. And onto my shoes.

"Wow," I say.

"Sorry," Veronica says. She looks up at me. "Now we're even."

I slide my feet back. "Fair enough." I put her arm over my shoulder. "We gotta get you off the dance floor."

"Maybe," Veronica says, barely audible.

"I'll come with you," Millie says. "I'll take her to the ladies' room."

"Thanks," I say.

"Yeah, way to step up, babe," Paolo says.

Everyone dancing around us has taken notice of Veronica's spew and moved slightly away from where we're standing, inadvertently giving us our own private circle.

"Wait, dude, what about Phil?" Paolo says. "Want me to talk to him?"

"Screw it," I say.

"Cool. In the meantime, sweet dance circle going on over here," Paolo says, doing some sort of frenetic hip-hop jig.

"Dude," I say, "watch out for the—"

Paolo slips on Veronica's vomit and lands on his back.

"Holy crap!" I shout as everyone around simultaneously gasps.

"I'm okay," he says. "However, I am lying in my sister's puke. Help V to the powder room, bro," Paolo grunts, waving me off. "I'll be fine."

"Be careful," I say.

"I'll try to get a spontaneous, unrehearsed dance

number going," Paolo shouts from the floor as Millie and I limp away with Veronica.

"Just let her take me," Veronica mumbles. "You gots to go, Dent."

"I'm not going anywhere," I tell her.

"I'm not flowing fanywhere," she says.

Millie takes careful and deliberate steps, trying to give Veronica the smoothest journey possible. In the past day, I've remembered why she and I used to be so close when we were little. She's strange, but sometimes she's awesome. And for some reason, she's chosen to see my life out to its very end.

"Hey, Millie," I say. "Thanks."

She looks over Veronica's head at me. "You don't have to thank me."

"Okay, but I appreciate this."

"Today's the first deathdate I've experienced. I'm glad it was yours."

I'm reminded again of Millie's undated status. "Does it make you wish you knew yours?" I ask.

She thinks for a moment as we approach the bathrooms.

"Nah," she says. "Days are more fun when any one could be the day you die."

As I wonder if that could possibly be true, the slight distraction gives my stiffer-by-the-minute legs the opportunity to get tangled. I almost fall to the ground, taking Veronica and Millie with me, but I catch myself.

"Whoa," Veronica says.

"Sorry about that," I say.

The men's room and ladies' room are next to each other. Millie takes Veronica in one, and I detour toward the other, more relieved to take a breather from the prom than I realized.

I limp in, and it's empty except for Mark Hofner, from my cross-country team, checking himself out at the sinks. He notices me in the mirror and turns around.

"Denton! Hey, man!"

"Hey, Mark, good to see you, dude."

"You, too, man. Love that suit."

"Thanks, thanks a lot."

"Is your skin, like . . . okay?"

"I don't really think so, no."

"Oh geez. Also your shoes have some . . ."

"Yeah, little mishap."

"It happens. Aw, so sorry about your death. I'll miss you, man."

"Thanks, Mark."

"Fantastic that you made it to prom, though!"

"Yeah, absolutely." I start to limp past him.

"So what else is going on?" Mark asks.

Holy crap, I'm going to die having an inane conversation with Mark Hofner. "Um. You know, not much else. The dying thing is pretty much consuming all my mental energy right now. I'm just gonna take a pee."

"Yeah, cool. What do you think about the vibe out there? It's more fun than I thought it would be."

"Sorry, I really gotta pee pretty bad, so I guess I'll just . . ." I awkwardly step around Mark to get to one of the stalls.

"Your legs okay, dude?" Mark asks.

"Yeah, they're fine, just a little stiff."

"Could be a buildup of lactic acid."

"Maybe," I say as I walk into the stall. Coach Mueller was always talking about lactic acid during our cross-country season.

I don't really have to pee that bad. I give it my best shot, which results in this piddling sort of pee stream.

"Are you a shy pee-er?" Mark asks from outside the stall. "I totally am."

"Yes," I say. *Leave, doofus!* "I am the shiest pee-er around."

Mark laughs. "Say no more, amigo. I was just heading out anyway."

"Great, thanks."

"Denton?"

Ohmigod, take a hint, Hofner. "Yeah, Mark?"

"I won't forget you, dude."

Something about the way he says it causes a lump to form in my throat. I try to say, "Thanks," but I can't.

Mark lingers outside the stall for about ten seconds, waiting for me to respond. Then I hear the door swing open and shut.

I am alone. I take a deep breath. I clean off my shoes. I stare at the off-white stall door. Someone has left a sticker that reads in angular red letters: DEATH BRIGADE.

I cry.

I lean against the stall wall, and I cry. My legs are feeling bad. Numb, stiff, weird. I'd love to sit down, but the toilets in this place—emphasizing the *faux* in *faux-fancy*—don't have lids. I bend over and lift up my blue pant legs to get a better look at what's happening.

My legs are red.

The area on my right leg from ankle to knee is no longer purple. It's the same shade of red as the dots that used to be there. The left leg is also red, but it stops about halfway up my calf.

I look closely. The crimson is very slowly expanding up both legs, like a painstakingly deliberate knitting project. It's so subtle you'd only notice it if you're really looking for it, but the red dots on the purple are interweaving in this complex way, transforming the purple into red.

Red seems bad.

It's making my legs all fucked up, I'm sure of it.

Red = dead.

I'm getting panicky real fast.

Breathe, Denton.

Own this shit.

I look down my shirt and peek at my arms. I'm relieved to see they're still just purple, which has somehow become the new normal.

I hear the dumb DJ making some announcement in the main room, and I wonder what time it is. I take my cell phone out. It's 10:21. The battery icon is red, like my legs, which means there's less than ten percent power left. We'll see who lasts longer.

I am going to die within the next hundred minutes. I don't want to. I want more time to stand in the woods laughing with Paolo. To kiss Veronica, and to know she's kissing me back. To sit in my room doing nothing. To get frustrated with my dad's sweet inability to speak. To feel stifled by my stepmom. To get better closure with Taryn. To figure out how Felix actually feels about me.

Everyone else gets so much time. I don't want to be at prom. I need to find my parents so we can get out of here, and I can have my Red Death in peace.

I put my cell phone into my suit pocket, and my hand brushes against the unread letter from my mom.

I'd completely forgotten about it.

I take it out and hold the envelope in front of me, staring at my name, written in my mom's handwriting.

My mom's letter is written on paper ripped from a spiral notebook. I smell it. It smells like paper.

I slide my fingers back and forth along its folded crease.

What if my mom was a bad speller? Or kind of boring? Screw it. I don't have time to waste worrying. I unfold the letter.

My Dearest Denton,

Hello, Bonjour, Hola, Shalom, Aloha, Hello! (I'd include more, but those are all the hellos I know. Learn other languages besides English, it's one of my biggest regrets in life.)

I've taken a moment away from all the hullabaloo to write to you, the little creature in my belly. It's funny writing a letter to someone who is, technically, closer to me than any other person has ever been in my whole life. (Besides your brother.) But, in every other respect,

I don't know you at all. And I likely never will. And you won't know me. I'm making myself get emotional, and I've barely started writing. Doesn't bode well.

First, let me say that I'm sorry. Bringing you into the world, knowing I'll be leaving you without a mother, isn't fair. I apologize. Please don't blame your father for that; it's not his fault.

And, while on the subject of your father, know that he is a great man. He can be quiet and hard to read, but never doubt his greatness. I love him very much.

I also love your older brother, Felix. Listen to him, learn from him, and if he gives you a tough time, give him a tough time back. He's the sassiest nine-year-old in the world. I can only imagine what he'll be like when he's older.

I'm sure you're wondering what I was like. Barring some personality-altering stroke, I'm assuming your father hasn't been very helpful in that respect. (If he has had some kind of stroke, I apologize for the insensitive nature of that last line.) Hopefully, he's at least told you a few things, and now that you're old enough (eleven? ten? maybe younger?), I'll share some more:

—I'm supersmart.
—I'm respected by everyone.
—I'm the most beautiful woman
 who ever lived.

Are you familiar with the word "hyperbole" yet? You should also know:

—*I'm not perfect.*
—*I like to laugh.*
—*When I start a project, it consumes me entirely.*
—*I hate rude people.*

Your father's mom is outside this room asking people where I am. Your grandma's a good but occasionally scary lady (which you likely don't know because she'll only be with you until you're two), and I should probably bring this to a close so she doesn't strangle somebody at my Sitting.

Whoa! You just kicked. Crazy. Either you're upset at me for not writing more or you're extremely against strangling. Both are legitimate positions.

I'm so proud of you, Denton. I know it seems ludicrous of me to write that, seeing as you haven't even been born yet, but I know you're destined for great things.

Whatever happens in your life, I love you. Feel free to imagine me as a happy angel sitting on your shoulder, if that helps. Or don't. Happy angels aren't very cool for boys. So imagine me as a happy truck on your shoulder. Or a happy dinosaur. A happy dinosaur. Please remember that. I'm with you, Denton.

> *All the love in the world,*
> *Mom*

I have no idea how my father could have withheld this note from me. That was the voice of my actual mother. Words written by her for me. She's funny. I like her.

Wait a second.

Happy dinosaur. Holy shit. Those two emails were from Happy Dinosaur. My mom laid out a code for me before she died. Which I never had any idea about because MY DAD NEVER GAVE ME THIS LETTER. Granted, those were both ads for erection pills, but still. Maybe that's camouflage and I'm supposed to write back. Happy Dinosaur could be someone my mom knew.

And Blue Bronto. My beloved stuffed animal, with me from my first day in the crib, a gift from my mom: a happy blue dinosaur. She was laying groundwork for a common language people could use to communicate with me once she was gone, but my dad shit all over it. Maybe my whole life I've been inundated with mysterious happy dinosaur references that I've never understood.

I want to reread this letter at least five more times, but I know the clock is ticking, and I don't want to die at prom. I pocket the note and unlock the stall, and I push the door outward.

It won't budge. It's jammed. I push harder.

"Nope," Phil's voice says, directly on the other side. "Sorry, Little."

No.

"You've got to be kidding me, what are you . . . You're holding the door shut?"

"Ha-ha, you were so busy crying you didn't even hear me over here." I push against the door with everything I've got. I get it to open a crack, but then my wobbly legs buckle, and the door slams shut. "Nice try, you smug piece of shit. Going around giving people compliments like you're some kind of saint or something."

"Jealous 'cause I don't have one for you?" I say, looking around, trying to come up with any kind of plan. "Lemme out, Phil!"

"Oh yeah, I'm really jealous. It's funny. In the end, I won't even need a gun, just a flimsy bathroom stall."

I step back as much as I can (which isn't much) to get some momentum, then ram myself into the door again. It doesn't work, and I bump my bad elbow.

"OW."

Phil laughs.

"HELP!" I shout. "SOMEBODY!!"

"Dunno if you noticed, but that music out there is pretty loud."

My parents are bound to wonder where I am soon. Paolo and Millie, too. And Veronica, if she's done barfing. It can't end like this.

"Phil, listen, I'm going to die soon. So you will get what you want. Just let me die not in here, okay?"

"Look, you won't die in there. I'm just keeping you here till my grandpa shows up. Which should be any minute."

"Keeping me here for your grandpa? Do you know how insane you sound? And speaking of that, why did you send your grandpa to spy on me and Taryn on the hill?"

"What the hell? What hill?"

"Oh. Never mind." Guess that had nothing to do with him. "But, I mean, why does your grandfather care where I am?"

"He can tell you himself when he gets here. And then I can stop holding this stupid door."

I hear the door of the bathroom open. "Hey, help!" I shout. "Help, this guy's trapping me in here."

"Yo, who is that? Denton?"

It's Rick Jackson. My Facebook football buddy.

"Rick! Yes! Can you get this guy off the door?"

"Why're you doing that?" Rick asks.

"Hey, man, please," Phil says. "It's really important that we keep him in there. It's, like, official business."

"Official what? That's my boy in there, Denton Little. Move."

"No, man, sorry, I can't. Get off me!" There are sounds of a struggle.

"I said, MOVE!" I hear a loud bang, and then a body thuds to the floor. "Oh shit."

I push the stall door and it swings open.

Rick is staring at Phil's body, which is slumped underneath the electric hand dryer. Phil's fedora is still on his head. He looks peaceful.

"Yo, I did not mean to throw him into that thing."

"No, Rick, thank you so much. Thank you."

"Do you think I should get a teacher or something?"

"I dunno. I'm sorry, just blame it on me!" I hustle away, wanting to get out before Phil regains consciousness. "Say I pushed him, say whatever! Much respect, Rick!"

I fling the bathroom door open, ready to find my family and leave, and I hobble right into Paolo.

"Oh, thank you, mother-of-God-lord-ball-sack, thank you!" Paolo says. His face is half purple, half regular, with the midway line exactly where a mustache would be. "You're okay!"

"Hey," I say. "We should go."

"Whoa, you gimpin' out on me?"

"Yeah, I don't know what's up. My legs are turning red."

"Holy . . . The STD is getting stronger or something? Can you walk?"

"More or less."

"Good. 'Cause, dude: you just won prom king!"

"What?"

"Yeah, man, he announced your name, like, a minute ago, and everybody *freaked* the eff out, went nuts. But then everyone realized they didn't know where you were, so people freaked out harder."

"Is Veronica okay?"

"Dude, did you hear me? You're prom king! That's insane! And awesome! You gotta claim your crown! And also show your mom you're still alive, 'cause she's starting to lose it a little bit."

"Starting to?" I say.

"Ha, yeah, your mom's crazy. Come on, Limpy."

We head away from the men's bathroom, Paolo leading, and everything feels unreal, like moving in slow motion underwater. My stepmom embraces me, my dad is low-key but concerned, you know the drill. Felix pats me on the back and congratulates me on winning an arbitrary award.

It isn't long before we've been noticed by everyone else. Soon the entire room is resounding with cries of my name and wooing and applauding as all my peers move to opposite sides of the dance floor to make way for me. I'd like to leave, but instead I limp up this newly created pathway toward the DJ's podium, high-fiving people.

Winning prom king is great, I guess, but at this moment, it feels more like an inconvenience.

I'm moving incredibly slowly. The celebratory wooing gradually diminishes into the awkward sound of concern. I finish my pathetic walk to the winners' circle or whatever it is. Standing there, smiling in a tiara, is Chantel Prescott.

"Hey, King," she says.

"Hi," I say. I'm not gonna call her Queen.

Standing next to her is Lindsay Feldstein, the class president and someone I've known since first grade. I'm assuming she was the one who read the ballot results. "Yay, Denton!" she says, her tiny hands making fists in the air.

"Thanks, Lindsay," I say.

"We ready?" the DJ asks Lindsay, who nods. "And here he is, ladies and germs," the DJ says into his microphone. "Your prom king!" Raucous cheers are back as Lindsay places the plastic crown on my head. The DJ holds the microphone to the side and asks me what my name is.

"Seriously?" I say.

"Um, yeah, kid, seriously." He seems confused. "I want to announce it for all your friends."

"You don't remember doing my funeral yesterday? You messed up my name, like, eighteen times?"

Heavy DJ Man looks at me, sweat dripping down his face, the sequins on his vest reflecting the room's neon lights. "Oh yeah, sorry about that, didn't recognize you with the . . ." He gestures to my purple skin. "You're still going, that's great, kid. Darren, right?"

"Are you joking? I feel like you're doing a comedy bit."

"It's not Darren?"

"DENTON. All right? My name is Denton Little."

"Isn't that what I said?" the DJ asks, followed by a quick wink.

"No," I say, even though he's stopped listening.

"Your prom king," the DJ repeats into his microphone.

"DENTOOOOOOOON LITTLE!" People cheer. A low rumbling chant of "SPEECH! SPEECH!" begins and quickly grows louder.

"We get to speak?" Chantel says to Lindsay.

Playing to the crowd, the DJ puts the microphone in front of my face, and everyone goes nuts. I don't take the bait. I smile and wave, trying to keep my balance as my legs shake beneath me.

The crowd turns on me in an instant, and the booing begins.

"Give him a break!" I hear my stepmom yell over the boos.

I take the microphone out of the DJ's hand. "All right, all right." The boos die down. "I, uh . . . This is really nice. I guess. Thanks. Even if it is just a pity vote." I pause for a second, in case someone wants to shout out that it's not a pity vote. No one does. "I've been lucky enough to make it this far in the day, but I'm gonna die any minute now. Well, *lucky* might not be the right word. I'm scared. I'm losing feeling, like, in my legs, and I'm very scared. You guys are the lucky ones, Livin' It Up at prom. I'm . . . Well, I should go. Take care, everyone."

Did I just tell my classmates to "take care"?

"Whoa, whoa, whoa," Paolo says, blocking my path. "Stay right there, Mr. Little." He gestures to the DJ, who shrugs back at him. "What we talked about!" Paolo says.

"What did you talk about?" I ask.

"Wouldn't you like to know . . . ," Paolo says.

A high-pitched organ resounds from the speakers, followed by the familiar opening lyrics: "Bone Bone Bone Bone . . . BONE Bone BONE Bone BONE." Everyone on the dance floor is looking at each other, most with an *Uh, what is this?* look. But it's definitely familiar to me and Paolo.

"Dude," I say.

"What, man? If there's not gonna be any spontaneous dance numbers, we gotta make our own! Louder, DJ guy!"

A long time ago, when we were in eighth grade, Paolo's love of old hip-hop led him to this song called "Tha Cross-roads," by a group called Bone Thugs-n-Harmony. The song is all about death, about a rapper named Eazy-E who died, with a chorus that goes, "I'll see you at the cross-roads, crossroads, crossroads, so you won't be lonely." Since Paolo and I knew we'd be dying right around the same time, we imagined that we'd literally be able to see each other at these proverbial crossroads, which cracked us up, and was also genuinely comforting. It unofficially became our song. (I know, we have a song.)

"Come on, man," Paolo says. "Get in ready position!"

We also came up with a dance that goes with the song. (I know.) It was mainly a jokey dance, but then one night that year, when I slept over his house, we got really seri-ous about making the dance good because we thought that would make it even funnier. We worked on it till three in the morning. (Get over it.) Occasionally throughout high school, Paolo would randomly start playing "Tha Cross-roads" off his phone, and wherever we were—supermarket, comic book store, car—we would break into the dance. I never intended to perform it for our entire grade at the prom, though. Nor did I intend for it to be the Grand Finale of my life.

"When judgment comes for you, 'cause it's gonna come for you," Bone Thugs-n-Harmony sings as the piano bass line climbs one note at a time.

"It's gonna come for you, man," Paolo says. "Ready?"

I sigh and get into position, both arms straight down at my sides. I try not to worry that my legs are barely working.

Much to my dismay, everyone on the dance floor is still focused on us. Time to go down in a blaze of glory.

We begin.

At first, people just stare, shocked, delighted, confused as to whether or not they should be into it or making fun of it. The dance is a series of synchronized jumps, pop locks, robot moves, and other jaunty arm maneuvers, and, in spite of my stiff, sore legs, I'm able to keep up pretty well. The dance is so deeply imprinted in my brain, I could probably do it in my sleep.

It should be humiliating, but it's not. It's calming.

Krayzie Bone sings the words *we pray* about ten times, and I notice that some of the more religious kids in our class, like Christian Fellowship Club president Paul Baylor, take in this lyric and nod their heads, at first in recognition, then along with the beat of the music. Then somebody shouts, "Oooohh yeah!" and in an instant, everybody on the dance floor is into it, cheering, moving along with the music, yelling our names.

Paolo looks at me as we do a spin around each other. "Yeah, bro, told ya! Our whole lives have been leading up to this!"

That can't be true.

It's taking more effort to dance, as I've used up almost

all of my energy reserves. Hopefully I can make it through this song, and then we can get back home, where I can literally rest in peace.

"Now we gotta get everybody involved!" Paolo says.

"Why?" I say, out of breath and barely able to get the word out.

"Because it's the prom, man! That's what happens!" Paolo takes a simple sequence of moves from the beginning of our dance—arm slices, a spin, and air pats—and goes through them emphatically, then repeats it. "Do this with me!" I do. "Everybody!" Paolo shouts.

"Everybody join in!" the DJ says into the microphone.

"We don't need your help, man," Paolo says. "This is gonna be spontaneous!"

"You think what I do is easy?" the DJ says, off the mic.

Funnily enough, several people have joined in, and like a rapidly spreading disease, soon most of the dance floor is engaged in this stupid dance we made up in eighth grade.

"It's happening," Paolo says. "It's happening."

"YES," I say.

It's glorious.

But then my eyes land on the entrance, where, just as Phil promised, Officer Corrigan is sauntering in, a serious, determined look on his face. He scans the room left to right.

A terrible feeling floods all the parts of my body that I can still feel.

It's the closest thing I've ever felt to a Spidey sense.

And it's tingling like crazy.

32

"Hey, man, hug me later," Paolo says, shrugging my arm off. "People are really doing it!"

It's true: our classmates are executing our dance with a verve and precision I never could have predicted.

But I wasn't trying to hug Paolo. My legs have just given out, and he's my only hope of staying upright.

"No . . . I can't really stand on my own anymore."

"Oh man," Paolo says, steadying my back.

"On it," Millie says, swooping under my left arm and hoisting it over her shoulder.

Their heroics happen to coincide with the return of the song lyrics about praying, and people mistakenly get the idea that we're doing some sort of arms-and-shoulders prayer circle thing. Within ten seconds, everyone is swaying back and forth to the chorus.

"Whoa, sweet," Paolo says.

"I think Officer Corrigan from this morning is looking for me," I say.

HorribleCop approaches Mr. Canzola, the Italian teacher, and asks him something. I'm not close enough to hear exactly what he's saying, but I swear his mouth forms my name.

"Whoa," Paolo says. "He looks intense, like he's looking for someone."

"Yeah! Me!"

"Oh. Then you may wanna lose the crown, bro," Paolo says. "Draws attention."

I slide off the prom king crown and roll it away. You can't take it with you, right?

"Can somebody, anybody tell me why we die, we die?" Bone Thugs-n-Harmony asks. "I don't wanna die."

Me neither, Bone.

"I think we need to do something, Paolo," Millie says, her body wavering under my left arm. "I'm superstrong but maybe not strong enough to keep holding Dent like this."

"I got this," he says. As the chorus of the song starts to fade out, Paolo flails his limbs around and gives a hard shove to his side of the circle, causing ten or so people to cascade into each other.

"Hey!"

"What the hell, dude?"

"Ow, watch out!"

"Sorry!" Paolo says.

Lucky for us, three of those cascading people are Mike Tarrance, Danny Delfino, and Andy Stetler. You know the kind of guys who will take any opportunity that comes their way as an excuse to homoerotically wrestle? Mike,

Danny, and Andy are them. Paolo's shove instantly sends them into wrestling go-mode, their tuxes guaranteeing it's the classiest fight they've ever had. Mike laughs hysterically as he holds Danny's arms up behind his head while Andy repeatedly jabs him in the stomach.

"Get off, dicks!" Danny shouts, contorting his body wildly and kicking his legs, flinging the three of them into another pack of dudes, who happily get into it. Soon there's at least fifteen guys in tuxes pushing, shoving, headlocking, and hurling each other across the room. Everyone else has moved to the perimeter of the dance floor, trying to avoid getting inadvertently smacked. Suffice it to say, I'm no longer concerned I'll be the sole focus of attention.

"Well played," I say.

"Yeah," Paolo says. "I was just trying to pretend that I was having a seizure so we could create a diversion, but this is way better."

HorribleCop is right near the melee, not really focused on it, still searching the room. What does he want from me? Still hung up on the deathdate statute thing? Taking precautions because of my splotch virus? Or just a douche with a badge, getting revenge for his grandson? I can tell he doesn't want to be involved in stopping the fight, but it would be weird for him not to. His eyes skirt over Paolo, Millie, and me, but I gently pull us down to the ground. Finally, I can rest my legs.

"I think those guys are all in love with each other," Millie says, gazing at the scuffle as she crouches down with us. "Like, actually in love."

"All right, evvvverybody," the DJ says. "Uh, you might want to break up the fighting because it's time for the last song! That's right, prom is coming to a close, so I wanna see everybody out here Livin' It Up! Right?"

A predictably sappy last song starts, but the fighting doesn't let up. Danny Delfino gets pushed directly into Brittany Bottinini at the edge of the dance floor, and they both fall to the ground. Danny is wearing my prom king crown.

"This is an insult to our collective intelligence," Shuwen Tsao says, to no one in particular.

The dance floor is a bed of chaos. With a frustrated grunt, HorribleCop at last steps into the fray and does his best to separate all the roughhousers. "Quit it!" he shouts. Mr. Canzola and Coach Mueller join him in the thick of the anarchy, which rapidly simmers down. We don't have much time.

"Let's go," I say, amping myself up to stand again.

"Yep-a-doo," Paolo says.

"Should I get your parents?" Millie asks.

"We're here," my stepmom says from behind me, where she stands with Paolo's mom, my dad, and Felix. "We wanted to make sure you weren't going to get trampled by those boys. Why are you sitting on the ground? What's wrong? Were you trampled?"

"No, uh, my legs are a little messed up. Unrelated to the fighting."

My stepmom gasps. "I knew we shouldn't have come here, I knew it."

"Raquel, it's okay," my dad says. "Denton, can you stand?"

"I think so," I say.

"Take my hands," my dad says. I do. "On the count of

three, we stand. One—two—three!" My dad gives a big pull, but I can't get my footing at all. I'm deadweight.

"I can't," I say. "I can't." He gently puts me back down on the ground.

"Are you paralyzed?" Paolo asks.

"I'm not paralyzed," I say. "I just can't, like, move my legs."

"That's what paralyzed is."

Ohmigod, I'm paralyzed. "Fine, whatever, can somebody get me a wheelchair or something?"

My stepmom looks devastated by this potential paralysis, but she pulls it together and springs into action. "Okay, we're leaving this place. Who wants to go get Denton a wheelchair?"

"Do they even have wheelchairs here?" Paolo asks.

"I don't know! Go!" my stepmom shouts. He runs off, pulling Millie along with him. "Sweetie, it's gonna be okay. We're right here with you; that's the most important thing."

My stepmom's behavior has subtly shifted into full-on emergency mode. She's acting, probably correctly, as if this is the beginning of the end. "Lyle and Felix, go get the car and pull up to the front."

"Yup," my dad says, already in motion.

"I should stay here with Dent," Felix says.

"We're fine, your father needs help. Go with him."

"But—"

"Go!" my stepmom shouts. He does.

"Raquel," Paolo's mom says, "if you want to go get the car with Lyle, I can stay here with Denton until Paolo brings the wheelchair."

"No, Mom," I say, avoiding eye contact with Paolo's mom. I don't want her anywhere near me.

"You think I'm going to leave my son right now?" my stepmom snaps. She crouches down and puts her arm around my shoulders.

"No, no," Paolo's mom says. "Of course not, Raquel. Of course not."

I look over to where HorribleCop was, but he's gone. The ruckus has dissipated, and the dance floor is filled with kids enjoying the last dance of prom. I lift my shirt and see that, in confirmation of my worst fears, the red has spread farther up my body, all the way to my lower belly.

Gradual red paralysis. And it's not just my legs I can't feel.

I can't feel my junk.

"How we folks doing over here tonight?" HorribleCop says, from behind me.

No.

"We're fine," my stepmom says without looking at him. I think she would literally fight this cop before she'd let him take me anywhere. For the first time all night, I'm glad my parents came with me to prom.

"Well, I'm glad to hear that. And you're still alive," he says to me, making a big show of looking at his watch. "Just about eleven and still tickin'. Not bad."

"Uh-huh," I say.

"I'd rather go at the very end of my deathdate than the very beginning," HorribleCop says, stroking his chin like an asshole would. "That's what I always say."

I don't care how I die at this point, as long as it doesn't, in any way, shape, or form, involve this horrible human.

"Not sure if you noticed," my stepmom says, "but this isn't the best time to chat."

"I actually came over to see if you folks needed any help. What with this young man sitting in the middle of the dance floor, I thought maybe you'd need a ride to the hospital."

People have started staring at us, talking amongst themselves.

"No. We're fine; we'll be taking Denton to our home."

"I have no argument with that. I believe I was there this morning." HorribleCop laughs, as if he's chuckling about a funny thing that happened at a party we all attended.

"Yes," my stepmom says, looking at him for the first time. "I believe you were."

"Well. You folks have a good night. Good knowing you, Dinton."

The way he says my name sends a shiver down my spine.

We watch him stroll out the door of the dance hall, grabbing at the walkie-talkie on his belt as he leaves.

"I can't believe they let him be a policeman," my step-mom says.

"Yeah," Paolo's mom says. "Shameful. If you'll excuse me a moment, I'm just gonna run to the women's room before we leave."

"Make sure you don't bump into Officer Senile in the lobby," my stepmom says. "They should take dinosaurs like that off the job as soon as they hit fifty. Keep 'em in the office."

Dinosaur. Happy dinosaur.

I pull my phone out of my pocket and open up to my

Facebook in-box. As I hold the phone out in front of me, I realize my right arm is getting stiff. Shit. My body is giving up on me. I scroll through my messages and find the one I'm looking for. *Happy Dinosaur says: Come to Bloom!!! 4 Huge Erections You Can Buy 120 Pills for Only $129.95!! !!* I click on Happy Dinosaur's name. The profile is almost entirely blank. No photo. Just a name and location: New York City. I click the SEND MESSAGE box. I need to fire this off in case I lose feeling in my arms next.

Hey, I type into my phone. *Who is this? Did y—*

"This should work," Paolo says as he rushes up to us, out of breath, pushing a dolly with a gold banquet chair on top of it.

"I'm dubious," Millie says, appearing next to him.

"That's all you could find?" my stepmom asks.

"I mean, it works," Paolo says, pushing the dolly forward and then back to demonstrate.

"Yeah, for boxes, for luggage, not for my son."

"It's fine, Mom," I say. "We can make it work. Lemme just finish writing this. . . ." I go back to typing.

"Finish writing this?" my stepmom says. "What, are you e-texting with someone? All your friends are here!"

"It's important," I say, typing the last sentence: *Did you know my mother?*

I quickly reread what I have and push SEND. The little Internet wheel spins, working hard to get my message to the mysterious Happy Dinosaur.

"Let's get you in this chair, D," Paolo says.

"Yup, okay, I'm . . ." I stare at my phone.

The screen has gone black.

I push the one non-digital button over and over again.

Nothing. The battery's dead. I have no idea if the message sent.

"Ready?" Paolo asks, extending his hands for me to grab.

"I'll get behind him," Millie says.

"Niiice," Paolo says.

The last song is over, and all around us, people have begun the migration from the dance floor.

"Thank you sooooo much, evvvverybody," the DJ's voice blares. "I'm DJ Gary P of Phenomenal Entertainment, and I hope you all had a killer time tonight. For everybody going to Project PROM, buses are waiting out front."

I grab Paolo's hands, and he's able to lift me up onto my feet, then, with Millie's help, maneuver me backward toward the makeshift wheelchair.

"Someone needs to hold the dolly," Paolo says as he and Millie awkwardly try to push me into the chair, causing the whole contraption to slowly roll away.

"I'll get it," my stepmom says, jumping into position like she's manning a tank.

Paolo and Millie work together to try to get me onto the banquet chair, but it is only when Danny Delfino runs up to help that they're successful. He takes the prom king crown off his head.

"Here, man, this is yours."

It's a sweet gesture, but the idea of sitting up here on this wheelchair throne with a plastic crown on my head is too pathetic for my dying heart to bear.

"All you, dude," I say.

"Oh. You sure?"

"So very sure. And, Danny."

"Yeah?"

"You're fantastic on the sax. Keep at it."

"Oh, cool, man, cool. Thanks." He walks off, a bounce in his step.

"That guy was so happy after you said that," Millie says. "His eyes were, like, twinkling."

"I'm just amazed he came over to help," Paolo says. "Unpresidented behavior."

"Ha, *unpresidented*," Millie says.

"We should get this show on the road, kids," my stepmom says. "Mr. Little is waiting for us. You good up there, Denton?"

Let's see: partially paralyzed, going to die any minute, sitting atop a weird, homemade wheelchair. I'm fantastic!

"Sure."

As we roll toward the exit door through the slow-moving masses of my peers, my stepmom pushing the dolly as Paolo clears the way ahead, I hold on to the chair tight. It wobbles back and forth a bit, and my arms feel weak.

"You're gonna be okay," Millie says from beside me, her hand reaching up and touching my knee.

"Thanks," I say.

We go over the threshold from the party room to the faux-elegant hallway, and I get jostled a little bit in my chair. I almost fall off, but I'm able to hold on.

"You need to slow down a little bit, Paolo," my stepmom says.

Paolo looks confused, like he's about to say, "You're the one pushing the cart, lady!" but Millie gives him a look.

"Hey!" I hear from way behind us. It's Phil. "You're lucky your sugar daddy showed up, Little! Come on back here!"

There's not even the sliver of a possibility that I'd be able to fight him right now. I can barely move.

All the heads in the hallway stop and turn back to look at him.

"No, you guys don't get it," Phil says. "I was knocked unconscious."

"Good," Ratina Jacobs yells. "You're an asshole!"

"Denton is eight billion times the human you will ever be," Melissa Schoenberg says.

"Just 'cause you run fast doesn't mean you're cool!" someone else says.

Phil gets lost in the crowd.

"King Denton!" Willis Ellis says, his hippie girlfriend, Jeannie, at his side. "Sweet ride, man."

"Sorta," I say.

"See ya around, dude."

"Bye," Jeannie says.

"Bye, guys," I say. I have the instinct to wave, but I'm afraid if I let go of the chair, I'll tumble off it.

We make it outside, where it's gotten a little chilly, with a crisp night breeze. In spite of all that's happening, I try to feel the sensation of the wind on my chest, cutting through the blue fabric of my suit.

"Do you see Dad's car?" my stepmom asks.

The parking lot is a zoo, with a couple of buses that will take kids to the alcohol-free Project PROM, six or seven limos that will take kids too cool for that to beachy places like Wildwood or Ocean City, and then a sea of cars, mainly student-driven. And—somewhere amongst all of this—my dad in the family minivan.

"Not yet," I say.

"Well, where could he be? He's been out here for fifteen minutes."

"I'm sure he's somewhere out there," Paolo says. "I'll go scout it out. You coming, Millie?"

"Oh, sure," Millie says, looking back to me for a moment as she follows Paolo into the parking jungle.

"We're gonna be home soon, sweets," my stepmom says, standing on her tiptoes, trying to see over the long line of vehicles.

"Can I help you guys?" HorribleCop says, appearing out of nowhere. My heart and stomach leap, but the rest of me doesn't. Moving is getting harder and harder.

"Are you kidding me right now?" my stepmom says. "Absolutely not. There is nothing you can do, and I don't understand why you keep thinking there is."

"Well, if it's your husband you're looking for, I believe I see his car right over there. Your other son's in there, too." HorribleCop points past the parade of limos. "A minivan, right?"

"Where?" my stepmom says, staring out along the trajectory of his pointing arm.

I start rolling backward, toward the banquet hall, and I'm about to call out for help when a hand covers my mouth. "I'm sorry, Denton," Paolo's mom says into my ear. "You have to trust me."

No. This isn't happening. I try to pull her hand off my face, but my arms have stopped working. I look down and my hands are red. My stepmom's too wrapped up in a parking argument with HorribleCop to notice that I'm drifting away. I should scream. But sound won't come.

Paolo's mom carefully threads me backward through the crowd, and I'm thinking someone will notice, someone will stop this from happening, but everyone's too caught up in their own postprom excitement. We move around the side of the building, then turn so that Paolo's mom is behind the dolly and chair, pushing me forward.

I should have listened to Veronica and left when I had the chance.

I crane my neck sideways to see if my stepmom has noticed we've gone, but she's still trying desperately to get permission for my dad to drive up closer so it's easier to get me into the car.

I finally attempt a scream, but it barely registers. The muscles of my mouth feel slack and marbly.

My stepmom fades into the distance. I can only see part of her face.

Then nothing.

That might be the last time I see her.

Paolo's mom steers me down the narrow side alley of the building, farther and farther from the cacophony of voices in front.

"Here we are," she says as we turn the corner of the building. Her station wagon is parked next to two big Dumpsters, its engine running.

She takes her hand off my mouth. "Please don't shout, sweetie, okay? Honestly, trust me." I couldn't shout if I wanted to.

She stands in front of the dolly chair, sizing me up.

"What's the easiest, safest way to get you into the car?" She puts her arms around me and tries to heft me off the chair. My useless arms flop at my sides.

"Oof, sorry, hon," Paolo's mom says, lowering me back into the chair. "Better call in the troops." She scampers over to the car and taps on the passenger-side window. "Gonna need your help."

The door opens, and Veronica comes out, still drunk. "I told you to leave," she says to me. "Why didn't you leave?"

"I don't know," I try to say, but it comes out a soft "Iuhohhh."

"Denton! DENTON!" I hear from the front of the building, sounding far away but still piercing through all the other noise. My stepmom. She'll come get me.

"Ohmigod," Paolo's mom says, putting a hand over her eyes. "This is heartbreaking." She gathers herself and crouches over me. "Denton, I promise this is for your own good. I'm sorry it has to happen like this, but I'll explain everything in the car. Come on, Ron. Help me here."

Millie and Paolo start shouting my name, too.

"Mom, I just—" Veronica says.

"Veronica," Paolo's mom says. "Please, sweetheart, you have to trust me, too. I need your help. Denton needs your help."

Veronica looks to me with bleary eyes. I look back at her. She helps get me down from the chair, wrapping her arms under my pits and around my chest as Paolo's mom grabs my legs. I feel Veronica breathing hard into my ear as she struggles to get a good grip.

I know my stepmom will find me. Paolo will find me. Felix will find me. Any second now.

After a protracted sequence of awkward maneuvers, I am more or less stuffed into the backseat of the car. I slowly topple over onto my side, but Paolo's mom picks me up and gently balances me against the back cushion.

Paolo's mom gets into the driver's seat, Veronica beside her. She shifts the car into drive, and we move forward, around the other side of Haventown Gardens.

As we move through the parking lot, I spot my parents' minivan. I grunt uselessly as we speed by. Paolo is standing near it, eyes searching, and I think he notices his mom's car pulling away. At least I hope he does.

Paolo's mom stares forward, driving with purpose. Veronica looks back at me. As we pull out of the parking lot, it finally sinks in. No one has found me. I've been kidnapped by Paolo's mom.

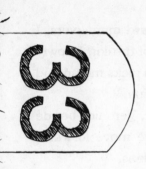

33

"The hard part is over, Dent," Paolo's mom says into the rearview mirror. "Thank you for cooperating. I know how confusing and scary this must be."

Like I had a choice.

"Are you okay?" she asks.

My head and neck are the last things left I can move, so I can nod or shake my head if I want to. But I don't.

"Believe me when I say I hate that it had to happen like this. I would have wanted you to say goodbye to your family. To Pow. But they never would have understood."

The town rushes by outside my window.

"Mom, I don't even understand," Veronica says, pulling her hood down.

"Denton, I'm an agent working for the DIA. That's the Death Investigation Agency. Have you heard of it?"

I haven't. I grunt.

"I think Veronica told you that I've been watching you

most of your life. Since you were five. I was the perfect candidate for your case. Not only is Paolo the same age as you, but he also has nearly the same deathdate. It was, like, fate. My son could be your best friend. What better cover for getting to spend a lot of time with you?"

I don't know what to do with these words.

"Not that Paolo knows about any of this. And I can't stress enough, Denton, how much I truly came to care about you. To love you like one of my own kids." I stare at the back of Paolo's mom's head as she speaks. "I don't want you to think all of our interactions were a lie. None of them were."

"You are full of such shit!" Veronica says.

"Please don't, V."

"Why shouldn't I? Do you even hear yourself? You just kidnapped him—and me—and you're saying it's out of love?"

"There was no other way."

"Oh, so when you were in our kitchen shoveling your pills down Denton's throat, that was out of love? What are those, actually?"

I don't want to know.

Paolo's mom looks at Veronica, then back at the road. "Those really were homeopathic pills! To deal with anxiety. I knew how difficult today would be for Dent; I was trying to help."

"Really," Veronica says.

"Yes."

"What about when you lied to him and convinced him that his girlfriend had dumped him?"

"Look, I'm not proud of that, but there was no other way to get Dent to stay over," Paolo's mom says. "And I needed a sample of his blood and hair as close to midnight as possible on the day before his deathdate, when the virus was activated. I feel terrible, but I had no choice."

Me and Veronica. All part of the setup.

"I did not think, however, that the two of you would . . ."

Okay, phew. At least us hooking up wasn't part of the plan. Because if my best friend's mom were the wingman responsible for getting me laid for the first time, that would be pretty embarrassing.

"I. Can. Not. Believe. This. Shit!" Veronica shouts into her window.

"Shhh. Please, V."

"What about lying about having a crush on Dent's dad? Your lies are all over the place. It's disgusting."

"I did once have a crush on Lyle! I always wished you kids had a father figure around."

"You're completely nuts," Veronica says.

"Is any of this making sense?" Paolo's mom looks into the mirror, waiting for me to give some sign of affirmation. I don't give her any. Almost none of it's making sense.

"Put it this way. It's"—she glances at the digital clock on the dashboard—"eleven-twelve p.m. on your deathdate, and you're still alive."

I'm also purple, mute, and immobile.

"I'm saying you might live, Denton. You might live through your deathdate."

Sound drops out. My breath catches in my chest. My head rolls back and forth on my neck. I might live. What?

"Mom, why are you saying this?" Veronica asks. "You're being insane!"

"It's true. Denton. The purple-red thing you've taken

to calling the splotch? It's a virus. Your mother injected it into you before you were born."

My mother.

"As far as we know, there's only been a couple of people injected. And you're one of them. And you're the first one to reach your deathdate." I look at the clock: 11:14. Forty-six minutes to go. "So what happens to you is obviously of considerable interest to certain people."

"But . . . ," Veronica says. "I have it, too . . . and Paolo. I mean, what does that mean?"

Paolo's mom turns to look at Veronica, then turns her gaze forward. "We don't know. Maybe nothing."

I stare out the window and try and figure out where we're going.

"DC," Paolo's mom says, like she's reading my mind. "We're headed down to DC, if you're wondering. The DIA will take good care of you."

I find it hard to believe any organization with *death* in its name prioritizes care.

"That is, assuming you do actually make it through your deathdate. If not, then I turn this car around, and the government and I come up with a believable story for why you were in the car with me when you died."

Paolo's mom looks into her mirror. "Oh shit."

The engine makes a revving sound as we speed up.

"This is exactly what I didn't want," she says. "Your parents have caught up to us. Not sure how, but they have."

They found me!

"Looks like your brother's behind the wheel," Paolo's mom says. "I just don't want any of them to get hurt. This has gotten so out of hand!"

We run a red light.

"Mom," Veronica says, gripping on to the armrest. "Can't we just pull over and talk with them?"

"Doesn't work like that," Paolo's mom says.

She executes a crazy, skidding U-turn, and I'm knocked onto my side. My view is limited to the gray fabric of the passenger seat in front of me.

I can hear the family minivan doing a similar screechy turn behind us, though. We take another quick turn, which swings me back up into a sitting position. My seat belt was never buckled. Paolo's mom looks in her mirror, and I can tell my family's still behind us. The sound of a police siren tears through the air.

Veronica looks past me. "Um, Mom, there's a cop."

"Yeah." Paolo's mom sighs. "He's with us. Unfortunately." She talks to me through the rearview. "I'm so sorry you had that idiot on your ass all week, Dent. Usually, I'd have another agent giving me backup, but that guy's the brother of my boss's boss, so I had no choice."

She's connected to HorribleCop.

"The power went to his head a bit. It's unfortunate."

"Is he gonna arrest Denton's parents?" Veronica asks.

"No, he's just gonna stall them."

We jolt forward, all three of our heads snapping back simultaneously. Felix must have rammed the minivan's bumper into us.

"What the hell!" Paolo's mom says. "I'm doing this to help your brother!" she shouts into the rearview.

"Mom, you're really scaring me," Veronica says. "Can we please slow down? Or just stop or something?"

"V," Paolo's mom says, looking right at her. "Please

keep it together. I didn't force you to go home and drink all that alcohol; that was your decision. And now I need you to—"

I see the car ahead of us before Paolo's mom does and only a fraction of a second before Veronica. But it's as if I can see not only the car but everything else that is about to unfold. I feel strangely at peace.

"WhoaMomMomMOMMM!" Veronica shouts.

Technically, I can't feel anything. But I am aware of everything.

Paolo's mom's eyes snap forward, just in time to see the stopped car ahead of us, patiently waiting at a traffic light. Heads up. If I could move my arms, this is the part where I'd attempt to buckle my seat belt.

Paolo's mom slams on the brakes. Too little. Too late. The brakes screech.

Then: A spine-rattling crunch. The whoosh of air bags.

As I'm propelled toward and through the windshield, I get a glimpse of the sporty yellow car we've collided with, and I know instantly who the driver is.

I half open my eyes.

I am horizontal. And not in a good way.

All around me, people speak in hushed, concerned voices. I feel nothing.

I hear an ambulance siren.

I close my eyes.

35

"I got this, fella."

"Excuse me, Officer?"

"I can take it from here. I'll wheel him into the hospital."

"I'm sorry, Officer, but that's not allowed. Someone with medical training needs to be with him at all times. Protocol."

"But I'd be wheeling him alongside these other folks on stretchers. And all of them seem to have escorts with medical training. One of their escorts can double for this guy."

"I don't make the rules, sir. And unless you got some legal reason why you need to come along, you won't even be allowed to follow us past the waiting room."

"I do, in fact, have a very good legal reason, son. This teenager is a criminal."

"Oh?"

"Damn right."

"Well, after somehow surviving being propelled out of a

car at sixty miles per hour, he seems to be paralyzed from the neck down, so I don't think there's much to worry about."

"He was already paralyzed before the accident."

"What?"

"You heard me. This boy's a criminal, and he was already paralyzed."

"Oh . . . No wonder he survived the crash . . ."

"So I can take it from here, you can . . . go do some other hospital stuff."

"I . . . No, sorry, I'll need to see the legal paperwork."

I hear the unmistakable sound of automatic sliding doors opening.

"You'll have to excuse me if I don't always carry around paperwork when I'm out in the field. Keeping this town safe."

We're inside now.

"You're excused. But I'm sorry, Officer, you won't be coming into the emergency room with this boy."

"Now you listen to me, and you listen to me good." The stretcher stops rolling. "You don't understand a lick of what's actually going on here, so why don't you just let the professionals handle this."

"No, Officer, I understand completely. Today is this boy's deathdate—I'm fully aware of that—so you think we should just give up. Some other hospitals may operate that way, sure, but we don't. We fight until the last minute, fight to make all our patients' endings as comfortable and easy as possible. Now if you'll excuse me."

We roll onward.

"Get back here! Stop right now, boy!"

"No."

"Don't you even get it? Don't you know what time it is? It's eleven-fifty-three p.m. You have seven minutes! Goddammit, what're you gonna do in seven minutes? Lemme take him!"

"No."

Chaotic hospital sounds surround us. I hear no further protest from HorribleCop.

I could open my eyes, but I'm scared. My gut tells me I'm better off if people think I'm still unconscious.

A quick recap of what I've learned since regaining consciousness:

There was a terrible accident. I was flung out of the car. Others were also injured. I am (still) paralyzed. Being paralyzed somehow saved my life. HorribleCop wants to kidnap me, picking up where Paolo's mom left off. Oh, and I have seven minutes left to live. Probably six by now.

I wonder how fucked up my body is.

"Is he okay?" Paolo! Out of breath. "Hey, sir, that's my best friend. Is he still alive?"

"Yes, he's breathing. Unconscious but breathing."

"Holy shit!! Seriously? That's awesome!!" Oh, Paolo.

"We don't have much time."

"No, but that is really awesome! What time is it? This is insane! And he looks good, don't you think, Doc?"

"I'm not actually a doctor yet."

"Oh, sorry, right, doctors don't wear scrubs, right?"

"No, they do."

"Oh. Well, anyways, he does look good. I mean, he's bloody, but not superbloody."

"Yeah, your friend is very lucky. But I'm sorry, you can't actually be back here."

"But we were in the accident, too. In the third car that crashed into the other two." Oh no. My family. "And, I mean, this guy's my best friend, so—"

"Look, if you want us to help him, we need to start working on him ASAP. Please, this is the way you would most be helping your friend."

"Okay, okay. Sorry." Paolo sounds a little emotional. "Denton." His voice sounds close-up and his breath smells like pickles. "You only have a few minutes left, and this hospital dude is making me leave. I don't know if you can even hear me, but . . . you're my best friend, and I'm gonna miss you like crazy. Even though I'll see you in a month, right? Aw, man, this is so intense, I'm not usually a crier. I'm so pissed at my mom for kidnapping you and everything. Hey, actually, Hospital Guy, have you seen my mom? She was in the same ambulance with Dent. With this kid. This teen."

"I think your mom was already taken into the emergency room."

"Is she okay?"

"She wasn't wearing her seat belt, so the air bag slammed into her face. She'll be fine, but she's unconscious."

"Oh. Um . . . Can I see her or what?"

"No, you really shouldn't be back here at all. I'm gonna have to ask you both to—"

"One more thing," Paolo says. "Have you seen my sister? Veronica? Angry-looking girl? Looks kinda like me?"

"No."

"No? Oh man. Guess that means she was wearing her seat belt . . . ?"

"I don't know. You have to leave."

"Okay . . . Love you, Dent!" The sound of Paolo scampering down the hall. "Millie, come on! What are you looking at?"

Millie also made it out of the crash unscathed. Good.

"I always liked you, Denton," she says quietly. "Like, really liked you."

"Hey, Millennium, come on! We gotta clear out so they can help him."

"I know, but—"

"Trust me," Paolo says. "I got a plan."

"That's unsettling." The light behind my eyelids darkens as Millie hovers closer. "Bye, Denton. Thanks for everything." She gives me a tiny kiss on the cheek, then her footsteps join Paolo's, echoing down the hall away from my stretcher.

The conversation from the car floods back into my head. My mother. A virus, injected into me while I was in her womb. Living past my deathdate.

I open my eyes as slightly as I possibly can so that I can see some things but still seem unconscious. White ceiling tiles and fluorescent lights whiz past. I try to get a look at my hospital protector, but it's hard from my angle, especially since we're moving at a surprisingly fast pace. He seems like he's in his midtwenties, black or Indian or Hispanic, I can't really tell.

"Almost there, buddy," he says. "Don't worry."

I reclose my eyes.

"Sean, Sean, wait, wait." A new voice. We slow down, but we don't stop.

"Dr. Hemler, this boy needs immediate attention."

"No, Sean. Stop. Stop!" We do.

I open my eyes just a bit and see that Dr. Hemler is a nearly bald man, with a mole on the right side of his chin. He's distinguished-looking but wrinkly.

"His time's up," Dr. Hemler says. "He has just two minutes to live, and he doesn't seem to be in any pain, so that's all we can do."

"I don't understand. He's still breathing; we should bring him into the ER."

"Sean, listen to me." The older doctor's voice gets very quiet. "This instruction comes from higher up. Much higher up. It is in the best interest of this hospital—and all of us who work here—to do as we've been told and hand this boy over to the police."

"Excuse me?"

"You heard him, son."

He's back.

"We're gonna hand a patient over to this cop? What about his parents?"

"Look, look," Dr. Hemler says. "The boy's parents are being treated right now for wounds sustained in the accident. His body will go back to them as soon as the police are finished."

"The boy's body? This boy is still breathing!"

"Yes, of course, but seeing as his deathdate will be over in one minute, it will no longer be our concern."

"I don't understand. This boy might live past his death-date, meaning some sort of medical miracle will have occurred, and you're saying it's not our concern?"

"That's exactly what I'm saying. It will no longer be within our jurisdiction. And if you want to continue to have any sort of medical career, Mr. Davis, I would let this one go."

I'm trying to listen to everything that's being said while ignoring the insistent countdown in my head. Less than a minute of life left. Maybe.

Unprompted, images flicker through my mind: Running through woods and sunlight. Getting dripped on by a slice of pepperoni pizza. Taryn smiling at me in the hall. Flipping through a comic book. Seeing my dad and stepmom waiting for me as I get off the bus, home from a summer away at camp. Sitting in a circle at preschool next to Sophie Heller. Trying desperately to reach the kitchen counter, but being too small. Following Felix into the backyard, excited that he's agreed to play with me.

My heart beats faster. This is what the end feels like.

"Okay," Sean says.

"Well, lookit that," HorribleCop says. "It's midnight. Deathdate over. Guess I'll take it from here, gentlemen."

He rolls me away.

36

The thing is, it's not the end. Because I'm still very much alive. My mom saved me. My mom's virus saved me. What the hell does that mean?

Maybe it's not actually midnight yet.

"Goddamn, I can't believe it myself," HorribleCop says, as if reading my mind. "But I see you breathing, and my watch right here says twelve-oh-one. This is really something."

The stretcher moves onward. I have no idea where he's taking me.

"You know, you hear stories like this, but you never believe 'em."

My body starts tingling. It is the first thing I've felt in hours.

"Urban legends, tall tales."

It starts in my face, then slowly moves down my torso, my arms, my legs, down to my toes.

"But here you are, living a day you aren't supposed to live."

Maybe this is actually what dying feels like.

"Up to me to get you out of here. I'm sure people are gonna wanna study you. Figure out how you did it."

How I did it?

I open my eyes a bit and see HorribleCop get on his walkie-talkie. "I got him. Still alive. We should be moving out soon. Of course I'll be discreet; who do you thi—"

"Stop right there." I know that voice.

"Sorry, Doctor, this boy needs to be taken to the ER immediately, he's only got—"

"Don't bullshit me, Officer." It's Brian Blum. "I know exactly who this boy is, way better than you ever will, and I know that I can't let him leave this hospital with you."

Holy crap.

My stretcher comes to a stop. "So you know, huh? You think 'cause you work in this hospital, you can stop an officer of the law?"

"This isn't my hospital. And, yes."

"Well, you're wrong. Now back off."

"No."

"Should I call for backup? Maybe come up with a reason why you should be arrested?"

Brian waits before responding, possibly sizing up whether or not HorribleCop is bluffing. "Before you do that, maybe you want to take a look at this." The sound of Dr. Brian Blum unfolding a piece of paper and handing it to HorribleCop.

Not a second later, I'm startled by Brian's voice in my ear. "Whenever you can . . . run."

He must not realize that I'm paralyzed.

"What is this?" HorribleCop says in response to whatever he's reading.

I feel Brian's hand at my waist, and I flinch. He slides something into the pocket of my suit pants.

Wait. I felt that.

"This looks like someone's prescription for something. What's this got to do with me?"

"Nothing," Brian says as I hear him grabbing the paper back from HorribleCop. "Absolutely nothing." His voice and footsteps head down the hall away from us.

I move my fingers. I move my toes. I adjust my torso. I can move!

"Don't have time for this bullshit," HorribleCop mutters. "Let's take a quick detour."

Our stretcher slows down. I open my eyes and see that HorribleCop is inspecting all the doors we pass, looking for something. I subtly flex my right and left ankles. They tingle.

"This'll do," HorribleCop says as he turns the stretcher left through the doorway of what seems to be a tiny medical supply closet. He parks the stretcher right in the middle.

I watch as HorribleCop takes a syringe out from God knows where, possibly from the nook underneath his balls. Ew. He holds it up to the light and taps it twice.

"Sorry to do this, but clearly you're in no position to mind."

I curl the fingers of my left hand into a fist. My heart is beating a million times a second.

"Just a little sedative, make sure you stay knocked out during all this."

HorribleCop grabs my right arm and gets ready to inject me.

"Never done this before. Heh heh . . . Here goes."

I spring into action, swinging my left hand into HorribleCop's wrist and knocking the syringe onto the ground.

"Wha?" he says.

Then I pull my leg back and send it soaring into his chest. He is pushed backward into a shelf, not as hard as I would have hoped, but it knocks him off balance and he ends up in a sitting position.

I stand up off the stretcher, and my legs are shaky as hell.

I go to pull open the door and race out of there, but the closet is too small, and HorribleCop's seated position directly blocks the door.

Shit.

He slowly lumbers up onto his feet. "You're not going anywhere, son. Especially after that little stunt."

I skitter to the far corner of the room, my back against the wall.

HorribleCop leans over, picks the syringe back up.

"Please," I say, my voice dry and raspy. "I'll come along with you. You don't have to do this."

"Yes, I do." HorribleCop reaches out for me, surprisingly quick, and is about to inject me when the door swings open and someone whacks him on the head with something hard.

It's Felix! Holding a bedpan.

"Get outta here, Dent! Go!"

HorribleCop is, for a moment, disoriented, and I take the opportunity to get the hell outta there.

Felix saved me. Again. One billion brother points.

I walk down the hall, fast as I can, as I go through what feels like the worst case of pins and needles ever experienced by anyone ever.

I'm keeping my head down and trying to play it cool, to come up with some sort of a game plan, when I'm approached by two people in blue hospital scrubs. I try to pick up my pace and avoid them.

"Holy shit!! You are full-on ghosting! What the hell are you doing still alive?"

It's Paolo and Millie, for some reason wearing scrubs. They hug me.

"Shh, I have no idea," I say.

"I'm so happy!" Paolo says.

"Why are you wearing those?"

"Paolo had a plan," Millie says.

"Yeah, it was a plan to save you, but I guess we don't need it anymore."

"No, you might. Felix bailed me out back there and is dealing with HorribleCop, but I doubt I have much time." I look down the hall to make sure no one is following me.

"Hey, you're not purple anymore!" Paolo says.

"Whoa, yeah, you neither."

"Mine, like, trickled away after midnight. It looked cool, right, Mills?"

"Eh," Millie says. "If by cool, you mean gross."

"I don't think I have much time before HorribleCop is back on my tail," I say. "Do you know which room my parents are in?"

"You got it, dude." Paolo walks us down a long hallway, up a flight of stairs, then down another hallway. I try to remain inconspicuous, just another alive person walking in a hospital. Not sure if it's working. I'm jumpy as hell.

"Speaking of parents," I say, "your mom . . ."

"Oh, don't even get me started. I'm freaking out hard-core. Veronica was telling the truth!"

"Yeah, I'm sorry, man. Your mom's been spying on me my whole life."

Paolo shakes his head in wonder. "I'm so pissed, but part of me also thinks that is insanely awesome."

"She knew I might live through my deathdate."

"What? Then why did she crash the car?"

"That was out of her control. I think that's just how I was supposed to die: in a car accident with Willis Ellis."

"*Cómo*saywhat?"

"Think about it: three separate times I was almost killed by him and his yellow car. But for some reason, it never worked. The purple virus saved me. Especially the last time."

"You lost me, man."

"I get it," Millie says.

"I was paralyzed, so when I was thrown out of the car, I couldn't, like, tense up my body or anything. So I didn't get hurt. I was just a rag doll flying through the air."

"Wow. Crazy theory."

"It's not a theory; it's what actually happened."

"Maybe the purple virus saved me, too."

"What do you mean?"

"I don't know, just 'cause I was also purple."

"Was Willis Ellis hurt, by the way? And Jeannie?"

"Nah, they stuck around till the police and ambulance came, gave the necessary info, then headed down to the beach for postprom partying. He was bummed about his mom's car. But it was still drivable."

"Oh. Yeah. That's too bad."

"Yeah. Here we are." Paolo stops in front of an open door. "My mom's in there, too. FYI. Our folks are roommates. Kinda cool."

"Oh."

"Don't worry, she's unconscious. I think."

Inside the room, there are four beds against the far wall. My stepmom is in one, unconscious yet maintaining a peeved expression. Her face looks fine, but she has a large bandage on the right side of her skull.

This is my fault.

My dad is in the bed next to her, also unconscious, his face also fine. His leg is suspended in some kind of cast above the bed.

Also my fault.

Paolo's mom is in the next bed over. Her face is all bruised and bandaged, and she, too, is unconscious.

Her, I feel less bad about. Mainly confused/terrified.

The fourth bed is empty.

I wonder where Veronica is.

As I scan back across the room, I see my dad staring at me, his eyes wide open. He opens his mouth, about to speak, but then says nothing. We look at each other, the beeping of various machines the only sound in the room.

He is looking at me, not with his usual cluelessness. Like he gets it. Like he's always gotten it. And he knows I can't stay here. He looks over to my stepmom, then back to me, and gives a little nod. I want to tell him I love him, but instead I just nod back.

Then Paolo's mom opens her eyes. She looks at me. My whole body freezes.

She stares at me for a few seconds longer, and I am convinced she is going to speak, but then her eyes close and her body relaxes.

Time to go.

I look back to my dad and try to smile. I point to my stepmom and blow a kiss in her direction, hoping this will be interpreted correctly as *Tell Mom I love her.*

He nods again.

I walk out of the room.

"How was it?" Paolo says.

My throat is filled with too many feelings to speak. "Your mom scares me," I finally get out.

"Sorry. This is pretty insane. You're, like, a wanted man. I'll come with you. This is so *Thelma and Louise.*"

I start walking down the hallway, and Paolo and Millie follow.

"I can come, too," Millie says.

"Yeah, babe," Paolo says. "You can be Brad Pitt."

"Can you give me your phone a sec, Pow?" I ask.

"Yeah, sure."

I go into his Facebook account and log out.

"Aw, man, don't sign me out of Facebook!"

"Why?"

"Sorry, bad time for jokes."

I sign in and immediately go to my in-box, looking for a response from Happy Dinosaur.

There is one.

I click it open:

Correct!! ! Come to Bloom!!!! 4 Huge Erections You

Can Buy 120 Pills for Only $129.95!! !! It's again followed by a link and a phone number, saying to click/call to find the address.

It says, *Correct!* Meaning the sender did know my mother? Or am I reading way too far into a boner email?

"What?" Paolo asks. "Already setting up hot dates in the afterlife?"

"Something like that."

"Dent!" Felix shouts, emerging from the stairwell door right near us. "You gotta get out of here! I injected him with that sedative, so I think he's out, but he had already called for backup. Lots of it."

"Okay, okay."

"Go all the way down the hall, take that last set of stairs all the way to the basement. There's a side door down there. Use it. And go somewhere far away."

"What?" I can't process what he's saying.

He shoves a wad of bills into my hand. "Take this."

"You're being weird, Feel, I don't wanna take your—"

"Yeah, well, I just assaulted a cop. It's a weird day."

"Nice!" Paolo says.

"I can get my bike from your house, Denton," Millie says. "It's a little messed up, but you can use it to go somewhere."

"That's perfect," Felix says.

"I'll go with you. We'll cab it. See you soon, Dent."

Paolo and Millie dash away.

"You think I should take Millie's bike?" I ask Felix.

"Absolutely not," Felix says. "I did that to get them out of here. This is dangerous enough as it is; they don't need to be involved. Were you contacted with an address?"

"Contacted? What are you talking about?"

"An address! You were supposed to be given an address."

"What? No, I . . . Oh, wait!" I reach into my pocket and pull out a scrap of paper. On it is written: *I'm sorry I couldn't tell you more in the car. Too risky. But you've survived. Go to 301 W. 53rd St., 2D, NYC. You will be OK. Brian*

"Oh good, you wrote it down," Felix says.

"No, this is from Brian Blum, he put it in my pocket."

Saying his last name aloud triggers a phrase in my brain: *Come to Bloom!!*

What the . . .

Come to Blum! Find the address.

I was supposed to click to find the address in Happy Dinosaur's message. But I didn't. So Blum came to me.

He always knew I would live.

"When?"

"Just before, when I was on the stretcher."

"Oh man, well, he got it to you, at least. You need to go to that address."

"But this is in New York City."

"Denton." Felix once again puts his hands on my shoulders, and I notice he has a big gash on his forehead, I'm guessing from the car accident. He peeks back to make sure no one is coming, then looks directly into my eyes. "I love you, but you don't fully understand what's happening he—"

"So help me understand! What is happening?"

"Listen to me. You have outlived your deathdate. Because of, well . . ."

"The virus, right? Paolo's mom told me our mom injected me with a virus before I was born."

"Oh." Felix wasn't expecting me to know that. "Yeah. Yes, she did. But the government found out. And they do not want you living through your deathdate. At all. Which is why, it turns out, Paolo's mom's been watching you your whole life."

"But why is this so bad for the government?"

"Long story. But suffice it to say, important people have lots of money riding on the fact that the deathdate system works. If you live, maybe it doesn't work. The whole system is undermined, and those important people lose lots of money. You get me?"

"Not really."

"It doesn't matter. What matters is that for all intents and purposes, you are dead. The government will list you as deceased, and the world will believe that Denton Little is no more. There will probably be some headline about the car crash and your death in the newspaper. So use that cash, and stay off the grid. And grab the bag in the stairwell. It has clothes to change into."

For a moment, I wonder if I would have been better off if I'd actually died.

"How do you know so much? Are you working with Brian Blum?"

"Something like that. Look, I'm sorry I could never tell you all this until now. We honestly didn't know if it would work, but—"

"They're coming," a voice says from behind me. Veronica has emerged from the stairwell door at the other end of the hall. Her hood is down, and she looks afraid. I'm so glad she's okay.

Felix spins around and looks out the window of the door leading to the stairwell behind him. "Cops, Denton! Go go go!"

I don't think. His voice is the starter pistol, and I take off. I make it to the end of the hall, where Veronica has the door held open for me.

"Veronica," I say. "I . . ."

"I know. I feel those things, too, okay? I'm really, really happy you're not dead. But you need to get out of here," she says.

I look back and see three cops emerge into the hall. They tackle Felix. I feel Veronica's hands on my back as she shoves me through the threshold.

"Go, idiot!"

"Okay!"

I go. Down the stairs. Pick up the plastic bag. Into the basement. Out the door. Into the night. And I run. The pins and needles are gone, and I run. I picture Coach Mueller whistling and cheering me on, and I run. I feel out of breath, but I run.

I run.

It turns out there aren't many trains after midnight. In fact, as I stand on the near-empty platform, feeling antsier by the minute, I'm starting to think there won't be any trains until tomorrow morning. I probably didn't need to dramatically sprint the whole way here.

There's a young guy in some kind of military outfit standing next to the machine, so I haven't bought my ticket yet. What if he's a colleague of a certain horrible policeman?

I realize I'm still in a suit. I grab a hoodie out of the bag of clothes Felix left for me and throw it on. As I zip it up, I hear the clanging bells that signal the train's approach to the station. Hallelujah. The military guy walks down the platform away from the machine—hallelujah squared—and I race over to it.

In my anxious state, I keep pressing the wrong buttons and needing to start over.

Finally, I get it right: one adult ticket to New York's Penn Station.

One-way.

The machine asks me how I want to pay. I choose cash and slide in a crumpled twenty. It slides back out as I see the train approaching out of the corner of my eye. "Shit! Come on, come on!" I smooth out the twenty along the side of the machine and try again. It slides out.

A woman with big hair and glasses who just got in line behind me sighs.

"Sorry," I say.

I so badly want to use my credit card, the one my parents pay, but I know I'm not supposed to. I need to stay off the grid.

Because the world thinks I'm dead.

I slide the bill in once more, and the machine finally decides to approve my lackluster twenty. As the train slows to a stop behind me, I wait for the machine to spit out my ticket. I hope it happens soon, before I have time to think harder about all of this and change my mind.

"This train to New York, Penn Station," the conductor shouts as he steps onto the platform. "New York!"

The ticket comes out. I grab it.

I turn around, ready to get on the train, when the woman behind me gasps.

"Sorry about the wait," I say, trying to get by her.

"No, you . . ." She holds up her phone, with the browser opened to our area newspaper's website. On the screen, there's my senior year photo, under the headline LOCAL TEEN DIES IN CAR CRASH. The article begins, *A 17-year-old teen died Friday evening in a three-car accident on County*

*Route 103 in Marstin. Denton Little died in the last hour
of his deathdate when the car he was driving in—*

I stop reading. I need to get on the train.

This newspaper says I'm dead. The woman stares.

"Oh, um, yeah, I know," I say, ducking my head away.
"Looks like me, right? People always got us confused. It's
very sad. The death, not that we were always getting confused."

I can't tell if this lady is buying what I'm selling. She
keeps staring.

"Last call, New York!" the conductor shouts.

"Well, see ya later." I slide past her and past the conductor and step onto the train.

My cover is probably blown. Sooner rather than later,
the police and Paolo's mom and whoever else is tied up in
all this will know I've gone to New York City. And they will
follow. I wonder if I'll ever see my parents again.

I walk down the aisle as the train starts chugging forward. I plop myself into an empty two-seater, scooting in
toward the window. The train car is mainly empty, with
one guy Felix's age sitting five seats ahead of me, wearing
glasses and headphones, and a mom and her threeish-year-
old daughter sitting two seats back on the other side of the
aisle. The little girl is coloring in a coloring book. It seems
strange for her to be awake on a train in the middle of the
night, but okay. I inadvertently make eye contact with the
mom, then quickly look away.

It occurs to me that any of these people could be following me, watching me, and it gives me the chills. It seems
insane, but then again, so does the idea of Paolo's mom
spying on me for my whole life.

I need to be careful.

In other news, I must be in shock, because I'm not feeling much at all. Certainly not feeling like I'm leaving my town and everyone I love behind, maybe forever. Certainly not feeling like it's a miracle that I lived through certain death. Not feeling insanely guilty that if it weren't for me, my stepmom and dad wouldn't be in the hospital, where I've abandoned them.

As the train pulls away, I gaze out at nothing in particular. I hear police sirens getting louder and louder, approaching the train station. Maybe they're onto me. Maybe it's unrelated.

Then a fast-moving blur coasts into the station's parking lot, and I see that it's Millie and Paolo on her barely rideable bike. Paolo stands up on bike pegs over Millie, who's pedaling. They brake to a stop and stare at my rapidly accelerating train as it leaves the station.

I involuntarily put a hand up against the glass, reaching out to them.

They are too late.

A second later, they are out of view.

Felix was right. I don't need to get any more people involved and injured on my behalf. And in Paolo's case, his deathdate coming in less than a month, I don't want him spending the last days of his life on some terrifying adventure that ultimately kills him.

Besides, I don't know how much time I have left myself. An extra day? An extra month? A year? Maybe my deathdate certificate just got the date wrong by a day. Who am I kidding? I know that's not true. My dead mother has somehow kept me alive.

I take out the crumpled piece of paper from my pocket and look at the address one more time. And it all hits at once, this time in my heart as well as my brain: I can't go home.

I think about my life till now, about how much of it has been defined by the fact that I would have an early death. Opportunities specially granted, dreams realistically reined in. Of course I never wanted that to be what I was all about, but how could it not be?

I'm Denton Little, the kid who's gonna die during his senior year of high school. That's who I've always been. But my deathdate has come and gone.

So now?

I'm Denton Little, and I am still, somehow, alive. And afraid. And alone. Very much alone.

My eyes tear up a little. I wipe them clean with my hood. I know this should be a gift, but it feels like a big, blank, scary nothing. I didn't plan for any of this. I scrunch my body up against the window and try to take a nap. I'll plan later.

"That's so good, Dylan," the mom behind me says. "Next time maybe you can try to color within the lines."

"I don't think so," the little girl says. "I like it better this way."

I fall asleep.

Strong hands shake me awake, and I stare into the eyes of the train conductor.

"Penn Station, buddy," he says. "Everybody out. Unless you're wantin' to go back to Jersey."

"Yeah, no thanks," I mumble, standing up and gathering my meager belongings. I'm only half awake, and it feels possible that the past few days have all been a strange dream.

I float out the door of the train car and onto the gray platform.

The one other time I went to New York City by myself, it was overwhelming and intimidating. But there's no space or energy in my brain for either of those emotions. I ride up escalators and walk down corridors. I follow signs with circles on them and find myself staring at turnstiles leading to the subway.

The slip of paper in my hand says Fifty-Third Street. The nearby exit says Thirty-Fourth Street.

I skip the subway and walk up the steps.

It's late at night, but the streets are crowded. I walk for three blocks, then turn the other way once I realize that the numbered street signs are going down instead of up.

I walk straight through Times Square. It's bright. I wrap my hand around the dead phone in my pocket. Even if it had a charge, I couldn't use it. It would lead the world straight to me. I toss it into a mesh trash bin.

I walk. Turning on streets, crossing at avenues. I make it to Fifty-Third Street, becoming more alert as I go. I don't know what I'm moving toward. I'm not even sure how I got here.

I look up at a building. Number 247. Getting close.

What if I walk into this place and immediately don't want to be there. Where will I go?

A huge truck passes by, reverberating down the street.

I arrive at 301. It's a blocky, nondescript building. I walk up the large stone steps.

The rest of my life starts now.

I buzz 2D. I wait. I hear the creak of stairs inside, and I want to run. I shouldn't be here. The door opens. It's an older woman.

"Denton," she says.

"Ohmigod," I whisper.

She has brown curly hair. She has my smile.

"Am I dead?" I ask.

She shakes her head.

"No," she says. "I'm alive. We're both alive."

I stare at my mother's face.

"We've been waiting for you, Denton."

For a moment, everything spins. Then it stops.

I nod at my mother.

I walk inside.

She closes the door behind us.

Acknowledgments

Thanks for reading this book! And also for feeling invested enough in it to want to read the acknowledgments. You are cool.

Huge thanks from all four chambers of my heart go to:

All of the early readers, whose thoughts, criticism, and encouragement were invaluable: Katie Schorr and Mariel Rubin (who both read the first two hundred words written and were so encouraging, as if they could really tell anything from that one paragraph), Zack Wagman, Ray Muñoz, Dustin Rubin (whose in-depth story notes were particularly amazing), Julie Harnik, Hannah Smith, David Smith, Rachael Weiner, Dayne Feehan (the book's first actual young adult reader), Erin Rubin, and Todd Goldstein.

Mollie Glick, agent extraordinaire, for her astute guidance, her refreshing honesty, and her general knack for getting shit done. Thanks also to the other superb humans at Foundry Literary + Media, including Jess Regel, Emily Brown, Sara DeNobrega, Emily Morton, and Katie Hamblin.

Nancy Siscoe, my terrific editor, for loving all the same things about this book that I do, having a hawk-eye for detail, and being so generous with her "Ha!"s. Thanks also to the rest of the amazing team at Knopf BFYR and Random House, including Angela Carlino, Katherine Harrison, Heather Kelly, Artie Bennett, and all the super people in sales, marketing, and publicity.

Zack Wagman, BFF of the century, who has supported my creative endeavors for decades and has been one of this book's greatest champions since the first draft. Thanks for all the sharp insights and enlightening conversation, and for talking up Denton all over the land. Rubber chicken vids 4eva.

Ray Muñoz, one of the most hilarious human beings of all time and an even better friend. You know the deal.

Stephen Feehan, MRHS, Lenny's on 9th Avenue, Fearless 15ers, Iconis and Family, BTTF, Argo Tea, Andy Hertz and TBBME:TM, the Gang, Birch Coffee, EST, Brown, the Tea Lounge, UCB, the NYC, and everyone who responded in a genuinely supportive way when I told them I was writing a YA novel.

Firecracker grandmother Minna Rubin, incredibly supportive in-laws Jenny and Larry Schorr, and happiness maker Sly Rubin (though he didn't exist when most of this was written, the idea of him was hugely motivating).

Mom and Dad, two wonderful, funny people, whose unconditional love and unwavering support of my creative career path have been two of the biggest gifts of my life.

And, above all, thanks to Katie Schorr, whose intellect, humor, love, ability to talk out this book for literally hours on end, and steadfast confidence in me, even when I had nothing of the sort, have meant the world. She made this book way better, and she makes life way more fun. Thanks, Kit.

DYING FOR MORE?
HERE'S A SNEAK PEEK FROM

DENTON LITTLE'S
STILL NOT DEAD

Now he needs to get a life . . .

LANCE RUBIN

author of *Denton Little's Deathdate*

I open my eyes and stare up at a crack in the ceiling.

I don't think this is my bed.

Waking up confused is my thing now.

I peer around at blank walls, and the lunacy of last night comes rushing back to me. Oh right, I'm hiding from the US government in my dead mom's apartment.

No big deal.

I hear the muffled sounds of my mom talking in the other room, a man's voice responding. Probably Crazy Dane. I don't want to go out there.

As my grogginess melts away, I remember everything I left behind when I didn't die.

Oh God. Paolo, my best friend. His deathdate is in twenty-six days. Wait, no, twenty-five days now.

Is it possible he could live, too? I passed him the virus on my deathdate. His purple splotch didn't have the red dots like mine, but he still got something.

I rip off the hoodie I've been wearing since the train station, followed by the button-down I've been wearing since the prom. I can practically see the stink lines emanating off my body, but even if I showered, I don't have any other clothes to change into. So, for the time being, I throw the hoodie back on. Now I'm in that and powder-blue suit pants. Ridiculous.

I move to the window on the other side of the room, pushing aside its green, scratchy curtain. It's morning. I wouldn't have minded sleeping till the afternoon, but oh well.

I met my mom last night. And she was kind of intense. (And I was kind of punchy and nonsensical, but I'm choosing to block that out.) I'm not sure I'm ready to face her frenetic energy again. I know I should be ecstatic to have met her—not to mention grateful, seeing as she saved my life—but every cell in my body is screaming that I need to find a way out of here. Nevertheless, I take a deep breath and swing the door open.

And I'm staring at my older brother, Felix.

"That's not what I do!" he's saying to our mother. They're sitting at the small table, laughing together as they eat waffles and bacon.

"It absolutely is," my mom says, turning her body toward me while her head stays with Felix so she can get in the last word. "I know you, so don't even bother trying to deny it." Her head joins her body. "Well, good morning! At last, he rises."

"Hey, Dent," Felix says, smiling as he stands up and gives me a hug. "Nice outfit."

"Hi," I say. Part of me is relieved to see my brother, but

the other part feels like I've stepped into some alternate universe.

"You sure you don't want to sleep some more?" my mom says. "Thirty hours may not have been enough."

"Thirty . . . what?" I ask. "Didn't I go to sleep at, like, three a.m. last night?"

"Try three a.m. the night *before* last night. It's Sunday morning."

I look to Felix, confirming that this isn't one of our mom's hilarious jokes. He nods.

"From what we've seen," my mom says, "living through your deathdate completely saps the body. We thought you might sleep longer, actually. After mine, I was so wiped, I slept at a Super 8 Hotel in Poughkeepsie for almost two full days straight."

"Oh," I say.

"To be fair, I'd also just given birth. To you!" She shouts that last part, like, *What're the chances?*

I must look terrified or, at the very least, befuddled, because Felix says, "I know this is a lot to process. But you were absolutely awesome on your deathdate."

"Thanks," I say.

"I was awesome, too, of course," he says.

My mom cackles at this.

"While you've been sleeping, I've been in jail for hitting that cop with a bedpan to save you."

"Whoa, what? I'm so sorry," I say.

"All good," he continues. "I got bailed out, and you got here, so it was totally worth it. Though . . . you don't seem too excited about the whole being-alive-instead-of-dead thing. I would think that might be a boon to your spirits."

"A boon?" I ask.

"Yeah, a boon."

"That's a word?"

"Yes," Felix says. "It's, like, a helpful addition. A lift."

"Sounds made-up." For pretty much my whole life, Felix was predominantly an absent brother, always busy, but then on my deathdate, he became this ever-present guardian angel, saving my life on at least two occasions. I was incredibly touched, but it's suddenly hitting me that he was probably just doing it because our mom asked him to.

It also occurs to me that Felix can probably provide information I desperately want. "Are Mom and Dad okay?" I ask.

Felix's eyes flick over to our mother, then back to me. "Um, you mean Raquel and Dad? Mom's sitting right here."

"You know what I mean," I say. He can be just as much of a fart-face in the afterlife as he was in the real world.

"You can call me whatever you want, Denton," my mother says, adoringly rolling her eyes at Felix, who sneers back at her.

"So, are they all right?"

"Yeah," Felix says. "I talked to Dad on the phone, but you know how that goes; we didn't actually say much. Sounds like they're fine, though. They were discharged from the hospital yesterday afternoon."

Thank God.

"Sweet of you to be concerned," Felix says, putting one hand on my shoulder, "but I'd say the bigger news here is that you're alive. And so is Mom." His face is barely able to contain the smile that's broken out. "Can you believe that?"

"Not really," I say. "I also can't believe you knew about this and never told me."

Felix scratches the back of his head as he nods. "Yeah, I apologize for that, I really do, but there was no way we could tell you. If you'd let someone know Mom was alive, you would have jeopardized everything we'd been working for."

"It's the truth, hon," my mom says. "Plus, we didn't know if the virus was going to work. We didn't want to lift your hopes up for no reason."

I'm sure they're right, but that doesn't make me resent them any less.

"Look," my mom says, getting up from her chair and walking toward us, "like Feel said, you're here now, which is all that matters." She's in a lime-green running ensemble: skintight shorts, T-shirt, and sneakers. "Oh," she says, glancing down at herself, "yeah, I ran this morning. Didn't know you got that from me, did you?"

Felix must have told her I'm a runner. And, no, how the hell would I know that when NO ONE TELLS ME ANYTHING?

"Mom is pretty hard-core," Felix chimes in. "She runs almost every day." He has this idiot glow about him, the same look he used to get when he'd tell me stories that painted our mom as a near-mythological figure.

"Yeah, I'm kind of an addict," she agrees. "Gotta stay healthy, you know?"

I obviously never knew my mother, but being here has the strange effect of making me feel like I don't really know my brother either. My chest tightens, and the room spins. I don't want to be here. "I might actually go for a run myself this morning," I say, looking at the floor and trying to get my bearings. "Get some fresh air, move around a little bit."

My mom and Felix share a look.

"Running isn't an option," my mom says.

"Sorry, Dent," Felix adds.

I don't understand. Does living through your deathdate make your body lose its ability to run?

"You can't go outside," my mom says.

"I can't—Wait, what? I can't go outside today?"

"Not only today," my mother says. "For the indefinite future. Until things settle down a bit."

The floor lurches out from beneath me, and I lean back onto the door frame to keep myself from falling.

"Dent, you okay?" Felix says, reaching out.

"I'm fine," I say, forcing myself to make eye contact to prove my fineness. "Is this a joke?"

"Look," my mom says. "It's for your own safety. The DIA came way too close to getting you, and you can be damn sure they have teams of people looking for you now. If anybody saw you get on that train, they'll definitely be searching New York City. So we have to be careful."

Oh my God. She's serious. "I can't leave here?" The place looks even sadder in the daytime, if that's possible. Other than the folding table where breakfast is happening, there's a gray, ratty couch; an old TV that's box-shaped instead of flat screen; a closet-size bathroom; and a kitchen with a yellowing fridge and a stove, three of its four burners rusted over.

"It's not as bad as it sounds," my mom says. "You can get on my laptop whenever you need to. I've blocked all the email and online phone call sites—don't want you to be tempted—but otherwise you can look up whatever you want to."

Because using Internet search engines all day is exactly how I want to spend my post-deathdate existence.

"I brought over my Wii for you," Felix says, pointing to a little black box standing up near the TV. "It's got Netflix." He gives me this grin, like fucking Netflix is going to make up for the fact that essentially I'm going to be a prisoner here.

"And," my mom says, racing to the kitchen cupboards, really pushing the hard sell now, "I have no idea what teenage boys are eating these days, but I tried to stock this place to the gills with tons of snacks you'd like. Ho Hos, Ding Dongs, Starbursts." Those are all foods my stepmom would never let us keep in the house. "And the fridge is packed, too. Peanut butter, jelly, eggs. Tons of frozen dinners. And there's ham. If you want to make a sandwich or something."

I'm not fully clear on what's happening here. Are my mother and I going to stay in this nondescript apartment eating ham and Ding Dongs for the rest of our lives?

"Here," my mom says. "Sit down. Have some food. You'll feel better. I made waffles and bacon, Felix's favorite, so maybe that's something you like, too."

I take a seat at the table with my mother and brother. As the two of them continue to engage in their cutesy mom-and-son-comedy-team bullshit, I chomp down on a piece of bacon. It pisses me off that my mom knows Felix's favorite foods and not mine. I know they had nine years together before she fake-died, but it still makes me feel outside of the world's best inside joke.

Ohmigod. I wonder if my dad knows, too. I mean, in the hospital, he saw that I had survived, and he hardly blinked an eye. It was like he'd always known I was going to live through my deathdate. So why wouldn't he know this, too? How messed up would that be? He knows his wife isn't actually dead, but he remarries anyway?

I wait for a lull in the banter and turn to my mom. "Dad knows you're alive, doesn't he?"

She looks at Felix, then slowly nods. "He does."

If Felix and my dad both know about my mom, is it something they talked about on a regular basis? Am I the only one not in on this secret? There's no way my stepmom knows, right?

"I don't—" I say. "I mean, Felix, how long have you known?"

A small smile curls on his face as he looks to his mom. "Pretty much the whole time," he says.

I'd thought my brain had already exploded, but I was wrong. *Now* it's exploded.

"Yup," my mom says. "He was nine, but I thought he was mature enough to understand. And to keep the secret."

In other words, nine-year-old Felix could be trusted, but I had to wait until I was seventeen and fake-dead.

"I know it seems crazy, Dent," Felix says. No wonder he was never around. Probably was too worried he'd accidentally spill the beans to me, the oblivious idiot. "But it wasn't like Dad and I ever talked about it. He refused. Just like he waited almost eighteen years to give you the letter Mom wrote."

"I'm so pissed at Lyle about that," my mom says. I have to agree. She wrote me a letter before I was born, and my dad didn't give it to me until my deathdate. "He knew the whole point of that letter was to establish a code, a way to communicate with you when the time came. *Happy dinosaur.*" (And here I thought the point was to let me know she loved me, even though she was about to die.) "That's also why I gave you that dinosaur toy, so it would further cement the code in your head." (She's talking about my favorite stuffed animal of all time, Blue Bronto. Who, apparently, was just a pawn in my mom's scheme.) "But thanks to Lyle, I'm sure you thought my top-secret Happy Dinosaur messages were actually real ads for erection pills."

"I did," I say.

"Geez!" my mom shouts. "I spent so much time on those, too."

"Anyway," Felix says. "My point is Dad wanted nothing to do with it. And for a lot of years, Mom and I were just communicating through old-school mail, letters sent back and forth. I didn't start seeing her in person until . . . I think . . . late in high school?"

"Right, yeah, because I helped you with that college essay, remember?" my mom says.

"But," I say, completely unable to wrap my head around the idea of my dead mother guiding Felix through the college application process, "if you guys were able to see each other, I can do the same, right?" My voice is all shaky. "I mean, like, I can see Dad and Raquel, right? And my friends?"

My mom looks at me, then Felix, then me again, her eyes apologetic.

"No," she says, "you can't."

I stare at my mom, unable to speak, as the abyss below me grows vaster. I don't think she's joking. This is my life now. I survived my deathdate for . . . whatever this is.

"It's just not possible, Denton," she says. "At least not for a long time."

"But . . . ," I say. "Then what's the point?"

"What do you mean?"

"I mean, what's the point of living if I can never see my family again? Or my friends?"

"The point is you're *alive*," my mom says, looking personally offended. "Most people think that's better than being dead."

Right. Without meaning to, I've crapped on the choice she made when she ditched my family for all this. I should probably feel bad about that. But I don't.

"Look," she says, softening her tone. "I understand. It wasn't easy for me when I survived. At all. But you *do* have family in your life: your mother and your brother. That's more than a lot of people have, Denton. You should be grateful."

"I am," I say. "I just don't get why it's not possible."

"It's too risky," my mother says, banging on the table and accidentally sending a fork clattering to the ground. "You're supposed to be dead. Someone happens to see you, they tell someone else, that someone tells someone else, and it eventually gets back to the DIA, who will find you and then, you know . . ." She lets the sentence hang in the air.

"Wait, no," I say. "I *don't* know. Find me and then what?"

"Well, any number of things, really," my mom says, leaning over the table and looking straight into my eyes. "None of them good."

"I was told the DIA would take me to DC and run tests."

"Sure, they'll definitely do that."

"But you're suggesting they'll also do other stuff to me?"

"Look," my mom says again, raising her hands in the air exactly the way Felix does. "I don't know for sure what they would do, but I'm pretty sure none of us would ever hear from you again."

My stomach drops.

"Yeah, Dent," Felix says. "This is no joke."

"How many people have lived through their deathdate like this?" I ask. "Has anyone been taken before?"

My mom grimaces. She looks away for a few moments

before turning back to me, incredibly serious. "Five of us have lived. One's been taken. Dane's wife."

I can't believe what I'm hearing. "What the hell? Why did they take her? Is she all right?"

"We don't know! This is what I'm trying to tell you, Denton," she says. "The DIA is not to be taken lightly. Don't you think, after I lived through my deathdate, I would have wanted to keep my life? To stay with your dad and Felix? And you, my new baby? Of course!" She gestures wildly. "But I didn't, because I'm not an idiot. At the time, there was a scientist doing the same work we were doing, trying to find a way for people to live past their deathdates. But, unlike us, he made no effort to keep what he was doing quiet. The *New York Times* printed an article about him, and the next day there was a huge fire in his lab. All his work was destroyed. A few days later, he went missing."

"But," I say, trying to process all this as quickly as I can, "what if that was completely unrelated to the DIA? What if he was sabotaged by some rival scientist or something?"

My mom looks me in the eyes. "Don't be naïve."

"Are you saying the US government would *kill me*?" I can't believe that Paolo's mom would purposely lead me to my death. But I also wouldn't have believed that my best friend's mother was actually a spy who'd been watching me my whole life.

"Denton," my mother says, her eyes boring into mine. "What I'm saying is that your existence is a threat to a multibillion-dollar industry that directly benefits many of the people *in* the US government. Would they go so far as to kill you? I can't be sure. But, honestly, no one would know the difference anyway. You're already listed as dead."

"Holy shit," I say quietly. I thought the whole point of living through my deathdate was that I'd escaped death for the foreseeable future. Incorrect.